GOING ZERO

GOING ZERO

A NOVEL

ANTHONY McCARTEN

HARPER

An Imprint of HarperCollinsPublishers

GOING ZERO. Copyright © 2023 by Anthony McCarten. All rights reserved. Printed in the United States of America. No part of this book may be used or reproduced in any manner whatsoever without written permission except in the case of brief quotations embodied in critical articles and reviews. For information, address HarperCollins Publishers, 195 Broadway, New York, NY 10007.

HarperCollins books may be purchased for educational, business, or sales promotional use. For information, please email the Special Markets Department at SPsales@harpercollins.com.

FIRST EDITION

Designed by Nancy Singer

Library of Congress Cataloging-in-Publication Data has been applied for.

ISBN 978-0-06-322707-1

23 24 25 26 27   LSC   10 9 8 7 6 5 4 3 2 1

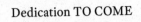
Dedication TO COME

GOING ZERO

PHASE ONE

7 DAYS BEFORE "GO ZERO"

BOSTON, MASSACHUSETTS

THE FULL-LENGTH MIRROR IN THE lobby, there to lend a sense of light and space to the cramped entrance hall, is spotted with age. The corrosive grime picks at the silvering like a scab. Still, it works well enough for the rent-controlled residents—teachers, low-level civil servants, the owner of a bakery, and half a dozen retirees just grateful that the elevator works most of the time. They can pause and check themselves before going out, take one final glance to make sure skirt hems aren't snagged in stockings, flies are done up, chins bear no toothpaste, hair isn't hysterical, toilet paper isn't clinging to shoes before they stumble into the street to be judged by their fellow citizens.

It's useful for the end of the day, too. As the residents shake off the chill of the windy streets, loosen their coats, and empty their mailboxes, it's the old mirror that will give them a first look at the damage the day has done.

The woman who has just come in glances at it reflexively. Here's what the mirror shows: midthirties; black hair in a bob; big glasses that became fashionable again last year; long, wide-fit trousers with sneakers; and, under her good late-spring last-season coat, a stiffly ironed black blouse with a swirling floral print. She looks a lot like what she is—a librarian, or someone's idea of the same. Bookish in her buttoned-up-ness, but independent-minded in the details: a huge pendant necklace, jangly earrings, a signet on her pinky. Could be on her way to a church bake sale, or to a #Resist event, impossible to say.

She unlocks her mailbox, pulls out a handful of envelopes, presses the little door closed until she hears the snap of the latch, which is when she sees that the mailbox label is slightly askew, so she squares it.

K. Day
Apartment 10

The *K* is important. Not the full *Kaitlyn*. Just that single initial to identify her: call it Single Woman Trick 273. Comes right after walking home with your keys (weaponized) in your hand. Write *Kaitlyn Day* on the mailbox or directory, and you're asking for trouble; every passing creep now knows there's a single woman in the building and could start hanging around just to see if she needs saving, mocking, following, fucking, killing.

She sorts the mail over the recycling bin. Junk. Junk. Junk. Bill. Junk. Bill. And then . . . Oh my God. It's here. It's actually here.

The envelope has *Department of Homeland Security* printed on it. There's even a frigging *seal* on the back; she thought that kind of thing went out with the Tudors. Inside, however, shitty government-grade paper where she had expected wedding-invite quality. Still, an invitation nonetheless.

Going Zero Beta Test, it reads across the top of the single sheet. That part is bold and underlined.

> *Dear Ms. Day,*
>
> *Congratulations! You have been selected as one of ten participants in the Going Zero Beta Test of the Fusion Initiative, a WorldShare partnership with the U.S. government.*
>
> *Per instructions, the Going Zero Beta Test will begin at 12:00 noon on May 1. At that time, you and nine other randomly selected participants will receive a message at the number on your application telling you to "Go Zero!"*
>
> *At 2:00 p.m. the same day, your name, photo, and address will be provided to the joint task force of the Fusion Initiative at Fusion Central in Washington, DC*
>
> *While this test is in operation, you are at liberty to take whatever*

steps you feel necessary, consistent with the laws of the United States, to avoid being detained by the Capture Team dispatched by Fusion Central to find you. Any participants of the Going Zero Beta Test who are still at liberty at 12:00 noon on May 31 will receive a tax-free award of three million U.S. dollars ($3,000,000).

We thank you for your patriotic efforts, and for playing an important part in making your country safer.

Special Notice: Upon penalty of disqualification, you are not permitted to declare, announce, or claim to be a participant in the Going Zero Beta Test until you are cleared, in writing by this office, to do so. Please refer to your application for further details of your nondisclosure agreement (NDA), legal responsibilities, and possible penalties.

Kaitlyn looks up and sees her own reflection in the mirror again. Just an ordinary woman, a dime a dozen. But for the next five weeks, she needs to be exceptional.

Are you ready to be perfect, Kaitlyn Day? she asks herself. For that's what she'll need to be now.

Her reflection gives nothing away.

Go upstairs, she tells herself. Check everything. When the order comes to Go Zero, then she must be ready to disappear in the wink of a knowing eye. Erase herself. *Vanish.*

Who does that? Vanishes? Well, it happens. Hell, *she* knows that better than most. People can just—*poof*—be gone.

She needs to rest. This might be one of the last nights she'll sleep easy in her own bed for a very long while. The reflection in the mirror doesn't move for a few moments as she considers what lies ahead. Then it moves fast.

7 DAYS LATER: 20 MINUTES BEFORE "GO ZERO"

FUSION CENTRAL, WASHINGTON, DC

ON MAY 1, AT TWENTY minutes to noon, Justin Amari is greeted by a welcome committee outside Fusion Central, a private complex that had sprung up near McPherson Square the year before with odd speed and mystery— "Silicon Valley Billionaire Cy Baxter Buys Block of Downtown DC, Spending More Time in City, Reasons Unknown."

Justin spots, among the faces, Cy Baxter's almost-as-famous-as-he-is right hand, Erika Coogan, cofounder, with Baxter, of Fusion's parent company, WorldShare. A powerhouse, too, if in her own subtle way.

"Nervous?" Justin asks her as he approaches.

The question surprises Erika into a grin.

"I have faith in Cy, and in what we're doing here," she says. Her voice is pitched low, just a trace of Texas left. "But today, for sure I'm nervous. It's big. Huge."

Along with other dignitaries, they walk across the lobby of glass and steel, then through a pair of high-security checkpoints, before entering the super-secure area, the no-digital-dust-on-your-shoes, no-cellphones-no-laptops-no-Fitbit-no-recorder-in-your-pen-cap area, whose atrium-like center and active hub, full of dedicated teams on the ground floor over-looked by a system of gantries, has been dubbed the Void.

The scale of it still shocks him. Ice-down-the-spine stuff. A vast hall of screens, within which are rows of desks occupied by the super-smart engineers, data scientists, intelligence agents, programmers, hackers, and myriad analysts from the private and public sectors who are the foot soldiers of the Fusion Initiative. And from a dais on the first floor fit for Captain Kirk, Cy Baxter, vibrating with nervous energy and pride, looks down on his mighty works.

I'm the one who should be nervous, Justin thinks. For one thing, it's my ass that's on the line here today.

All the screens—desktop, tablet, cell phone, even the huge ones on the rear wall—are black, sleeping, waiting . . . waiting . . . waiting to be woken.

Justin checks his watch. Fifteen minutes and fifty-nine seconds to go . . . fifty-eight . . . fifty-seven . . .

When he is waved forward, he walks up to the dais where Cy waits, formally suited for once, sparing today's crowd his usual adolescent and stubbornly unretired uniform of sneakers, baggy jeans, T-shirt bearing some inspiring quote like WHY THE FUCK NOT?

Also waiting, Justin's boss, Dr. Burt Walker, CIA deputy director for science and technology, he and Cy up there looking like they've just discovered the Theory of Everything. Also with them, less pleased, clearly not so convinced that all this is such a great idea, is Walker's predecessor (now CEO of some threat analysis start-up), Dr. Sandra Cliffe.

To Justin, Walker looks like he's trying to spot a ribbon to cut. Wrong era, Burt. No ribbons here. What will initiate the launch of this all-important beta test will be something as inauspicious as the click of a single mouse, which in turn will fire the ten chosen candidates in this secret trial to Go Zero, to get lost. Rapidly, they must disappear off the radar, leaving no trace. But this will not be easy: Cy Baxter and his team of cybersleuths are equipped, as no others in human history have ever been equipped, to find them, and find them rapidly.

Each of the ten participants—or Zeros, as the team knows them—has two hours, and two hours only, to get a head start: to activate their strategy, whatever it may be, after which the pursuit by Fusion will begin in earnest.

"A few quick words," Cy says with amplified solemnity—at forty-five, he is boyish still, with a slightly forward-tipping body, weight on his toes as if poised always to take a run—"before we begin. First, thank you to our friends at the CIA for this truly historic public-private partnership."

His eyes pass over Justin to settle on Drs. Walker and Cliffe, giving each a meaningful nod. "I'm also grateful, of course, to all of the investors who have placed their trust in us, some of whom are here today." A nod to the array of suits at the front of his audience. "But thanks mostly to all of you, the Fusion team, for your tireless hard work and genius."

The Fusion personnel applaud. Made up of experts in their respective fields, and equipped with immense technological weapons and wide jurisdictional powers, they number nearly a thousand here at headquarters but are augmented by thousands more personnel in the field, Capture Teams sprinkled all over the map and ready to pounce. Cy Baxter has drummed into each of them that it is the *speed* of these successes, as much as the *means* by which they will achieve them, that everyone has come to witness.

"We have serious business ahead. The next thirty days will determine the fate of a ten-year commitment from the CIA to fund this relationship, the fusing of government intelligence with free market ingenuity." He pauses then, and seems to weigh his next words carefully. "Everything you see . . . all this"—he waves his hand to encompass the atrium and indicate the three floors of basements beneath them full of thrumming servers coddled in air-conditioned racks, the 932 handpicked personnel (each one rigorously background-checked by the CIA) stationed throughout the ops rooms, VR suites, drone bays, research facility, food court, and offices—"will be nothing if we fail. For me personally, this project is the most important work I'll ever be part of. Period."

Applause greets this.

"When I was first approached to see if I could imagine a public-private partnership that might lift this country's security and surveillance powers to a whole new level, to an incomparable level, I looked at the deputy director here . . . and Dr. Cliffe, who may remember my reaction . . . I believe it was . . . right? . . . 'You must be shitting me!'"

Laughter on cue.

"But I guess—I guess Orville Wright must have said something similar to his brother, right? Or Oppenheimer when ordered to make a bomb, or Isaac Newton when asked to define which way is up."

More laughter.

He grins, a surprisingly winning smile. "You don't know you can till you can. Right? 'No way' precedes 'of course.' But despite our confidence, and all the hard work put in by everybody in this room, we still don't know, one hundred percent, that we can. Hence this beta test. So let's all get to it. Light the touch paper and see what we've got here."

Extended applause. Cy loves these people and they love him right back, for ample reason.

Justin's eyes stay on Cy as he wonders, Just how rich is this guy? No one is quite sure. His biography is opaque. Details scarce. Born where exactly? Over this there is even confusion. Cy says he's Chicago-born, but no birth certificate has been offered to answer rumors that his Slovakian mother brought this only child to the United States at seven. Recently, when the Ravensburger jigsaw people approached Cy, releasing a thousand-piecer of him—arms akimbo in front of a Bezos rocket ready to set WorldShare security satellites in orbit—folks finally gained a forum, with avid fingers and searching eyes, to do what up till then had been a purely mental challenge: assemble a clear picture of this man.

Justin has studied him from afar, collected the facts. Magazine profiles, invariably flattering, reveal a slow developer, one late to learn which fork to use, the right way to say words like *niche* (Cy: "nitch"). IQ of 168, though. A lonesome kid, often bullied, almost good-looking, although his small eyes were slightly asymmetric, his elbows and shins blotted with eczema. Got into computers early, then rode the tech wave. Built the garage start-up into a business valued at twelve billion dollars by the time he was twenty-six, and was off to the races. His thing, initially, revolutionary tech and social networks. Grew WorldShare from a small, friendly information exchange—"Wanna hook up?" "Sure, why not?"—into a *global* friendship ecosystem and from there fanned out fast, in all directions, sinking the profits into riskier ventures as if betting on swift greyhounds.

Wall Street fell in love at first sight with this future-seeing whiz kid, pipelined money into his escapades: cybersecurity, home protection cameras, alarms and public surveillance tools, even communication satellites. Midas-rich after a decade but never one to flaunt it (never photographed at Paris Fashion Week, no Hollywood friends, no giant yacht or private jet), he quietly, without undue publicity, also bet big on a green, wholesome, earthly, and even interplanetary future. Now he funds solar power research, battery life extension, and transparent cryptocurrency for the Federal Reserve, while also digging modular nuclear reactors to finally end the era of oil. What makes some people love Cy, find him so appealing, beyond his brilliance and despite his wealth, is how he truly seems to want to use who he is, and what he possesses, to aid the world when he could just, well, surf. Or rocket into space.

And not just a workaholic, he makes time for his private life: plays bass guitar in an indie four-piece and sweats at his local Palo Alto public tennis court twice a week. He has never been romantically linked with any other woman than Erika Coogan. He told *Men's Health* he finds much-needed balance in meditation. He can endure the lotus position for hours, and perform 'the plank' exercise for well over fifteen minutes. (When the media disputed this, he livestreamed a twenty-three-minute retort.) He has emerged, ultimately, a cult hero: head and heart in twin good health.

Quite an act to pull off, concedes Justin, that in this unadmiring age a billionaire can acquire and achieve so much and yet engender so little disdain. Further proof, he is forced to conclude, of the abiding benefits of keeping whatever the hell you actually do way, way, way under the radar.

18 MINUTES BEFORE "GO ZERO"

89 MARLBOROUGH STREET, APARTMENT OF KAITLYN DAY, BOSTON, MASSACHUSETTS

THE CLOCK SEEMS TO HAVE stopped. Time crawls, collapses, and just when she's sure that something is wrong, that there is a wrinkle in its weave, the second hand ticks forward again. She curls up at the far end of the sofa, a blanket over her knees and a book in hand, a book she can't even remember picking up, long ignored on the overpiled coffee table, slippery with magazines twisted over one another like strata after an earthquake—the *Atlantic*, the *New York Review of Books*, the *New Yorker*.

But she isn't reading, she's debating: This is a bad idea, this is a brilliant idea, this is insane. This is her best chance, her last chance, roiling like waves, crashing and receding.

Forget. Remember. The thoughts break and shatter over her too quick to latch on to.

Backpack
Sleeping bag
Hiking boots
6 T-shirts
1 extra pair of jeans
Anna Karenina

Breathe, woman, she tells herself. Breathe slowly. Remember who you are. I am Kaitlyn Day, she whispers, like a mantra. Thirty-three years old, birthday September 21, Social Security number 029–12–2325. These familiar facts are a healing oil, a balm, a prayer wheel, a tether to hold on to, and finally she can feel the air filling her lungs, reaching her blood.

Road maps
Pup tent
Gas stove
Cooking pot
Face mask
Phone K
Phone J
Compass
Canned food
Cutlery
Trail mix
Can opener
Tampons
Soap
Toothpaste
Flashlight
Batteries
Water bottle

Kaitlyn Elizabeth Day. Born and raised in Boston. Parents gone. Two brothers—but she doesn't talk to either of them much. They like sports, she likes books. They got jobs in construction, she became a librarian. They shout at the TV, she writes to senators. They have no imagination, Kaitlyn has too much. In fact, Kaitlyn has way, way too much imagination. Sometimes so much that her brain spins too hard and has to be regulated with little white pills.

She has a plan. And it has to work. It *has* to. It's gonna be fun, she tells herself. It's also gonna be terrifying.

2 MINUTES BEFORE "GO ZERO"

FUSION CENTRAL, WASHINGTON, DC

"LET ME FINISH WITH A thought. One last thought." Cy Baxter pauses to survey his audience. How good he is at this, thinks Justin, how controlled. A little awkward but endearingly so, the remnants of a friendless childhood still apparent, too much time coding, unresponsive to the distant playground squeals, and then a few years later, already with a hundred grand in the bank but no date for the prom.

"Today is not just about a proof-of-concept trial or even an opportunity to show our partners"—he turns to nod at the two esteemed CIA PhDs sharing the stage—"what we can do when we pool our resources and work together . . . though it is, and we will. Today is really to welcome in a partnership years in the making, drawing together, and this is so cool, the combined resources of law enforcement, the military, and the security industry—NSA, CIA, FBI, DHS—integrating them for the first time with the hacker and social media communities, all coordinated by the brilliant intellects of the crew here at WorldShare."

A smattering of applause here from the corporate sector.

"There they are, Fusion's parent company! . . . And all combining to form a bleeding-edge, three-hundred-sixty-degree intelligence data-sharing matrix unlike anything the world has ever seen. So pretty cool." Here he glances again at his CIA paymasters with a friendly collegial grin that shows just how unbelievably smoothly this has gone thus far. "So in conclusion, our almost ridiculous aim has been pretty simple: make things a whole lot tougher for the bad guys and a whole lot easier for the good guys, using the best technology we have to do it." As if running for office, he concludes with something slightly unexpected: "May God bless America and our troops! And now . . . let's roll."

With this, he points to a digital representation of a large analog clock projected onto the wall behind him, the final seconds before noon expiring with the sweep of a second hand climbing to join, like a clap, the hands of minute and hour.

On the stroke of noon Cy speaks the vitalizing words "Go Zero," and synchronous with this a single mouse is clicked somewhere in the bowels of the building and a message sent to ten cell phones across America: a small two-word phrase that almost rhymes. The hiders now have two hours before the seekers set out to find them.

ZERO HOUR

89 MARLBOROUGH STREET, APARTMENT OF KAITLYN DAY, BOSTON, MASSACHUSETTS

BRRRRRRR BRRRRRRR BRRRRRRR BRRRRRRR

As she scrabbles for her phone, she knocks it to the floor and it skitters under the sofa, where a dried-out, un-sprung mousetrap waits, tense with force, craving a visitor. But her searching fingers merely brush the contraption aside to close on the vibrating phone. With shaking thumb, she opens the text message. Reads:

GO ZERO

She immediately flips over the phone, takes out the battery.
Showtime.

SEVEN MINUTES LATER SHE'S ON the street, swimming in the current of humanity. Need to hotfoot it now. Only two hours to get lost. She's buried her features under a Red Sox baseball cap, large sunglasses, and an N95 face mask. She's done her homework, knows all about facial recognition cameras and how to outwit them. She's also wearing so many clothes that she might even elude anyone (or any bot) on the lookout for a thin bookish type.

Furthermore, she's read up on gait recognition technology, knows she needs to *not* walk like herself but can't walk erratically, either, which would in itself set off computational suspicions. What she must do—and is right now trying to do, which is requiring serious concentration—is to walk like *somebody else consistently*, to create a distinct persona and give that persona its own gait, a unique style of comportment she can also maintain. She cannot have, in the first hour, some computer somewhere pinging with an alert that there is a suspicious woman on a Boston street right now walking like three different people, either because she's a drunk or is trying to fool them. Hence, she is trying to walk like a singular invention, Ms. X, someone her age perhaps, but more confident than she is, happier, less burdened, with more of a skip in her step and roll to her hip. Down the street she moves in the manner of this Ms. X, but this is harder in practice than she thought it would be, as she kicks out her ankles, swings her free arm, arches her back, and steps like a runway model in an immediately exhausting ordeal of fabrication.

What is she doing anyway? This elaborate game of hide-and-seek? Kaitlyn's a librarian. A librarian, for Pete's sake, about whom—in two hours from now—they will already know more than even she knows—*far* more. Habits and patterns she's not even conscious of. Blood type (Does anyone know their own?). Star sign (okay, Virgo). Relationships (not much to learn here). Bank account number, bank balance (nothing to write home about). Children (zero, that's an easy one). Mental health (fragile, records available). Fuck, she thinks as her knees knock. Walk, Ms. X. Stay in character. PS: Walk faster.

CAPTURE WINDOW: 29 DAYS, 22 HOURS, 21 MINUTES REMAINING

FUSION CENTRAL, WASHINGTON, DC

ONE HOUR AND THIRTY-NINE MINUTES after Go Zero, the Fusion teams are at their posts, waiting before their rows of darkened screens, obedient to the order not to tap even a space bar until the ascribed two hours of lead time have elapsed. Only twenty-one minutes remain before the most high-stakes challenge of their professional lives begins. *Tick, tick, tick . . .*

Dr. Sandra Cliffe waits among them. At sixty-eight, a feisty veteran of many battles. Seen it all and seen off many rivals. Way back in the 1990s, Sandra had been the first to successfully encourage the CIA to pursue partnerships with the private sector. Even personally designed a proposal to procure technology at the development stage from the tech giants. They gave her the CIA Director's Award for that, the Defense Intelligence Agency Director's Award, the CIA Distinguished Intelligence Medal, the National Reconnaissance Officer's Award for Distinguished Service, and the National Security Agency Distinguished Service Medal. She resigned in 2005, satisfied with her contribution. For nearly a decade afterward she resisted public office, until the new (friendlier) president made her a member of the National Science Board and the National Science Foundation in 2014. The next president (more hostile) ignored this position, before his successor (friendly) reaffirmed it, and so it is in this capacity she has been dispatched here today to put Oval Office eyes on the Fusion Initiative in general, and on her successor at the agency, Dr. Bertram "Burt" Walker, a

George W. Bush appointee, in particular.

Sandra Cliffe's big worry is this: Back when she first encouraged the CIA to work with the private sector, there was no question that the assets the agency procured were to be owned and operated by the CIA, the DIA, the National Geospatial-Intelligence Agency, and/or the wider governmental community. They were specifically *not* to be either co-owned or entirely operated by an unelected entrepreneur who had sworn no oath to anyone other than his shareholders. As a result, she is suspicious of this project and will not cry a river if this beta test falls flat on its way-too-expensive face.

When she turns to look at Burt Walker, he smiles; wowed by so many blinking lights and screens crammed with data, he seems much happier about all this than she is.

Fusion is Burt's biggest roll of the dice as deputy director *by far*, and is his own attempt to do for the agency in the 2020s what Dr. Cliffe so elegantly and successfully achieved three decades earlier—namely, to expand and modernize the agency's activities. With the CIA largely prohibited from operating at all on U.S. soil, and only then against foreign threats, Burt sees in Fusion, and in Cy Baxter, a way to quietly expand the agency's domestic operations without triggering a big, multiyear, committee-choked argument in Washington about overstepping its charter.

Fusion can therefore do, on the CIA's behalf and *very discretely*, what the CIA cannot do directly.

The backroom deal Burt has struck with Cy Baxter is as simple as it is fragile: should this beta test prove a success, then Fusion will be bound by an annual contract with the CIA that will thereafter pay all the Fusion Initiative's bills, roughly nine billion dollars a year for the next ten years. Under this secret charter, Fusion will have access to all the agency's *relevant* intelligence data from the country's national intelligence network, with strict guidelines on its use. In return, the CIA will enjoy unfettered (and undisclosed) access to Fusion's massive library of private information on everybody who ever installed WorldShare: currently more than two billion people. In addition, Fusion will make available to the CIA its brilliant tech partners around the globe, plus their cutting-edge surveillance assets, both on the ground and—in the form of WorldShare's constellation of low-orbit WorldOne satellites—in space.

Burt sold the deal—the exact terms of which have been kept from Congress—by persuading his bosses and the Pentagon that the government faces an existential choice: either a partnership now with Baxter's WorldShare or a risk of falling perilously behind China and Russia, both of which are state sponsors of cyberweaponry.

Under cross-examination in a classified Pentagon approval hearing, he was asked how it had happened that an organization as mighty and established as the CIA could fall so far behind *a social network* in intelligence-gathering capabilities.

Simple, Walker replied. WorldShare, unlike the CIA, faced no constitutional, legal, or regulatory constraints. "These Big Tech giants have had it all their own way, been granted a license to basically steal and manage and manipulate and sell human experience and personal data for nearly two decades, and no one on the Hill has really said *boo*. So is it really any wonder that they now exercise almost total control over the production, organization, and presentation of the world's information?"

Thus, the most secretive branch of the world's largest superpower has no choice but to set a place at the big-kids' table for Cy Baxter, who is at least a guy the CIA can work with.

No surprise, then, that Cy is smiling down from the gantry on the first floor as the final seconds count down before the beta test begins, as excited as a champagne-bottle-heaving princess at the slipway launch of a new ship of state. He and his generation are effectively declaring victory today: victory for his young industry once considered so frivolous, now entrusted with mighty work. In addition, it's a more personal victory for Erika and himself, scarred as both are by a tragedy for which this project is, in no small part, a profound response.

Should the beta test succeed, and no one except perhaps Sandra Cliffe doubts that it will, the era of total information will have arrived—for better or worse—and can be put to work making the country (and world) a safer place.

Three.

Cy makes fists of his hands, raises them aloft . . .

Two.

How great if it all works out. For everyone. Really.

One.

Everyone except for the bad guys.

"Showtime!" Cy proclaims.

And with this, in the same instant that all the computers and myriad screens spring to high-res life, the old-fashioned clock projection goes dark, and in its place on the huge LCD screen, appears a large backward-counting digital clock—with old-fashioned block numerals—proclaiming in blazing red:

29 DAYS, 21 HOURS, 59 MINUTES REMAINING

29 DAYS, 21 HOURS, 59 MINUTES

BOSTON, MASSACHUSETTS

THE RULES WERE THAT THE candidates had only two hours to Go Zero. How quickly two hours can speed by! Two hours and one minute after the Go order, Kaitlyn *knows* that her super-smart pursuers will surely have her address, her bank details, her cell phone, her biography in large part, her tax returns, her medical records, her emails, her photos. She can *feel* them crawling all over her, inspecting her, scanning her, invading her as if conducting a physical pat-down, as if harvesting lint from beneath her nails, tugging a strand of hair to break down her DNA. She flinches as she thinks of the limitlessness of these digital violations. But now is not the moment to lose her nerve. Just follow the plan, she tells herself. Adapt if necessary, but stick to the plan. She knows this is all one hell of a risk, this little day one strategy she's cooked up, which is to not run too much, or too far, just slowly make her way to the local bus station at the appointed moment and then take it from there. She's done her homework and she's said her prayers. Holy Mary, Mother of God. It *has* to work. She goes through her mom's favorite saints in her head. She's not really a believer, but she needs all the divine help she can get. Should have lit more candles, she thinks. Asked for an angel or two to look out for her. What would it hurt?

Boston. Home. But suddenly it's enemy territory. Eyes everywhere. She's been watching the cameras on familiar streets for a while, but she feels these same cameras are all now watching *her*. Somehow there seems to be far more of them than before, at every crosswalk, appearing on nearly every bike messenger's helmet. These cameras, they don't bother you when you know they're not looking for you, but when you know they are, how insidious they become. Everyone and everything now appears to be a possible informant, the entire world around her hostile.

Her core strategy right now is to do the wrong thing, smartly. Upset their expectations. They are expecting from their contestants craftiness and guile, brilliant ruses and wild misdirects. So what if she doesn't try too hard to escape? In trying too hard, she'd probably play into their hands.

For instance, nothing in the rules says you can't fly to Honduras or Patagonia, but to do that you'd invariably along the way encounter the state's methods of surveillance at their most intense. The very attempt to put yourself beyond their reach would prove your undoing. So, having decided there'd be no airports or border checkpoints in her plan, she started to think about actions that might be truly unexpected from a woman like Kaitlyn Day. What could she undertake that would definitely *not* fit with their predictive model? What would jar with her personality profile and background, and so would not be anticipated?

She'd read up about the behavior modeling the new surveillance society had developed to stay one step ahead of criminals, to know before the bad guys did what they were going to do based on past behavior and the human truth that no one basically changes, not *really*, apart from the odd spasm and flourish. *Qui non mutantur.* So for sure they'd be making models of Kaitlyn right now, and from her track record be able any second to figure out, and with a high degree of probability, just what she was most liable to do next. So, what if she upset that whole apple cart? Threw a wrench in their works? What if she not only walked like someone else but also *thought* like someone else, *acted* like someone else, *reacted* like someone else, *became* someone else?

Approaching the bank, her life for now something of a masquerade, she studies her fellow citizens, all of whom are engaged in their own performances of self and selfhood, their own mini masquerades. Who among them is a spy? Is a fake? A fraudster? And which of them is out to get her? This young male approaching, like all his phone-clutching generation walking around as hunched over as *homo habilis* was 2 million years ago—is he the enemy? Or this other en-phoned person, a woman posting her Twitter update perhaps, or tracking her steps, checking the calorie count in the average muffin, or getting notification of a discount voucher for the coffee shop she just went by, and all of it recorded, reordered, mined for consumer insight by data conglomerates, insurance companies, political campaigns? Warren had explained all this stuff to her back in the day, and when he finished she canceled all her accounts the same night. *Bam.* Everyone else suddenly looked insane. The way they were living their lives was clearly pure madness. And yet they call Kaitlyn crazy!

Kaitlyn loves detective stories, classics but also the new stuff; they line the walls of her cramped little apartment, and in pride of place sits the stories of Edgar Allan Poe. Now, you can forget Sherlock Holmes. That endlessly recycled *Masterpiece* sociopath was a cheap copy of the one and only C. Auguste Dupin, hero of Poe's "The Murders in the Rue Morgue." What a story. Yeah, the one with the ape in it. Dupin can astound his friends by reading their minds, replying to their unspoken thoughts. He knows what someone's going to do before they themselves know. He has a thirst for detail, a way of seeing, and of remembering and interpreting what he sees. Dupin deduces, extrapolates, infers, predicts. Just a made-up story of course, and a cool idea, but no one can see that much and remember that much and predict what is going to happen before it does. Till now. Now? Now everyone carries a little oblong form of C. Auguste Dupin in their pocket; it analyzes their sleep cycle, their heart rate; learns their schedule, their commute; overhears their conversations; deduces their next moves. This miniature sleuth knows just when a news alert should reach you, just which advertising slogan to hit you with so that it steers you in through the appropriate shop door at just the right moment.

Okay. Okay. Here we go.

She walks up to the bank. Asks Warren, mentally, to wish her luck, then stands at the ATM, awaiting her turn. In broad daylight. Cap. Sunglasses. Over her face this whole time (no one bats an eyelid anymore, will ever again) has been the Covid mask. But now, oddly, she takes it off. Breathes deeply. Her turn. Hail, Mary, full of grace. She steps forward. Punches in a knowingly telltale PIN, and even glances up to the where she feels sure a hidden camera is capturing her, recognizing her. She offers her unmasked face to this unseen eye, holds it there, calm, nice and still, before she takes the regurgitated cash, pulls up her mask again, and is gone.

29 DAYS, 21 HOURS, 14 MINUTES

FUSION CENTRAL, WASHINGTON, DC

SO FAR, SO GOOD.

Cy is in his tech-filled office on the first floor as the first alert comes in. His glass desk lights up. The librarian, Zero 10. The Boston gal. Great. They have a Capture Team in that city. Cy doesn't run out of his office; he strolls. Of all the Zeros whose identifying details he has been studying for the past sixteen minutes, Zero 10 immediately announced herself to him as the one most representative of an unsavvy citizen, a beautiful bungler happy in the delusion she lives in a world where everything she does is still private.

But he had hoped that even the librarian would offer more of a challenge than this. She has apparently gone up to an ATM and used her own debit card. No fun at all. He sure hopes that his technology, vast and various, gets a far better test drive by the time this is all over. In order for the CIA to be impressed, and so to approve a ten-year, ninety-billion-dollar package, he needs them to see his teams work through hard problems, really get their teeth into tough-to-solve situations, dig deep into the digital detritus that the ordinary person leaves behind, and demonstrate unimagined capacities of physical detection and capture, because the Zeros of the future will be not librarians, but state-backed cyberenemies of America: Russian and Chinese hacker gangs deploying elaborate, nearly undetectable and totally indefatigable strategies; North Korean cryptocriminals; Iranian blackmailers; anonymous terrorists loosed on real American streets.

So picking up Zero 10 in under an hour will not be really as great as it seems. In fact, he regrets his own insistence on being left out of the Zero selection process, a process largely the work of his CIA partners, tasked under the agreement with recruiting five representative civilians and five professionals. A librarian, though? Representative? *Really?* A *book* person? When the rest of the world had gone digital a generation earlier, some fuckhead on his team chose *a book person*, an antiquarian, to stretch Fusion? He makes a mental note to complain about this lost learning opportunity, before realizing that analog people (haven't thought about them in a while) actually hold advantages in the modern surveillance world, their boo-boos far less likely to set off digital alarms, making their capture more reliant on traditional means. Still, and too soon even for his liking, this analog butterfly has been nabbed in his flashing net.

He comes out onto the elevated walkway over central control and looks down at the big screen.

"Visuals?" Cy calls down.

Erika is on the floor. He waves, she waves back.

Without Erika, none of this, he thinks. How much I owe her. Some relationships bust you up. Some make you. Rare ones inspire things like *this.* Looking down on all that he, with her help, has built, he affords himself a compliment also: not too shabby for the son of a single mom who sold empty soda bottles for pin money on the poor blocks of Portland, Oregon, but who is now an essential part of the internal security apparatus of America and beyond, in charge of a facility that might detect the next strange viral outbreak as soon as it starts, pick up chatter at the planning stage of a soundwave attack on U.S. embassy employees, repel ransomware shutdowns of vital services, stop another Jeffrey Epstein in his tracks, not to mention what happened to Michael! Poor Michael. Thinking of you today, dude, he reflects as his eyes turn upward in a secular prayer to the ceiling and the universal spaces beyond.

The low-res footage lifted from the ATM is now ten feet high on the giant screen. A program, one of his own creations, automatically freezes the video on its favorite frame, draws green lines across the planes of the face, measures the distance between the eyes, the shape of the ears, the generous slice of Kaitlyn Day's mouth, and runs it against a still from a video taken during the interview phase. Perfect match. Now they have a choice of angles from the ATM, so they can track her face anywhere. He watches as Zero 10 turns and walks out of the frame. Cy glances at the time stamp: fifty-three seconds ago. A person, now a pulse on the map. Washington Street. She doesn't stand a chance. At this rate, he bemoans, they won't get to play with any of their best toys.

"Can we get Medusa on her?" Cy asks. He means the superdrone hardware that can cruise as high as twenty-five thousand feet, carry multiple cameras, and use exceptional optical engineering to enable them to get a perfect close-up of Zero 10 while still keeping an eye on the surrounding fifteen square miles.

Erika shakes her head. Negative.

He gets it. Boston is one of *those* cities. You'd have thought that after the marathon bombing they'd have clamored to have a Medusa drone circling up there, but no.

Erika turns back toward him. "But we have compact drones moving to the scene, as well as CCTV. She's heading toward Chinatown."

As Erika listens in on the operators of the fleet of next-gen minidrones, each no bigger than a paperback, Cy comes down the spiral staircase. "Where's the Capture Team?" he asks.

"Her apartment. They were just setting up to conduct the initial sweep. Four minutes out."

Cy rolls his shoulders to relieve the stress that accumulates both there and in his neck. "After they pick her up, they can join the alert teams for Zeros Seven and Four. And do I have a yoga appointment tonight?"

"Drones in the air, and yes, we flew Kuzo in."

"What would I do without you?" Dating her is like dating reliable software.

As Cy takes his seat on the dais, Captain Kirk once more, the main screen fractures into half a dozen Kaitlyns walking down the street from the ATM, three from fixed cameras, joined now by three others, more distant but closing fast, a little flock of aerial shots.

"Who is piloting?" Cy asks.

Three hands nearby shoot up briefly, and he issues instructions.

"One of you get in front of her, feed her stride through the gait analysis and cross-reference it with the static cams." There's no point really, she is in the bag, but it will train the algorithm and keep the gals and guys in the Void on their toes until the Capture Team shows up.

One shot on the screen swoops and spins as a drone speeds ahead of the others, then flips around. Following events on the screen and also glancing at the operator at the controls, he thinks, is like being swung on one of those kids' teacup rides. It's smooth, though—the gimbal in the camera makes it easy, and the processing speed and the 5G connectivity make every little thing frictionless. Cy leans forward, selects a couple of options from the drop-down menus on his own screen so that he can monitor the real-time analysis of how Kaitlyn moves, how her hips roll, her legs strike out and extend, her arms swing, each of these common in the human catalog but here represented as spiraling lines of cold numbers standing in for something intimate, personal, specific. He is watching a machine *think*. It is beautiful, one of the human mysteries being encoded, *Homo erectus* in motion. Then it stops. No Kaitlyn on any of the six screens.

He looks up.

"Where is she?"

"She went in there," Erika says. One of the drone cameras is showing a sad little bodega.

"CCTV inside?"

"Nothing," one of the teams specifically assigned to Zero 10 calls. "They aren't linked in. Do we wait?"

Cy breathes. Realizes they are actually looking to him for an answer. Still has things to learn about being a general on active duty in a combat situation; this moment feels very far from chairing a board meeting or signing off on an annual report. "Does this store, by any chance, have a back door?" it occurs to him to ask.

One of the drones skips niftily over the roof and descends right into the back alley, hanging there like a hummingbird, waiting. It captures a fire door, just then swinging shut. The alley is empty, though.

Cy twirls his finger and the pilot turns the drone in an agonizingly slow circle: dumpster . . . fire escape . . . garage doors . . . There! "The garage!"

As Cy shouts, the drone jerks then steadies and races down the alley like a gundog, reaching the street just in time to see Kaitlyn Day . . . stepping into a cab.

"Talk to me!" Cy shouts. Suddenly, he's not bored anymore.

"Capture Team at two minutes. And we have the cab ID'd."

A taxi driver's license comes up on the screen with a badge number, followed shortly by almost everything known about the visa-overstaying Moldovan father of three who owns the medallion.

The other Zero teams are watching the big screen now, too, pulled away from their own work in the Void and elsewhere by the twitching excitement of the chase.

The drone pilot who caught Kaitlyn getting into the cab is still in pursuit, using his generation's gaming skills to jog the hand controls this way and that. He dodges the street furniture, arcs around trees, lurches low under the overpass on Washington. Then, in the moment his view is blocked, the cab turns into a stream of traffic, of other cabs, so that the entire chase team is now vicariously dodging between lanes on Stuart Street, then north on Charles, veering round a bus, swinging away from the sidewalk while a second drone takes a shortcut under the trees and swoops over the heads of up-gazing tourists ("There ought to be a law against these drones")—in time to see the cab ahead pull a hard left to the wail of horns. The drone twitches. Responds. Renews the pursuit.

"There!" Cy shouts as, finally, the cab pulls up fast next to the stairs of the Park Street T, choked with student traffic sprawling down into the subway. He catches a glimpse of a slight, dark-haired woman diving down into the heaving mass of teenagers.

With that, she's gone. The drones sit uselessly over the entrance to the subway as the Capture Team screams up in a blacked-out SUV and all but two pile onto the street in their black uniforms, anonymous jackets. The two who remain pull the driver out of his cab, flashing their badges. The driver does not look exactly happy to see them.

As the Capture Team gives chase, Cy smiles and slaps his palms on the tabletop, mostly in appreciation of the librarian's unexpected skills and his excitement that she is presenting a decent challenge after all! How cool is this? The team's body cams give Cy eyes on the pursuit as they (unarmed of course) stumble down the stairs and push past the kids on the narrow escalator.

"Facial recognition in the station is getting nothing," one of the Zero 10 minions says. "And she hasn't used her CharlieCard on the turnstiles."

The screen flutters with a wide array of images from inside the station as his people plug into the station's CCTV network. A mass of Bostonians. All shapes and sizes and colors. All moving, veering, mingling. Cy bites his lip. There are too many of them—too many Red Sox caps and winter hats and turned-up coat collars (even in May), the urban hurly-burly, and his facial recognition algorithms scramble to keep up. Park Street. Two subway lines, four directions to choose from. Blind spots. Pillars. For the first minute he's hopeful, but as the second minute expires he starts to think she's gone. She got away.

That merits another smile of appreciation. Well waddaya know? "Split the team. Send half back to her place to complete the scans, keep half in place, and keep the recognition running on all downtown cameras. Hell. Run it over the whole city."

He heads back to his office, still smiling, thinking perversely, Go, Kaitlyn.

29 DAYS, 20 HOURS, 47 MINUTES

BOSTON, MASSACHUSETTS

SO THEY HAVE MY FACE, she thinks. Almost certainly. Her unique mug is now certified on national databases: Kaitlyn Day, Zero 10. As a consequence, she must conceal this face very well from now on, wherever she decides to take it.

Back during the interview process, after she signed the NDA, the Fusion folk had surprised her by taking no fingerprints, not even a copy of her driver's license. This was all part of the challenge that the Fusion people had set themselves, they explained—namely, to know as little as possible about their prey beyond what was necessary to determine their professional suitability and mental fitness. They needed a good cross section of types and abilities so as to test their own preparedness against real-world threats, but they also wanted to make it hard for themselves. An assortment of candidates would be chosen, they promised, with varying worldviews and perspectives and skill sets. She has to assume she was selected to test their armory against all future single, childless, nearsighted female book lenders likely to pose a threat to the nation's security.

She hustles along the Winter Street Concourse to Downtown Crossing and hangs from the strap on the train to Back Bay. She spots a dozen others wearing their Covid masks—perhaps for some this will become permanent now, no matter what the future holds, some old perplexity about viral loads pumping in their imaginations, a base-level fear about the threat other people pose, one that obliges self-protection, and she thinks, How quickly the world can become a hostile landscape. Perhaps she is feeling this so sharply simply because the best-trained people in the world are now actually out to get her. But she also has felt for a long time that she has somehow fallen, fallen through the social fabric and numbers herself not just among the hunted but also among the unwanted, the exiles and renegades in an underworld of the undesirable.

She switches direction, heads for State Street, pulls up her hoodie as she jogs up the stairs and onto the red-brick pavement, stopping at a newsstand to buy a copy of the *Washington Post*. No mistakes, she instructs herself. She must maintain her vigilance. Who among these strangers walking past might pose a threat? The older woman who frowns at her? The teenager, his hair spiked and his fluorescent puffer jacket bulking out his thin frame, giving her a nod as if they have a kinship? The white-haired old guy, his face pink with cold, recoiling immediately from the danger he sees in everyone? And what do the cameras that seek Kaitlyn Day see? What do they recognize?

As she passes by the bank of CCTVs on Congress Street, she knows that, far off, the Fusion Initiative software will right now be trying to work out if this woman in the hoodie in the subway station lobby could be Kaitlyn Day, whether they have a match, whether the person she is now presenting to the camera moves like Kaitlyn Day, behaves like her. And so she focuses her mind—her only rival weapon—on *not* being Kaitlyn Day. *Not* Kaitlyn Day. *Not* Kaitlyn Day. Not walking like her, not thinking like her. She repeats this mantra to herself as she passes under the leering cameras, unable to know if the invisible matrix, calibrated to detect her, recognizes that which is unique in her, that irreducible thing she cannot ever conceal, the mark of the self.

Surfacing into daylight, she heads for the bus station—for a century the favorite hangout of runaways, addicts, fugitives, the poor, the desperate, and all those hoping that a better future is waiting in some place other than this one. She picks up her ratty backpack from Left Luggage (a key element of her preplanning) and uses cash to buy a ticket from the machine. Her bus is waiting. It's one of the budget lines, ratty seats, no cameras onboard. She changes her top. Shoves the hoodie into the backpack. Breathes deep. Feels almost like a new person. The bus pulls out of town.

29 DAYS, 20 HOURS

FUSION CENTRAL, WASHINGTON, DC

THEY ARE ONLY TWO HOURS in!

Since the chase began, only 120 minutes. Or 7,200 seconds. There is so much fucking time left it's ridiculous, a whole galaxy of time: 30 days' worth of time no less, or think of it as 720 hours, or think of it as 43,200 minutes, think of it like that, or go all the way and think of it as 3.25 million heartbeats. They have heartbeats *to burn*.

Back in his office Cy tinkers on his laptop, and right away the calm spreads through his limbs and permeates his bones. In his case, technology soothes better than Xanax. Only when his fingers dance on a keyboard, and when worlds leap into sudden life at his touch, does he feel that the world is truly *in Ordnung*. Yes, he likes nature, is himself helping prop up the finite planet in significant ways (electric cars; carbon-neutral homes; development of floating cities; grants to stall the chainsaws in the Amazon, Daintree, and Congo; investing in next-gen small modular reactors), but what really pleases him, excites him, rouses him, is the manufactured world, the intelligent product of artists at drafting tables. If he had his way, the universe would have a new-car smell.

Ultimately, it's all about control. He admits he feels jumpy when this is denied him. How do you ensure you have control? By being excellent, by rising to a position of command, whereupon you are in a position to order the world as you see fit. He believes winning—and he is surely a winner—is just the by-product of truly knowing yourself and harvesting your special gifts, those acuities, those tiny grains of genius that everybody possesses in some measure but that very few properly refine and turn into an empowering isotope. Cy has *made* himself what he is. Built this thing that is himself. He's very far now from the playground runt who once lost a tooth (baby tooth, luckily) to a bully's elbow. This year *Forbes* has him slipping up eight places to number 47 on their rich list—he'd be higher still if he didn't dream so big, pump so much cash into high-risk ventures that go belly-up, or discreetly give so much away to charity. He hopes to be about as good a person as someone as ambitious as he can be. Perfect? Certainly not. Trying? Yes, and again yes. *Vincit qui se vincit.*

And, he believes, Fusion is the next step, maybe the final step, toward the kind of world that folks deserve. Sure, he knows all the arguments against it, that privacy once sacrificed cannot be recovered, that future abuses might yet occur, but he knows that the benefits of protection vastly outweigh such concerns. People, when monitored, are simply nicer, he believes, and when they step over the line, expect a swift countervailing response. Is this the dark fascist fantasy of a police state? No, no. He rejects that. Think of a fairer world in which the impulse to do evil just got a whole lot less attractive. Was there a better gift he could give?

Curious about their near miss, Cy turns back to his laptop, goes through the file being built on Zero 10. A ton of stuff already. Interesting-ish. Few surprises. Certainly a *type*, and rather unremarkable in her own way: a frustrated person, an unhappy person, not a very successful person, unstable (based on her medications and mental health history), a loner, finds the world a hard nut to crack. Found sanctuary in the world of books. A shame, then, for Kaitlyn Day, that her slithery escape into the bowels of Boston won't save her; winning three million dollars would surely be a life-changing event. Well, maybe there was something he could do for her when this was all over.

Second mental memo on the subject: Why *did* she get selected? If this were a chess match, then this novice from Boston just managed, out of all the possible opening moves (1,327 according to *The Oxford Companion to Chess*) to luck out on a classic (Ruy López, for instance, early knights, aggressive king's bishop), which is a good opening move only if you know how to then develop it. No small feat. He wants another crack at her *himself.* She intrigues him now, this ghost across the invisible chessboard. Were the reasons for her selection more mysterious than he knows? Still, his prediction: mate, in three more moves.

He leans back from the screen, tries to remember the last time he rode public transportation. Would've been New York in the first days of WorldShare when he and Erika were rattling into Midtown every morning from Williamsburg, trying to explain to the moneymen what he had made. They'd stay out too late drinking overpriced cocktails on maxed-out credit cards and then rattle back to the rental, where he'd sober up with energy drinks and Adderall and then code until dawn while Erika slept.

Erika quickly learned to speak the language of the moneymen. She'd translate for him, and translate *him* to them, explaining all about data draft and digital exhaust in a way the Street could understand. She showed them the huge amount of information the eager adopters of WorldShare were creating as they wandered around in their digital wonderland, their likes and wants, recipes and knitting patterns, conspiracy theories, sexual preferences. Everything they touched, looked at, searched for, and shared, created a digital wake she could explain. This wake, or trail, could be bundled and even traded as a commodity, she would explain. You could then target individuals with ads tailored to their tastes, vastly increasing your chances of generating a sale. The pitch worked.

Erika was soon too busy to keep up with the tech side of things; she detached herself from it, learning just enough to wield a meaningful vocabulary but otherwise focusing on hiring the right people to get granular. Hire she did—lawyers, financial analysts, publicists, a sleek yet geeky sales team—while Cy did what he did best, turning their golden data mountain into predictions of future purchasing patterns or political affiliations, with world-changing impact. Hey, no harm no foul, he argued, just discovering your audience for you. How did you come by all this personal information? they would ask. Simple. We found gentle ways to get ordinary folks to give it to us of their own accord. Click, done. Nobody reads the fine print. As a result, they paid a great price for entry to Cy's addictive playpen of apparently harmless friendship groups, geotagged photo and video and news sharing, facial recognition, to this massive depository of information that documents the public's reaction to events and its evolving customs.

Of course, it could be used to make people sad, angry, hopeful, hopeless, greedy. Due to too-eager fingers on personal computers, human psychology cracked open and offered itself up for scrutiny. Turns out we aren't as complicated as we thought we were. We were just pretending to be complex. Really, we're a herd. Now WorldShare was legitimately riding that herd with bullwhip and stirrup and rolled-tongue whistle. Yee-haw.

"Cy?"

Erika's voice buzzes. She is the only one with the clearance to jump right into his ear. "The VR team is set up in Zero 5's apartment. Wanna drive?"

FIFTEEN MINUTES LATER HE'S WEARING a VR headset and standing (or seems to be) in an ordinary suburban living room in Boise, Idaho. The Zero 5 Capture Team has gained access to the actual house and is scanning, for Cy's benefit back at Fusion, the hall and bedrooms: oversized TV, slightly shabby sofa, food stains on the cushions, floor thick with kids' toys. And Cy is there, right there, looking left, looking right.

"What are the details on her?" Cy asks as he moves about his illusory version of the same room, hundreds of miles away, VR headset over his eyes.

Erika's voice replies in his earpiece. "Zero 5. Rose Yeo. Single mother. Two kids."

That would explain all the stuff lying around. Cy walks right through the ghost-sofa to the ghost-mantelpiece. Examines the ghost-family-photos. A second civilian type, he thinks, on the surface of it devoid of unique talents: So what inner complexity had secured her selection? Well, perhaps some mysteriousness had been identified, something atypical that marked her out as even harder to read than the average person in the street, and so, finally, a fitting adversary in this monolithic game of hide-and-seek.

The VR interface isn't working as well as Cy would like, and the images flicker, resolve, flicker again. The headpiece, for one thing, is heavier than one would want it to be, a faulty proprioception as your body tries to work out why your head is suddenly too large and unbalanced. Engineering should have sorted that out by now. It needs counterweights, thinner glass.

He lifts his hand, and the sensors on his wrists draw a version of his fingers into the simulacrum of Rose Yeo's living room to stop his subconscious from freaking out. It's a little crude, a mist of blue bubbles, but good enough for his brain to go "Okay, that's my hand now" and orient itself.

"Do you know how to tell if you're dreaming?" he asks the nearest Fusionnaire, causing a heart to flutter, the figment of a face to turn toward him, thrilled to have been addressed by the great man and almost in person.

"No, sir. I . . ."

"Look at your hands. In dreams, our brain finds them hard to draw. Your palms will look weird; you may have extra fingers. And if you look at your feet, half the time they won't quite reach the ground."

Cy looks down, as does the acolyte. Their feet might be blue fuzz, but they sit squarely on the carpet.

"Needs work, but at least we're doing better than the average dream."

Okay. To business.

Half the pictures on the mantelpiece are of the kids. A boy and a girl. As he focuses, their names and ages appear in the air next to the photos. Seven and five, respectively. He drags a finger through the air to scroll deeper into the intel. This new interface works well. Good school reports. Girl needs braces.

He moves then to a pic of Rose, taken in a bar with a couple of girl-friends, glasses raised to the camera. The info on the other two women instantly hovers in the air above the photo. Both are friends of Rose on WorldShare, so they were data-scraped in the first moments of the pursuit. Gabrielle and Kaisa. One married, one single. Neither with kids. Both employed at the same local data entry firm as Rose.

Next photo. Older Asian couple, Rose between them. Mom and Dad. Local. Mom's on WorldShare a lot. She hasn't posted as much over the last few days as she usually does, which may or not tell the analysts something. But then they find something clearly noteworthy—the detail pulses orange in the air, an amber flag, the equivalent of the algorithm pausing, and saying "Hmm, interesting"—Mom's grocery bill. It was higher than usual last week. A lot higher. And she didn't go to her knitting group on Tuesday evening. The orange slashes across the data are building up. Nothing to trigger an automatic red-flag alert yet. How about Dad? Dad is a digital gray space. An email account he shares with his wife. No social media. Doesn't have a smartphone. Such people do exist. Cy watches the processing of the man's financials, looking for the orange glow of significance. He picks up the documents out of the air, scrolling and screwing them up and throwing them over his shoulder with his cartoon fingers. Likes his coupons, does Daddy Yeo. Gets loyalty points whenever he fills his car. The algorithm has highlighted the last three entries. Not the usual weekly gas run. He's been going every morning, keeping the tank on his Ford full to the tippy top.

"Home address," he says. "Show me."

The map hovers in the middle of the room, complete with a blinking red dot.

"Route from here."

A neat red line, from house A to house B.

Cy has his hypothesis. "The parents."

Moments after this, in his ear: "We have Grandpa's car."

"How?"

"From his registration, we traced the car's onboard computer and hacked into its ECU. Tracking it now."

A new map, on it a blinking dot sent by the car's engine control unit. Route 84. "Is he alone in the car?"

"We presume so."

"Why?"

"He's listening to John Denver. Loud. Would you like to know the song?"

"Sure."

"Country Roads."

Cy starts crooning to his team: *"Almost heaven, West Virginia, Blue Ridge Mountains, Shenandoah River."*

Adds Lakshmi Patel, ex-FBI, assigned early to Fusion, a thirty-something woman with ironed black hair, intones: *"Life is old there, older than the trees—"*

Less amusing somehow.

Cy interrupts: "Can we get a local drone on him?"

"Already deployed."

"Keep your distance. Don't spook him. He's leading us to them."

Meridian, Idaho, ten miles outside of Boise. That's where Old Man Yeo leads the Fusion team. Fifteen minutes later he arrives. They're watching him from above as he pulls into the back of Big Daddy's BBQ. Fusion accesses the history of the restaurant, going back years. A link is found. A cousin's ex-husband on the wife's side of the family is the manager there. The Yeos clearly thought this would be a distant-enough connection. Wrong.

The Capture Team finds Rose and the two kids holed up in the storage room. Her plan, it is soon revealed, was for Pops to pick them up here and then head up to Snakey, the Morley Nelson Snake River Birds of Prey National Conservation Area. Do a bit of camping. Not a bad plan—would've been pretty tough to find them out there—but they didn't get that far.

As the family files out the back of Big Daddy's behind the Capture Team, one of girls stops and waves up at the drone hovering overhead. Cy, in Washington, looking down, catches himself waving back. Cute kid.

"Nice work, Cy," Erika says. "One down."

Cy puts his VR headset back in the rack, yanking the Velcro to release his wrists from the sensors. Wonders where Rose made her first mistake. Maybe she'd figured on leaving the kids with her folks but couldn't do it in the end. Cy's mom had always been happy enough to leave him behind with a sitter she hardly knew when they went on trips. Mama Rose should have taken a leaf out of her book. The first family Cy had ever really felt part of was the Coogans. Their house was as full of random stuff as this one. He spent countless nights there, with Erika studying at the table while Cy and Michael talked code. Long time ago. Yeah. Did strange stuff to your head, family.

One down. Nine to go.

28 DAYS, 5 HOURS

MILWAUKEE, WISCONSIN

AS THE SECOND GO ZERO day draws to a close—noons now replaced midnights on every player's mental clock—Ray Johnson, Zero 1, suddenly feels his age like it has crash-landed on him. He can smell the stiff old scent of defeat on his own skin. Still tough, able to run for half an hour every morning and enjoy a round of golf with the guys (can blast it 185 yards), he is better preserved than most of his vintage, the beer-bellied, the fissure-faced, the combed-over. He has developed plenty of hobbies since he retired, and he and his wife have discovered that as long as they spend at least five hours apart every weekday, they still have a pretty good marriage. Any fewer than that? Don't ask.

He'd been reluctant to sign up to this crazy venture, but that old familiar pull of duty, boy oh boy. They needed men like him, they'd said, men who had never felt even the twitch to share photos on WorldShare, who didn't trust email, a man who still—Christ, they must have had a job finding someone like him, now that he comes to think of it—used checks. *Checks!* A man who liked to do his banking in person with someone he recognized across the desk, someone who knew his first name, his kids, the car he drove. *That* was the kind of personal data he wanted certain trusted people to know about him. He *required* this kind of data sharing. It made life (all forty-five hundred heartbeats an hour of it) worth living.

Marjory, his wife of forty-three not-bad years, is staying with her sister till all this is over. Thank Jesus in heaven. To her credit, she accepted off the bat that it was his duty and knows not to expect to hear anything from him: no great hardship on either side after forty-three rounds of "Auld Lang Syne."

He doesn't hold out much hope for the big prize. He accepts that the surveillance capacity of the modern state is a mystery to him, so he assumes he has little chance of taking effective countermeasures. He's too steeped in his old-fashioned ways. The type of guy to rely on his wife to tell him what the kids are up to, how their friends are, remind him of birthdays. It's only since he went in for the Fusion interview that he even noticed that she gets her information from the phone rather than the computer now. He's learned how to use Wikipedia (which he guesses has killed Britannica pretty much), but it all feels too fast, too slick, and he doesn't trust it since he learned that any kid can change the entries once they learn how. You couldn't pull that shit with Britannica.

The fact that Fusion hasn't picked him up already is honestly a surprise. He hadn't expected to last more than a couple of hours. The Go Zero alert pinged on his Jurassic-era phone, as his grandkids call it, while he was in the parking lot of Home Depot at noon. He'd meant to be back home before it started, but an accident on the highway had slowed traffic to a crawl. He left the car and remembered to take out the battery from his cruddy handset—his wife's idea, something she'd seen in a documentary—then caught a bus into the middle of town. Put on his disguise. Not much of a disguise. A woolen beanie rolled low above the eyes and an old pair of reading glasses that blurred his vision, which he had to wear low on his nose, looking over the rims. He'd stopped shaving when they told him he was a finalist. Hey, it was something.

In the bus station for more than a day now, holding a ticket for Florida (no ID needed), he's been snoozing on and off in the corner like a deadbeat. When asked from time to time if he's okay, says nothing, just shows the ticket, they leave him alone again. Hobo Hilton.

Florida's where some old navy buddies live. They're gonna get the crew back together and make a top-secret project of this Fusion. If Ray can just get his ass down to Orlando without getting caught, they told him, they'd take over from there. "Not even the devil hisself will find you, guarantee you that, hombre," Scooter McIlleney had said, laughing.

Well, then, so far, so good, thinks Ray as the bus hits the interstate, rocking and rolling its way southward toward both the sun and maybe, just maybe, three million bucks. He harbors images of himself wearing shorts and a cotton shirt, lazing by a pool with a beer, watching all the pretty things float by, and having steak dinners with the guys. . . .

28 DAYS, 1 HOUR

FUSION CENTRAL, WASHINGTON, DC

THE TEAM ASSIGNED TO RAY Johnson works fast. Spider maps of his known associates, past and present, are already on full display, clustered across different parts of the States but with a notable preponderance in Florida. Orlando, specifically. Highlighted, a cluster where three of his assumed BFFs reside. Their model is good; one of the NSA kids had come up with a nice way to map the navy buddies and weigh them according to years served together and mentions of joint action in the military files in order to reveal which of them Ray is likeliest to reach out to. His top pick: Petty Officer First Class Scooter McIlleney, retired.

Cross-referenced with all this are the times his wife's cell phone googled "Florida retirement homes" at those very moments when her gym log showed her to be in an Aquafit class. Whoops. The Zero 1 team can now give a probability of 73 percent that Ray will catch a train or a bus—most likely a bus—to the Sunshine State at some point in week 1 of the operation and so advise that they move the Capture Team up from Chicago now, ready to move on short notice to the train and bus stations in Milwaukee as soon as the facial and gait recognition algorithms throw up a fit. The gait analysis is already scanning every side street, road, shop, and sidewalk. The traffic cameras they "own" already. On top of this, some bright spark has slaved in the collision alert cameras from the rear ends of post-2016 cars. The algorithm tears through the firehose glut of video data, swallowing up the crowd and discarding the strider, the tiptoer, the shuffler, the back curver (likely an office worker), the power pumper (clearly a soccer mom).

Cy is being a good boss, saying affirmative things, enough to make their little faces glow. Then *ping*.

Gait recognition has a suspect. Milwaukee Central Bus Station. Taken ninety minutes earlier.

Cy returns to his office, watches as his team members hit their stride, assembling imagery from various sources that, in almost no time, place Ray Johnson on the 9:35 bus to Orlando via Nashville. They're scheduled to stop for a comfort break and refuel just before Nashville in seven hours. Teams are scrambled.

FOR THE ZERO 1 TEAM, tasked with prioritizing Ray Johnson until his capture, the hours pass with mounting sports-level excitement. When it's time, Cy comes to the wall of his office to look down at Ray, on-screen, in glorious HD color, disembarking the bus, stretching his old bones. The other teams also draw around to silently cheer on this looming capture.

A café right by the station has its security cameras on Wi-Fi for the convenience of the managers, who want to keep an eye on the staff when they're not there. The footage is shared with a number of interested parties, which results in a nice discount for the purchaser, and a very convenient data set for insurers, food manufacturers, and customer behavior analysts eager to refine their up-selling techniques, not to mention the security apparatus of the United States. The nation thanks you, Cornbread Cafe.

Fusion Central watches Ray settle into a booth, scoot his butt around to get comfy, and then treat himself to Nashville's best hot chicken.

"Shall we pick him up now?" Erika asks Cy.

"Wait. I like this guy. Wait."

The waitress pings Ray's order by Bluetooth to the kitchen and thus, at the same time, to Ray's gang of recording angels back in Washington. Ray's not worrying about his cholesterol this evening. Hot chicken, fries, *and* apple pie with whipped cream *and* ice cream with chocolate sauce and a walnut sprinkle—a far cry from the salad-and-baked-fish diet he gets at home, according to his wife's debit cards. This order gets a round of applause from the Fusion team. Everybody's liking this guy.

"Now?" asks Erika.

Cy still shakes his head. "Let the man eat."

Erika smiles. It's moments like this that remind her why she loves Cy. She tries to file the certainty away for the next time she feels in need of it.

27 DAYS, 17 HOURS

CORNBREAD CAFE, NASHVILLE, TENNESSEE

RAY GETS TO ENJOY HIS dessert. He has savored his last spoonful and scraped the bowl clean. A minute later it's Benson, leader of the Tennessee squad, who enters the diner to let the old guy know he's a busted flush. Just sits down opposite him in the booth, flashes his badge.

"Good evening, Mr. Johnson. How was the chicken?"

Ray, captured on Benson's bodycam for the folks back home, doesn't look shocked. In fact, he nods, half expecting it.

"How'd ya find me? I paid cash."

Benson laughs. "You did great."

"Was I hard to find?"

"Not bad."

"Not the first one ya caught, though, am I?"

"Well, second."

"Fuck. Okay. What can you do?"

"Not a lot, sir."

"So it's over, then?"

"Pretty much."

The waitress offers Ray coffee, but he shakes his head. He pulls a napkin from the dispenser, one of those vintage Coca-Cola ones, and wipes his fingers carefully. \

"So what happens now?"

"We'll get you back home." Benson then holds his hand to his earpiece.

He has a question coming in. "One question, sir, from the head office. We'd like to vet our predictions about your future behavior. Were you planning to stay in Orlando during the exercise?"

"More or less the plan, yeah. Got good old friends down there."

"We know."

"Course you do."

A simple bit of paperwork on Benson's iPad asks Ray to affirm he has been caught and to honor the NDA. Ray makes his mark with great care, the digital pen slippery and unfamiliar in a hand used to real ink, real paper. Then he clears his throat and looks at Benson, his eyes full of rheumy appeal.

"I've got a question for you too, son. Do we . . . do we have to tell my wife this little exercise is over?"

27 DAYS, 13 HOURS

UTICA, NEW YORK

"PASSENGERS FOR UTICA, PASSENGERS FOR Utica!" The driver's mike crackles and fuzzes, and is answered by a variety of responses from the waking passengers: resigned groans from those who have arrived at their destination, resentful yawns from those with hours of stale air and dull fluorescent lights and hard seats still to go.

The woman in seat 14A rolls her shoulders. It's four hours since she left Boston. She hasn't slept. Mostly just phased in and out of a semiconscious state tinted blue by the lights of other people's screens, head against the cold window, eyes strafed by passing headlights. She's read about the effects of too much adrenaline in the human body. It's not good. It sends a fight-or-flight boost to the heart and head; a million years ago it would have gotten a hunter-gatherer up a tree, out of the crocodile-infested river, out of the tiger's mouth, or away from the bigger human with the bigger stick, but it's triggered again and again inside the modern human for hours and days at a time by the *buzz* and *zing* of your phone. The steady pump of cortisone and dopamine eventually corrodes your joints, fizzing out the connections in your overwired brain until things swell and eventually snap.

Score triple points if your answer to the following question is yes: Are you currently being actively hunted by a joint initiative of a social media titan and the most powerful and well-resourced government on the planet?

But it's worth it, right? she asks herself. Again and again. Yes, it is worth it. It's the only thing she can do. A few years off her life expectancy? So what? Her brain going smudged and confused a bit earlier than her contemporaries? Fine. Her heart weary and worn out slightly before its time? Whatever. It's a steep price, sure, but what exactly will more time benefit her if she doesn't do this? Who needs more of the kind of life she's been living? Her life needs exploding. Well, here she is, living in the smithereens.

She checks her watch. She's eleven hours into her third day of Go Zero, so time for the next stage of the plan.

As she watches the first of her fellow passengers disembark, she opens the backpack at her feet, and takes out her cell phone. She reinserts the battery and switches on the device, and the little screen lights up. In a couple of seconds it finds a strong signal. She's back on the grid.

27 DAYS, 11 HOURS

VOLTA PLACE NW, GEORGETOWN, WASHINGTON, DC

THE ALERT BUZZES SOFTLY ON Cy's watch at 1:00 a.m., so he sleeps right through the news that a Capture Team has been mobilized, following receipt of a ping from Zero 10's phone somewhere in upstate New York. At 5:00 he wakes, checks, sees it, grunts. Kaitlyn? Kaitlyn? he thinks. Oh, *that* Kaitlyn.

Rolls out of bed, pushing away the one-thousand-thread-count chemical-free sheets that come with the luxury rental (pool, garden, gym, home theater) that WorldShare has taken for him in DC Erika sleeps on, elegantly, discreetly. He stretches, touches his toes, prepares his body for the day ahead. Erika says what he really needs each morning is someone to turn the mechanical key that protrudes from his back and must be wound very tightly if he is to perform the challenging daily task of being Cy Baxter.

He turns to look at her. He likes to examine her while she sleeps. She is Instagram-ready even in repose, hair in soft waves, clasped hands pillowing her cheek as if in prayer. Sometimes it's a little too like *Town & Country* magazine. He seldom doubts that he loves her. Is he doubting it now? No, he does not. They are immensely well matched, soul mates even. Their sex, rarer of course than it used to be, is still good. Laughter comes easy. But his commitment phobia remains, a briar between them. Souls need not always marry in the legal sense, he argues. Why can't souls just do Monday, Wednesday, and Saturday nights? Besides, love is way down on his list of priorities; 90 percent of his fulfillment comes from his work. And so, except for the marriage thing, they're good, and in lieu of that he can at least give her the best sheets on earth.

By the time he emerges from the shower, steamed, scented, and medicated, and gets himself dressed in pressed, coordinated, subtle, unassuming luxury—the Capture Team has eyes on the bus Zero 10 is riding. The team members have planned to intercept it at the next scheduled stop, in the next ten minutes. Wonderful. Perfect. Splendid. He's glad she made it to the third day. Still, probably good to get her out of the way; a librarian at large for too long isn't the best look.

Cy summons the car and relaxes into the cool, richly upholstered back seat. He sets the massage function to work on knots no shower or stretch can reach and begins to mentally plan his next, glowing, progress report to Burt Walker.

But, by the time he enters Fusion Central, he's told there's a problem: they don't have Zero 10 after all.

The librarian was not on the bus. The Capture Team waiting at the bus stop found her phone stuck between the seats, left behind, clearly intentionally, so as to mislead them. Zero 10 might in fact have gotten off at Utica, or at any earlier point on the journey. Further analysis of CCTV footage of every drop-off on the route is inconclusive. The driver has no clear recollection of this passenger or her departure. It was late, the bus was full, he never does headcounts. "It's not a school bus, buddy."

"Trick a twelve-year-old could have pulled," Cy tells the woebegone group he assembles in his first-floor office. They stand. He sits, scrutinizing the faces of the Zero 10 team. They look like what they are—people who spent the small hours learning bad news in poisonous little drips and now fear for their futures. They have disappointed him. They know it. They *feel* it. And, honestly, he wants them to feel it. To sweat the moment. Usually everyone wants to catch Cy's eye, get an extra nod, an extra moment of connection, but not today. No one wants to look at him.

"Okay," he sighs. "What else?"

"We missed something," Zack Bass, the Zero 10 team leader, offers. "Yesterday. Back in Boston. After pulling the historical tracking data on Kaitlyn Day's phone over the last six weeks, and then cross-referencing it with the store's CCTV footage and cash receipts, we now believe that she . . . well, that she purchased at least eight different phones in three different shops in downtown Boston. They are actually registered online with slightly misspelled versions of her name." She clears her throat. "Seven of the phones are live, moving, scattered. One is dead. Battery out."

Cy stands up now. The benefits of his morning shower, the careful dressing and perfuming, the massage in the car on the way in here all fall away a little, his nerves suddenly exposed. Not that he is yet finished being amused by the resourcefulness of this librarian—she's really very clever—but what he doesn't like at any time is sloppiness on his end. He feels his anger rising a little, and sees a value in showing it to this team at this early point.

"Okay. So. The second she disappeared into the subway, you should have assumed she is smarter than you had previously factored. All the information you now have about the extra phones should have been gathered yesterday afternoon. Yesterday. *Afternoon.*"

He turns his back on them theatrically, making them feel his displeasure, intentionally letting them squirm while he concentrates of the natural miracle of a beautiful sequoia forest growing up the far wall of his office in perfect colors at a resolution of 1,200 pixels an inch. Finally, he turns back to face them.

"Who is this woman? This is a simple question. Here at Fusion, we need to be able to ask ourselves this question *and*, faster than ever before in human history, *answer it*. That's what we're doing here. That's it. Nothing more. That's your job. *Who is this person?* Yes? Good. Now, which of you has any ideas? Let's go. Talk to me. Someone." He waits, looking at one fearful face then the next. "Nobody? Okay. Relax. Everyone just relax. Simple one to start: *What is she up to?*"

"Jerking our chain." A woman's voice.

He puts his eyes on her. She's new.

"What's your name?" Cy asks.

"Sonia Duvall."

"So?"

Sonia is pretty. Twenty-seven'ish. East Coast private-school type. Ninety-five pounds of ambition wrapped around a fine-boned frame and, he assumes, an ice-cold heart.

She continues: "She didn't want us to find those phones right away, but she *does* want us to connect them to her once we get our shit together. Hence the misspellings."

"Okay. What else?"

Zack Bass, mustache like a bar code, wants to offer something valuable, but he's dry.

Sonia beats him to it: "I, uh, I went through all of the CharlieCards used in a one-hour period through downtown from the moment Zero 10 left the cab."

All Zack can do is sneer, and try to shoot this down: "Why would she use a registered card?"

Cy looks at this soon-to-be-*not* team leader–that shuts him right up–then returns his attention to Sonia. "Go on."

"She wouldn't. But I thought I might see something that the algorithm would miss. And I did. Find it, I mean. A card that went through the barriers at Downtown Crossing three minutes after we lost her was registered in the name of . . ."

"Of?"

"Of . . . Cy Baxter, and the associated email account is . . ."

"What?" Cy asks.

"CyBaxterknowswhereyouare at gmail.com."

Fifteen seconds of silence. Fifteen long seconds. Cy is trying to process this bit of news. And then he smiles. The librarian is playing with him. Toying with him. Fucking with him. "You don't say."

Sonia pipes up again. "So this woman is obviously clever. And cheeky."

Her tone has a note of admiration in it, a tone Cy can no longer summon as his brain stutters, freezes for a moment: such a thing hardly ever happens. The mechanical key in his back, Erika's joke, could evidently use a small turn. He nods at Sonia. "The phones she bought, where are they?"

Sonia looks to a teammate who has this information.

"Five are in the Boston area," the teammate says, glancing down at the tablet he's holding. "One is switched off, no battery. One has been in New York since last Friday, one is in the UK, in Central London. Whoever is carrying that one, we suspect unwittingly, went to *The Lion King: The*

Musical last night and is currently in the . . . in the Egyptian Gallery of the British Museum, actually." He pauses. "Looking at the statue of Thoth, the god of writing."

"How splendid. Conclusion?"

Sonia is the only one brave enough to risk an answer. "I suspect she's been surreptitiously planting these phones in other people's bags so as to create a diversionary data cloud."

"And she is . . . where?"

"I assume she is in the same place as the one phone with no battery," Sonia replies. "Keeping one for emergencies, we think."

Cy taps his fingers on the desk. His brain is finding its rhythm again. "First prize to Sonia! So, it seems we've got a joker in the pack. Good for her. And good for the selection panel. I wondered why she was chosen. Clearly, they knew something, saw something. Anyway, this is what we wanted. Right? So let's double our efforts on this one. Have we got her apartment scanned and logged?"

"We have," Sonia says.

"I'd like to inspect it. Ready the VR. As to these dummy phones of hers, split up the teams to gather them. Interrogate the London lead for clues, a prior relationship to our Zero. Let's calm the landscape. In short, in *short*, just do your fucking jobs. Oh, and, Sonia . . ."

"Yes?"

"Good work."

Sonia glows.

27 DAYS, 5 HOURS

SHREVEPORT, LOUISIANA

SUDDEN SINGLEHOOD AT HIS AGE was like zero gravity. Freddie Daniels, Zero 4, forty-six, formerly handsome—his face showed the beatings he'd taken—felt giddy, floating, corned-beef-brained. That's when the mistakes at work began, costly ones. His partners at his construction company urged him to take serious time off. He did. Spent weeks just watching TV, getting fed up about this, that, and the other, but it did him no good. Then an FBI buddy mentioned this weird thing to him: Fusion, Going Zero—three million bucks if he takes on the forces of the "deep state" and lies low for thirty days. Thought, Fuck it, how hard can that be?

The idea for this hideout came from a movie. Can't remember the title, but he liked it. About a lone rebel socking it to the system. Had Denzel in it, maybe. Or that other dude, what's-his-name, who was in . . . Ah, fuck it, doesn't matter. Anyway, as soon as he read the official letter confirming that he'd been selected, he knew what he was gonna do. Got the lumber in, the paint and plaster, took a chance. When the Go Zero text dropped he was ready.

Day 1 had been exciting. It was a Superbowl-level thrill hearing the Capture Team moving around the house, little fragments of their conversation, while he sat there, inches away and completely invisible behind the fake wall on wheels he'd drawn in on himself like the stone door on a sepulcher before power-screwing it all to the floor with, like, five hundred screws. Had repainted the whole room before that so the new paint didn't stand out against old stuff. The wheels averted leaving scratch marks on the floor. Pretty much thought of everything. And with each passing hour he grew in confidence, figured, Look, if they haven't cottoned on by now, they're not gonna. So it's just a waiting game.

He'd never done time, but he'd heard enough stories about what it was like to be cooped up. He was prepared. Strict regime of exercise and activities in a super-confined space. Photos of family and friends stuck up on the walls. Three fresh sketch pads and an old AM radio with headphones for silence. Day 3 now, and he was hanging in there. Mostly. Canned food for his rations. Fruit and juices and thirty cans of beer in his mini fridge. Peeing into old juice bottles, crapping in a portable toilet he got a beer buddy to pick up at BigShopper. Evenings his radio whispers to him as he cracks open a celebratory can. Cheers to three million bucks.

One hundred grand per day—the thought of the prize was keeping him going. The money, the money, the money. Every evening, at beer time, he'd run through what he was going to do with it. Go back to Janey, ask her to give him another try. Maybe take some cash to her in a suitcase and say, "That's your half, baby." Make pledges. No more drinking. Two vacations a year guaranteed. If all else fails, even agree to IVF like she always wanted. Give her two kids, even though he dreads the idea. Also, the wedding she'd always wanted, which first time around he'd denied her, opting for a courthouse rush job followed by a backyard party at her parents' place, fairy lights hanging off the clothesline, barbecue and ice cream. This time she'd have the dress, he'd wear the suit, they'd do it at a hotel, eat tiny snacks, drink champagne, and a real photographer, not Janey's cousin, whose shots were off-kilter. And the rest? After the honeymoon a big-ass new house, a better van. Business cards thick as toast and a receptionist maybe to make his bookings on a computer, send out the invoices, call him "Mr. Daniels" rather than him doing every blessed thing himself.

VOICES.

He must've dozed off. He hadn't heard the front door open, but now there are two men talking, close by. He holds his breath at times like these, makes sure the toilet lid is shut tight, the mini fridge off, killing its soft hum.

"Looks empty to me." A deep voice, like that one actor.

"Yeah, that's confirmed." The second voice is higher, sounds younger, almost prepubescent. "Something's been drawing that electric, though . . ."

Freddie, in the dark, touches the mini fridge. It was already a big mistake to have agreed to that smart meter. Still, he jerry-rigged power into this cubby so that they'll never find his tap-in point. He was careful—but maybe no more cold beers from now on.

"Okay," the other guy says.

Long pause. Freddie's heart rate picks up.

Voices.

Deep voice: "Yeah, I got something here."

Higher voice: "Tell me. Show me."

Freddie in the dark: What?

"If you generate a 3D model from the pic of him and his wife with the Christmas tree, and then compare *that* room to the laser scan the capture guys did of this room, we got . . ."

"Right."

". . . different dimensions, here."

High voice whistles. "A big disparity."

"See?"

"Big."

"We're talking, what, eight feet difference."

Freddie, hearing all this, thinks: You sons of bitches.

The voices come right up to his dummy wall, press against it, talking, close, close . . .

Deep voice: "Mr. Daniels? You in there? Mr. Daniels?"

Ah, shit. The voice sounds so close it's like the fucking guy is sitting in Freddie's lap. But Freddie's not answering. Not giving up. What if he says nothing?

"Mr. Daniels? If you're in there, listen to me. You can surrender to me or we can break down this wall. Your choice. Mr. Daniels? Can you hear me?"

Nope, Freddie's still not talking.

"Okay. We'll just have to break down this wall, then. Your call, Mr.

Daniels."

High voice: "I'm phoning this in, Chester. Set up a perimeter. How 'bout you do a thermal scan first, make sure if he's back there."

"Oh, he's back there."

Freddie hunkers, racked ed with regret. This was sure a shit option, should never have gone for it. At the very least shoulda built an escape route, a hatch through the floor for just this situation, coulda scrambled under the house right now, got away, not just sit there like some chambered fool waiting for a sledgehammer to make ingress.

A few minutes later, more voices, new voices, and one of these warns him: "Mr. Daniels? Keep your head down and your eyes covered, we're coming in."

26 DAYS, 18 HOURS

FUSION CENTRAL, WASHINGTON, DC

PING.

Cy shifts his laptop aside to touch the glass desk: Magically, it becomes opaque, then a map of the United States, then more than that.

Los Angeles is flashing red, red, red . . .

He taps the desktop, scrolls, and selects. They have only just closed Zero 4, and now a possible hit on Zero 3, Maria Chan, a former student activist from Hong Kong recently granted asylum in America. That's a cool choice. A professional challenge, given her years of avoiding arrest. This young woman will know all there is about leaving her regular cell phone at home, taking a burner instead, swapping SIM cards, never re-using handsets since each has a unique international mobile equipment identity number that is traceable; also switching among different VPNs—virtual private networks, which can mask a user's location—and paying with cash or untraceable prepaid credit cards, with voice calls made only as a last resort.

Cy thinks it's far too early for someone this savvy to have slipped up. Why had Maria been spotted so soon? He learns that all her devices went dead at midday on Go Zero, as you'd expect, but the Zero 3 team mapped her friendship network and identified a guy she'd been spending time with in the last months in L.A. whose phone went offline *at the exact same time*. If the two were really buddying up, it meant good news for any spy network; two suspects meant twice the likelihood of a slipup. Guy should have left his own phone on, thinks Cy, but it's hard to think of everything.

The teams then went after this guy's friend network. When three of them met in a Koreatown Starbucks, Fusion was listening, the loose-tongued conversation recorded by a specialist from across the street via a new sonic technology that, when aimed like a laser pointer at a certain object, say a plastic coffee cup (such as the one right then being used for a Frappuccino with extra cream), miraculously turns said object into a veritable microphone. Language-translating software provided a transcript of a hushed but excited chat that gave up details of Maria's get-lost plans and confirmed that she was working with the male accomplice. Fusion tracked the boy's vehicle through the L.A. traffic cams: how he had driven as far as San Bernadino and parked.

Cy speaks into his headset: "Do we have eyes?"

Lakshmi, ex-FBI, is on this: "L.A. surveillance drone is airborne."

In due course Cy receives on his desk poor but real-time images of the vast green swath of the San Manuel reservation. "She have friends there?"

The answer: "Our other subject's brother-in-law flies a light plane, general aviation, out of San Bernardino. He's just filed a flight plan for Seattle."

"So she's making for the airport?"

"We predict so, sir."

"Call me Cy." Government people are so uptight.

"Appears so, Cy."

The map before him plots a three-mile radius around Maria's position, showing, at its limits, San Bernadino Airport.

Cy: "Action report?"

Told: "We have notified airport security, detained the pilot, and im-pounded the plane."

"Great job." Cy rises and goes to his glass wall, looks down on the teams and the big screen, which reveals, in extraordinary detail, the facts of Maria's secret life, present and past, an intimate and animated record not even she could have assembled, all being dissected, pored over, ana-lyzed. What a fearsome weapon they have built here, Cy reflects, its po-tential barely tapped thus far. He gets the dangers better than anyone: a life opened up, akin to open-heart surgery, he thinks, the breastbone cut, the ribs spread, the living raw contents laid bare, to then be itemized, analyzed, manhandled. But whatever the sense of indecent trespass, he knows—*knows*—it is offset by the greater moral good they are endeavoring to do here. Were the world gentler, then perhaps what they are doing would be wrong. But the world is less gentle all the time, the evidence everywhere, and so up to the elbows the surgeon must be prepared to plunge his arms into the blood and maw. If they do not, the patient sickens and dies.

In his headset he hears, "Medusa visuals up now," and the right-hand side of the giant screen refreshes into a high-altitude but crystal-clear image of houses, playing fields, a creek, until the screen flickers as the camera zooms in and refocuses, flickers again, zooms in and refocuses, and Cy is staring down from twenty thousand feet on the image of a man and woman, running along a dried-up riverbed. The super drone whose development his investor pool had funded at huge cost is replete with multiple cameras and exceptional optical engineering, and so able to prove a perfect close-up of Maria Chan and her partner, while still keeping an eye on the surrounding fifteen square miles.

"Sound," requests Cy.

With this, the innocent blue water bottle in Maria's sweaty hand becomes—courtesy of a laser on high—a sonic spy.

Clearly audible, the heavy breathing of Maria Chan, almost her heartbeat. *Incredible.* Even the briefest exchange.

Male voice: "Okay?"

Female voice: "Yeah."

Cy smiles and exits his office, goes to the handrail, looks down on all the society-improving activity below. "How long till intercept?"

"Twenty minutes. They'll be waiting for her at the airport gates."

Just like that, he thinks. Surveillance at its very best. And American-style, not the blanket capture-everything-everywhere-anytime Chinese model, in which if you simply try to download WhatsApp, travel abroad too regularly, grow a beard, exit by the back door, or attend a mosque too often, then an algorithm will see you arrested and send you to join a million other miscreants at a "reeducation" camp in Xinjiang to help you "concentrate." No, no: In America, vast technology such as this will be deployed *only* as the need arises, always respectful of a citizen's right to privacy until a clearly offensive action by said citizen strips them of that right, as in the case that haunts Cy, and will always haunt Cy—*the* case that, in many ways, has spawned all this. Love you, Michael, he thinks. Love you, bro . . .

Looks at the clock counting down. Three days gone, three Zeros down, seven to go. And then? Brave new world, baby. Brave new world.

26 DAYS, 16 HOURS

MOOSE RIVER PLAINS, NEW YORK

AS THE SUN SETS ON her fourth successful day at large—at which point she is forced to admit to herself that she half expected to have slipped up by now—Zero 10 is absolutely sure of only one thing: that despite following all the instructions, damn well putting pole A into slot B, the dull green fabric of her tent still sags. She sits down on a foil-lined tartan picnic blanket and stares at the sad contraption until she realizes that, for a whole minute there, she wasn't actually thinking at all.

The woods are so quiet, she knows she would hear the fizzing hum of a drone above her, or the growl of an engine cresting the tree line, even the tread of a hiker long before they actually spot her here, off the beaten track. She's wild-camping. Two miles away from where she dumped the little trail bike she'd picked up in Utica. She was tempted to keep it, the neat little machine, like riding an angry hornet over the trails. But she's a million miles now from Keyes Pancake House, in Old Forge, where she ate her last real breakfast. No more pancakes for a long while for Kaitlyn Day.

The lockbox she left here in a brush pile a month ago hasn't been tampered with, so she's got the survival tent, and her rations (freeze-dried macaroni and vitamins), along with water purification tablets for the stream half a mile away and down the slope from her campsite. Also, a copy of *Anna Karenina*. It's a shame about the bugs. She pulls out her notebook from the pocket of her coat. More of a scrapbook than a notebook: her brain dump. Somewhere in the back is tucked the leaflet explaining the easy setup of the tent.

She reads it again, rolls her eyes when she sees that the colors of the flanges between pole type 1 and pole type 2 are different. She closes the notepad, sets it on the blanket next to her, and begins to get up, when she hears a voice—louder than normal—in her head: *What are the rules?* the voice says. (The voice is male. Clear. Not unfriendly.) *Come on, what are the rules?* She picks up the notebook and replies out loud, "Always carry the notebook. Always carry the cash. Fire at night. Heat pack during the day. Stay nowhere more than three nights."

Why?

"Noticed on day one, wondered about on day two, reported on day three."

Can a voice in your head nod? Yes, if the voice in hers belongs to Warren. *Concentrate, baby. Or you'll never make it even halfway. Maintain vigilance.*

"Okay."

Attagirl!

The notebook goes in the thigh pocket of her combat pants, and she returns to the titanic struggle of woman versus tent pole.

It goes up in the end, but the ground is hard and it turns out that chemically reheated mac and cheese does not sit right with her innards.

SHE WAKES IN GRAY HALF-LIGHT, her exhaustion doubled by a restless night. "I've gotten soft," she says aloud. If feels like someone has swapped her body with that of an eighty-year-old grandma. A grandma who'd been out drinking. She gives up trying to sleep further. Sits up in her sleeping bag with haystack hair.

Now that it's light outside, she goes through a couple of outdoor-survival magazines she picked up at the bus station, makes some notes, finishes her water. Thinks of the bookshelves back in Boston. Complete works of Hemingway. Decides she doesn't like Hemingway; the guy made all this woodsy, in-the-wilds, "Big Two-Hearted River" stuff sound romantic. All this uppin'-and-leavin', the all-American story. Fuck him. And thank you, Jesus, for the industrial revolution. All hail the internal combustion engine. In this moment she worships clever Michael Faraday and the emancipation of central heating, washing machines, coffee percolators. Home delivery? Uber! Grubhub! Praise be, praise be!

But she must be disciplined.

I know, Warren, I know. I can hear your deep voice, your gentle reprimand and advice, to stay disciplined, slow down to the speed of nature, to be one with the damn thing, as we are all just slightly more than sophisticated beasts in our deepest nature. What was that fancy Latin thing you used to tell me? Ah yes, I remember now: *Homo homini lupus est.* Man is wolf to man. And so true, baby, we *are* wolves to one another, and wolves ourselves, which explains why you are not with me right now. You were beset by predatory, cruel creatures who treated you with a disregard actually below that of an animal. Be alive, baby, be alive.

And with that her thoughts return to the present: How will she spend this day? And the next? And the next? What will she do? What will she do with her mind, her wild thoughts?

The answer, the only sensible one: Nothing. Nothing at all, if she can. Eat, drink, sleep, wash, pee, maybe dig a little latrine. Today, what her plan requires, and what she is determined to deliver on, is a whole lotta nothing.

24 DAYS, 17 HOURS

FUSION CENTRAL, WASHINGTON, DC

AT 5:00 P.M., THEY CALL him into the VR suite again. Wrist sensors are crunched into place, headset lowers like a diving mask. As the system tracks Cy's eyeballs, a spiral of pinprick lights syncs them with the software, and *boom*, like stepping into a painting on the wall, he's in a book-lined apartment.

He looks around him. So this is how a Boston librarian lives. Another overstuffed sofa with a tartan throw over it. Cy wanders to the window. Notes the view: Beyond the window and the fire escape, the rain is beginning to fall, graying out the eastern skies.

"Cozy," a voice behind him says.

Erika has joined the session. The VR program, in response to her presence in the scene, has drawn an approximation of her body mass next to Cy in a person-shaped cloud of blue dots. It means they can point to things in the apartment if they feel the urge, and won't walk into each other back in Fusion Central, which is the easiest way to feel like a total loser while playing on your personal eight-million-dollar holodeck.

Cy nearly expects to feel the damp Boston chill in the air and has to remind himself he is inside a digital reproduction. He walks into the kitchenette area. Mismatched junk-shop china in the drying rack. A cereal bowl, a coffee cup.

"Do you think she washed up as soon as she ate," Erika asks, "or cleared up when she got the Go alert? That would make her one cool customer, no hint of panic or urgency."

"She was ready to go when the alert came," Cy says dismissively.

Classic Erika, thinks Cy, the person who knows me best in this world, and is trying now to warm me up, after I lost my shit a little over the phones fiasco. How she knows, also, the best treatments for my maladies, senses my condition and is ever on hand to address it. Bless this good woman.

Cy walks ghostlike through a wall. His body is getting used to this, and his subconscious's instinctive panicked squawks about striding through solid objects at a nose-crushing pace recede into a mild grumble and a jerk on the amygdala. The bed is neat: patchwork cover, squares of rosebuds and gingham. Thus far, a woman who lives alone, and has done so for a long time. Kaitlyn probably made the bedspread herself; the uneven stitching looks amateur. A trendy artisanal type, cheap clothing and organic everything, insistent on making things herself, badly and expensively (possibly wastefully)—smocks, skirts, endless knitted bunting, beeswax candles—and it reminds him, with a jolt, of his own mother's efforts to get by on a shoestring, the sole breadwinner driven to similar remedies, not to save the planet or her own health, but to survive and raise a son. Nothing fashionable in his mother's handiwork and homemaking, and yet, from a pauper's home where the electricity might or might not flow when you turned on the light switch, a creature like himself emerges. Extraordinary. Love you, Mom.

Cy blinks. Tries to stop himself going off on a typical mental detour. Walks back through the wall into the main room, where Erika's blue cloud is studying the shelves, full of books in several languages: Baudelaire in the original, Virgil in Latin, travel guides in several tongues. This place, he thinks, is actually right up Erika's alley. She still finds the time—even though she's at least as busy as he is—to read fiction. Her side table is always piled high with novels, earmarked and only fractionally read before yet more books arrive, ordered online. He often jokes that she'd have done better to have invested in Amazon than in WorldShare, but it is a weak joke; her net worth puts her twenty-eighth on the *Forbes* "Richest Self-Made Women" list.

Where odd bits of wall space have escaped the clutter of books, they are filled with art posters in midrange frames. Great overblown flowers in cluttered pastels, thick forests with cartoonish tigers peering through the foliage. That painting of a pipe, with *Ceci n'est pas une pipe* written underneath it. Such bullshit. Surrealists annoy him almost as much as crafters. This part of Cy's character, the twitchy, impatient, quick-tempered and sharp-tongued side of him, can slip out of his control when he is superpressurized. In these rare moments, there is nothing his PR people, or even Erika, can do. It's as if something else takes over, some vengeful inner child compelled to settle some historic wrong. He feels an impulse to shout from some rooftop "Get real! Get real!" matched by a desire to do harm, to wreck what has been carefully wrought—and it's difficult to find the kill switch within himself sometimes. But he knows, also, that it's ever more important that he find it, that he gain mastery of these destructive moods, especially now that they exert an actual force on the markets. On any given day, if Wall Street got wind that he was losing it, misbehaving, or just feeling a little off, WorldShare could shed ten to twenty points before the final bell. His moods have a verifiable economic impact. Hell, they are *insurable*.

But more than that, he's mindful that the security of the country is also now vulnerable to his moods, and the CIA is also aware, and so is the NSA and the military and to some degree Congress. He lives his life under klieg lights, monitored closely, but still he finds it hard to realize the consequence of his own importance. He must now keep a lid on these moods of his, not just to protect his share prices, but for the good of the country, *literally*, because the trouble is—and here's the fatal flaw in his master plan—just as he *is* WorldShare, he *is* now Fusion. Without him, it all goes away. For all the sophistication of the network, its myriad unprecedented capabilities that he has meticulously built, there is a bug in the system, a known bug, and that bug is himself.

"Cy?" Her voice cautious. She clearly knows he's gone off somewhere.

"Sorry, babe. I just . . . It's so important we get this right." He not only needs this woman but also knows he will never *not* need her. "I know I'm getting kinda uptight. I just need it to work."

"It will work, Cy. It is working."

"You still believe we can do this, right?"

"I do, Cy. Yes. Absolutely."

He appreciates this. "I don't want anyone else to go through what . . .

what *we* went through," he says. The blue cluster of her hand approaches, and he feels the touch of it in the real world, the haptic sensation of actual Erika. "This is Michael's legacy."

Her voice catches slightly as she replies, "I know it is, Cy."

"I couldn't do it without you," he says.

"I'm not going anywhere. You know that." She drops to a deeper pitch when she is moved.

The walls, even the virtual walls in this place, press in claustrophobically on Cy. You can't do this VR shit for long. You get nauseous. He's got to get out of here soon, but he isn't done yet.

The TV is smaller than a laptop, has an actual wire antenna. No cable. A record player. Jazz records. Of course Kaitlyn listens to jazz. The place is dirty.

Physically not even really here, Cy is responding nonetheless. He wants to cough, his skin itches, he wants to put on gloves, wear a mask.

"Tell me about her. Tell me everything."

24 DAYS, 16 HOURS

MOOSE RIVER PLAINS, NEW YORK

AFTER TWO DAYS OF CAMPING, she's run out of drinking water. No biggie, she planned for this.

She tries to move around, to thaw the stiffness in her bones after her third night of sleep on too-hard ground. She crouch-crawls out of the tent, into the sun-seeping sky, then sets off through the leaf mulch, making for the stream, empty water bottle in hand.

The silence is beginning to freak her out. The lonesomeness of the wilds is a challenge. She skitter-slides down the hill to the creek, then crouches at water's edge, washes her hands, and feels the fierce grip of the cold water wake her up a little. By the cupped handful she splashes her face with the purest H_2O she ever saw. Thinks of another trip long ago, with Warren.

He was not a camper, either. Oh, he always *said* he loved the outdoors, and it was true he was up for a little hiking, a little night swimming, but what he enjoyed most on their trips was retreating to the cabin at night, the open fire, the bottle of scotch, the fur rug. A little touch of luxury when they had the cash.

But don't think like that, she tells herself. Focus. She lifts her head and looks around. The trees are thick with spring growth. No sign of sun yet. She fills the bottle and drops in a water purification tablet, shakes it, then starts her journey back to her camp. All this quiet makes her head buzz, a kind of tinnitus. Or is it her own blood talking to her? Her own heart? Tough place to be, in her state of mind, but what more can she do? A prison-sentence countdown of days, hours, minutes . . . Maybe she should have just headed for Las Vegas and caught a show. No, no. *Discipline*, lady. Get back to camp, get a grip, make a schedule—she likes a schedule: when to eat, to sleep, to exercise, read, light her camp stove, cook, wash her pots, her clothes, sleep, sleep if she can. This idea of a routine gives her a bit of lift, fills in a few of the blanks, reduces the psychological threat level. She must marshal the mind and keep things in order if she is to win.

Reaching the top of the incline, she follows the trail of her own footsteps in the mulch back toward her camp. Transecting her path are the earlier tracks of dirt bikes. She apparently shares these woods not only with squirrels and deer, birds, and battalions of insects but also with teenage joyriders who recreate in these pathless backwoods.

Be aware, she reminds herself. Be careful. She must not allow anyone a sighting of her. Leaving behind the dirt bike tracks, she soon walks where only she has been. She says aloud, "'Two roads diverged in a yellow wood / And sorry I could not travel both / And be one traveler . . .'" Ah, she used to know that whole poem. But her choosing, of all the options, "the one less traveled by," that's the point. And yeah, she's on that road for sure. For now, at any rate. And that is what she's thinking—I'm safe here, I'm safe—at the exact moment the world disappears.

Wham. Lights out. Thereafter, all is black.

24 DAYS, 16 HOURS

FUSION CENTRAL, WASHINGTON, DC

"PUBLIC LIBRARIAN," ERIKA BEGINS HER digest to Cy. "Been living in this apartment five years. It's rent-controlled. She's had some mental health issues." Her loose blue form moves toward the bookshelves. "Big fan of detective fiction and thrillers, as you can see . . . Probably where she got the phone idea from. But currently reading *Anna Karenina*."

"How can you tell?"

"She has it on loan, but it's not in her house, so we assume she is carrying it with her."

"Why would she bring a book?"

"For pleasure, we assume."

"Let's get an analysis of the book. Find out what it might inspire her to do."

"Throw herself under a train?"

"What?"

"Anna throws herself under a train. In the book. At the end. I read it a couple years ago, remember?"

"What happens before then?"

"She leaves her husband for her lover."

"Does Kaitlyn have a lover?"

"Not that we know about."

"Back to the mental health issues."

"Diagnosed with bipolar disorder in her late teens, hospitalized twice.

On and off her meds ever since. She turned up barefoot at the airport a year ago complaining she'd lost her plane ticket and saying that the president was in her apartment. Looks like she is off her pills again now. Last prescription was filled six months ago. Supply was for four weeks."

"I thought they were supposed to weed out the crazies?"

"By design, the selection team chose a wide variety of types. Maybe they felt we need to be ready for crazy. Our enemies will occasionally be on the crazy side."

Cy shrugs. "You're right." He surveys the librarian's book-choked shelves. You'd think she'd get enough of books during the day. He sees lots of orange and green covers, burred with age; paperback editions of classic British and American novels; and the sort of wrist-breaking Russian numbers he occasionally name-checks in those "What I'm Reading" listicles but never has actually read. Spines all cracked and roughened. Cy, by contrast, busy as he is, time-compromised, listens to his books—strictly nonfiction—in digested versions at 1.5 speed while he's working out. Way more efficient, and he gets the gist.

The VR re-creation here is perfect. You almost believe you could reach out and pick one up and turn the pages.

"What else?"

Cy walks through the sofa again, looking for family photos, anything they can reverse-image-search for people, places. Nothing. Just more art postcards. The room has been data mined, of course. The books cataloged, the prints identified, anything to thicken their files on Kaitlyn the renegade bookworm.

"She's crazy smart," Erika says. "We have her school records, college transcripts. Her IQ is off the charts, which is probably the reason she was ultimately selected."

Cy nods. This makes more sense. She's a savant. But then why the hell does such a genius waste her time in a library?

The Zero 10 team has new information they are ready to pipe through to Erika. "Cy, the FBI is just now with one of the carriers of Kaitlyn's decoy phones. They can VR it for us. Want to jump into it?"

"This is who?"

"A woman who agreed to take one of the eight burner phones. Knows

Kaitlyn."

"Sure. Pull it up."

And with this, holographically, Kaitlyn's Boston friend, name of Wendy Hammerback, in a shiver of pixels and haloed in her own secondary location, digitally enters this primary simulation, a window of a world within a world. Wendy looks flustered and worried she's done something wrong. Maybe forty years old, is fishing around in her handbag. Her hair is curly, streaked with gray, half crushed down under a woolen cap in rainbow colors.

"Yes," she is saying as the arresting agent (whose bodycam provides these live images) flips his FBI badge into view. "Kaitlyn gave it to me a couple of weeks ago. She just asked if I could keep it with me for her. Play a game of Candy Crush or take a photo from time to time. She said someone might turn up and take it from me."

"That didn't strike you as strange?" the unseen agent asks.

The woman laughs, rich and throaty, making her seem instantly younger.

"Of course, it was strange, but Kaitlyn *is* strange!" She shakes her head. "I mean, she's lovely. Looked after my kids every other day when my husband was going through chemo. And not just sticking them in front of a screen, either. She taught them how to cook lasagna, took them camping in the backyard. She loves that sort of stuff. But she has weird ideas. Like"—she looks a bit embarrassed—"there was that whole White House thing."

"You let this woman look after your kids?"

Wendy bristles now; her brow furrows, and she looks straight at the man in the body cam. Shoulders back. Her data appears on the screen: married, two kids, architect. Lots of pictures on WorldShare of her at protest marches.

"She was stable, took her meds. Frankly, sir, plenty of people believe some pretty strange things. Look, Kaitlyn asked me to do her a simple favor. I was happy to do it."

"Ma'am," the agent says after a pause, "your phone records indicate you haven't been in touch with Ms. Day recently. Have you seen her in person?"

"No. She hasn't been at the library in a couple of weeks. And how come you have my phone records? I didn't allow that."

The data will soon confirm that half of the protest groups that Wendy is aligned with meet at Kaitlyn's library.

"If we could just take the phone Ms. Day gave you, ma'am. It's part of a Homeland Security operation."

Wendy holds out the phone, but when the agent puts his meaty paw on it, she doesn't let go.

"Sir, I want you to understand that I'm giving you this phone because Kaitlyn told me to hand it over to anyone who asked me for it. Otherwise, I'd need to see a warrant. When she asked me to hold on to it, I worried of course that she was having an episode, so I made a note to keep an eye on her. Every time I've spoken to her since, she's been fine." Her eyes drift down till she is looking directly into the agent's body camera, at Cy, at Erika, at the kids in the Void who are watching along on the big screen. "And now here you are with a badge and a camera and my phone records, so it seems to me Kaitlyn wasn't being that paranoid after all."

Cy has seen enough. He disconnects the feed. "The other decoy phones? Who has those?"

"No live images, but I can give you the details."

"Let's see it."

Again, in the air, the information appears. He reads the short digest on several of the other phone holders. They are either friends or neighbors or else met Kaitlyn through a book club she runs or a social action group that meets at the library. Similar story with the holder of the phone that wound up in London. Cy drags through the data. *They* connect with one another all over the place, live crossing, multiple points of intersection, whether the library or their WorldShare pages, PTA groups, chat groups, Twitter, Instagram. But Kaitlyn is on none of these platforms. She herself is nowhere. A life lived in the real world. How very strange to see.

24 DAYS, 15 HOURS

MOOSE RIVER PLAINS, NEW YORK

COLD. COLDNESS AND SHADOWS. SHE'S dreaming. Then a klaxon blare of pain. A shuddering scream of it tears her into full white-bright consciousness. What the fucking fuck? Where am I and what in the name of all that's holy is happening? She forces herself to take deep breaths until the pain and the first wave of panic subside a little.

I am Kaitlyn Day. I am hiding in the woods.

I am Kaitlyn Day. I am hiding in the woods.

It actually helps.

She has something in her eyes. She blinks, rubs them. Her brain takes forever to come up with any explanation of where she is, and when it does, she doesn't like it very much. She's in a hole. A deep hole. Literally. She groans and shifts her weight, and the pain rockets up her leg from her ankle and Fourth of July fireworks blaze behind her eyes.

"Now you're screwed" they spell out in sparkles.

Just look at it, babe, that voice in her head says to her. Firmly.

Her imagination spins images of gushing arteries and a splintered femur sticking through skin. No. She wouldn't be conscious if that had happened.

Just look.

She does. She bends forward from her waist and pulls up the leg of her combat pants. No white flash of bone, no dark stain of blood. Just skin red and angry, and it's beginning to puff up. Okay. Danger of death in the next ten minutes through blood loss: minimal. Unless she's landed on a spike and hasn't noticed yet. That can happen.

Now, why is she in a hole and what sort of a hole is it? Very carefully, she gets to her feet, pressing against the earth walls and trying not to put any weight on her bad ankle. The hole has been made by a human, no doubt—it seems to be brick lined, like a cellar or an icehouse.

What the hell?

The area is roughly ten feet in diameter, like a chimney. She vaguely recalls a mention of an old mine when she was researching these woods. Nature's been at work since the miners left, apparently, roots searching and shoving their way through the walls, and a good number of the bricks they displaced scattered across the bottom. She looks up.

She takes a step forward and her ankle makes her hiss, but the first shock of the pain has worn off at least. The air is damp and cold. Smells of compost. Part of the side wall has slumped and caved opposite from where she fell, blocking the way into the rest of the mine. No problem. She's not here to spelunk. She knocks against something in the shadow at her feet, maybe a foot from where she landed. It's a welded net of rusting metal. Right. It's the grill they put over the top of the chimney to stop, I don't know, maybe paranoid librarians on the run from a government/Big Tech partnership from falling down it. She thinks of some guy mortaring it into place and sauntering off thinking his job well done, and not for one second pondering the action of water and time rusting the joints away till their nice safety measure turns into a perfect trap for whoever inadvertently trusted her weight to the mesh of twisted steel.

Christ, if she had landed on that! She shudders, examines the walls again and the circle of gray light at the top. Can she climb the broken brickwork? She reaches into her pocket for her water bottle. Nothing there. She checks her other pockets, panic sweat beginning to gather at the back of her neck. Nothing. She looks up again and shields her eyes. It's there, just hanging over the edge of the chimney. Okay. Okay. No problem. Just climb out of the hole, woman. All will be well; this is just a glitch. She puts her good foot into a crack between the bricks, reaches with her right hand, pulls herself up. Both bricks pop out of the earth wall as soon as they feel her weight. Nothing is holding them in place but habit. She slips, stumbles, plops back on her behind. The breath is knocked out of her; then she stops breathing entirely. Her hand is half an inch from the twisted metal spike of the grill. Half an inch from blood loss, gangrene, lockjaw. She closes her eyes. Job number one: That thing has got to go.

THREE TIMES SHE TRIES TO climb, three times she falls back, pleads for help from the silence. Her throat is raw, her head pounds. Then she almost brains herself throwing rocks at the water bottle high above in the attempt to knock it down to join her. Doesn't work. It occurs to her that she might die here. Be found only months, even years, later.

"I'm so sorry, honey," she says to the blank walls of her living grave. And maybe it's exhaustion or fear, or she's gone woozy after that last fall, but she swears it's Warren's actual voice that speaks back to her.

It's okay, babe. Save your strength. This may take a while.

He used her name only when she'd done something to really piss him off. The rest of the time that one syllable, stressed to be funny, chiding, loving, passionate, surprised, mildly exasperated, pleading, enquiring.

She takes the phone out of her pocket. And the battery. Looks up one last time in case there's a last-minute, million-to-one miracle, a fox with a rope ladder between its teeth, a blackbird trailing a golden thread, some fairy-tale creature to help her out of this goblin pit. But it's not a goblin pit. And it's not a fairy-tale woodland.

"I've failed you."

Do what you need to survive. Don't worry about me.

She sighs, like she can feel the weight of his hand, comforting, on her shoulder. She knows what she must do now. Give up. It's over. Her tears come. It's over. Say it again . . .

It's over.

It's over.

It's over.

And with the acknowledgment that survival now is her primary problem, she is about to click the battery into place and switch the phone on.

BUT SHE HESITATES. SHE RESISTS Warren in her head, has a little debate with him.

And so begins two *more* hours of rock throwing and six more increasingly futile attempts to climb out, all of which leave her weaker and more frustrated.

In the end, she is rapid in her insertion of the battery into the phone, doing it fast so that she doesn't change her mind again, doing it as if someone else were doing it for her.

Snap. There. It's done. The phone is turned on. In her palm, she stares at it. The screen glows, and the low note of its waking sounds like a death knell. Then. Nothing. No signal. She stares for a moment in disbelief, then starts to laugh. No signal down here. Of course. All that drama and debate, and the fucking thing is dead. No signal! Of course there is no signal. No signal. No way to be caught, which also means no way to be *found*. She is lost to the world. A zero. For all intents and purposes, she's won the game.

IN THE END, OF COURSE, there's only one thing left to try, and you don't have to be Monsieur Dupin to figure it out.

She struggles to her feet, her back pressed to the wall, her sprained ankle sending thunderbolts up her spine until she settles into an agonizing position that will at least allow her to fully swing her right arm. Calms herself. Prepares. Height of chimney? About fifteen feet. More or less. She can do it. Must do it. Has a reasonable throwing arm. If she fails, then she fails.

First time: not even close. The phone sails only halfway up, slaps the clay walls, falls back. She thankfully manages to catch it. So try again. You can do it. You must do it.

Second time, better: It rises almost all the way up, but the angle is bad and it bounces off the wall just below the lip, the rebound sending it dancing and slipping out of her outstretched hands, into the mud. Has she broken it? It's facedown, lying there like a little body. She wipes off the mulch, her fingers shaking. Still glowing, it's alive.

Her third attempt is not as good as the second. Huge pain in her leg by now. Fuck. Feel like crying. Her arms already feel like overcooked spaghetti. There will soon come a point when she'll weaken. The next few attempts will be her last, best chances. A fourth attempt, nope. Please God. A fifth, better. A sixth, worse. The sky grows darker. And each time she thinks she's going to shatter her phone, kill off this last hope. Getting the right angle and the distance necessary to clear the hole and settle aboveground is just so damn tough, so little room for error, and she risks smashing the phone against the walls each time. At least she had some practice throwing rocks in vain at the water bottle. The muscles in her arms are twitching and burning, and her heart has started beating faster. She doesn't believe in God. Not really. Not like she did as a kid. No more than she believes in foxes with rope ladders, but she prays anyway. And throws again. This time, it doesn't come back down.

It didn't come back down, she repeats in her head. She doesn't trust the thought at first. She checks the mud at her feet with her hands. Feels in the dark, the wet loam between her fingers. It's not there. No, it's up there *somewhere*. Has it cleared the hole or has it simply found a little ledge halfway up, nestled there, about to fall back on her head any moment? So she will surely be driven crazy before she dies of thirst and starvation. Finally, she screams. A scream, sent up and out of the well into a sky that suddenly relents as heavy clouds part and allow a column of silvery moonlight to penetrate a third of the way into her tomb, making visible—balanced on the edge of the rim—the metallic glint of her phone. There it sits, on the rim of the well, her last tenuous, teetering lifeline. Is she saved? There is no way to answer. *If* the phone is not damaged and *if* it has found a signal, there is now at least a chance that her hunters will soon come.

24 DAYS, 7 HOURS

PHOENIX, ARIZONA

CATHERINE SAWYERS, ZERO 6, IS pissed. Someone should've told her. They'd told her lots of other things: how having a career as a police officer would screw with having a family; how once you make lieutenant you effectively become a politician; how being a woman meant she'd have to be 3.5 times as effective as any man of the same rank, even while everyone acted like she only got the stripes to make the mayor look good. They'd even warned her that the pay sucked. Got that part right.

No one told her, though, that a day would arrive when the universe flipped a switch and you went from bright, ambitious up-and-comer to old, bitter has-been, floundering through your forties, up to your eyeballs in car payments and property taxes, wondering if every time you break a sweat it is a sign of early menopause and the crest of a downhill slide into obsolescence. Also, they had forgotten to mention that as the world got grayer and more complicated, and as getting the containers out on trash day felt more and more as solid an achievement as her best arrests, that some of the felons and bad guys she'd taken down in Alhambra would end up living in nice suburban mansions in Paradise Valley with landscaped yards and brand-new SUVs in the driveway. Just like this one. Justice? Where? *Where?*

For five days George Rivera had kept her waiting, saying he wanted to consider her proposal—which broke down as an even one million dollars of her prize money in exchange for hiding her for thirty days. He kept her waiting, watching crappy TV in a by-the-hour hotel off the I-17, sweating and fighting the ice machine, before the text message came in on her burner phone.

"Come by," he instructed. "Anytime."

Asshole.

So here she is, an hour later. George Rivera's house has a decorative pool out front. And a flagpole flying Old Glory. The pool is surrounded by pink and red flowers. Here are the fruits of criminality.

Catherine rings the doorbell and waits. Inside she can hear George shushing a yapping dog, and when he opens the door, he's holding it in his arms. It's a white bundle of fluff with vicious black eyes. Reminds Catherine of her former sister-in-law.

"Lieutenant. Welcome to my home."

She steps inside, wipes her Timberlands on a mat marked WELCOME and follows him across a pink marble hallway into an open-plan kitchen with views of the back gardens. More decorative planting. There's a fire pit in the patio area and a pool beyond it.

George sets the dog on the floor, and it skitters off into the interior of the house. He pours her lemonade from a jug in the fridge.

It's delicious.

"Who says crime doesn't pay, right?"

"Lieutenant, I thank the Lord every day that, despite my early misdemeanors, I've been able to use my entrepreneurial talents to the best of my abilities so as to provide my family the American dream."

Drugs, in other words. And stolen cars. Then, after he got out, strip clubs and bars, then construction and charity work, seats at Symphony Hall and two kids in private schools. Catherine finishes her lemonade.

Stop being surly, she tells herself. You need him. "So do we have a deal?"

He half shrugs, gets up on a bar stool, leans his elbows on his granite island top. His shirt is brilliant white with a thin red stripe. She joins him there, takes a stool, places her mobile phone on the countertop. His eyes fall on it.

"Obviously, I wouldn't do anything illegal, Ms. Sawyer," he says. "But in light of our long relationship, and with your assurance that this secret 'project' you're involved with is for the national good, then yes, I'm ready to hear your proposition."

"Not because of the million dollars?"

He laughs. "Well, there is that. Like I said, I'm an entrepreneur." He pulls her cell phone toward him. "And this is?"

"A burner. Just picked it up. I know what I'm doing. Emergencies only," she replied.

"Lesson number one. Criminal to cop."

She notes the dismissive look in his eyes, telling her that he deems her an amateur in this realm.

"It's not *your* phone that's the problem, it's whoever you *call*."

His looks say he expects her to acknowledge this criminal tutorial, and she obliges with a nod.

He continues: "They're into *all* your contacts' phones. All of 'em. Get rid of it. You're in my world now. Take it from me, they're bugging every motherfucker you ever met."

"You and I never met."

"Oh, you were with me every day, officer. Every day for seven years."

A vengeful look in his eyes, one she expected but still doesn't appreciate. Seven years served for a car theft operation across eight states. More than six hundred cars by the end. Even after she began to suspect George, it took her four years to figure out how he was doing it and to pin it on him. Toughest case she ever had to crack. For the longest time just couldn't work out the scam, until finally she did. A scam in two parts. The first part of the racket, any decent criminal mind could think of—renting cars from rental car companies, then switching the plates and selling these hot vehicles to unsuspecting private cash buyers on the secondhand car market. But it was the second part—*that* was special, and allowed his larceny to go undetected for so long—marking George out as a dark genius. After completing the first half of this scam, he'd steal the *same* cars back from their new private owners—grabbing them from driveways and garages—then switching back to the *original* plates and returning the cars to the rental car company before the rental period had even expired! Rental car company? Witless and happy. Private owners and cops left scratching their heads, for who would think that these missing cars would be rightly slumbering among the fleets at Hertz or Avis? That was good. That was *wow*.

"Lesson number two," he tells her as he pours her a coffee from a glass pot, pushes it over. "Think. Think like your opponent will think, and then think different. They don't see it, because they can't. We all think in patterns. Go outside that pattern, and you can stay off the radar."

As much as she resents his superior tone, this is the reason why she is here, why she has chosen him, why she has come to face this man she incarcerated: he knows as few do how to evade detection.

"One million dollars?" he confirms.

"In cash. That's forty large a day. That's one new SUV every day. A new pool every three."

"Just to hide you?"

"Right."

"You in trouble?"

"I wouldn't say that, no."

Finally, he shrugs. "Fine. Your money. But you better do exactly as I say."

"Or what, you put a sack over my head?"

"Now? First, finish your coffee. I've enlisted some help. Friends of mine."

"Okay. When do I meet these friends? Where they gonna hide me?"

"You'll see." Prepared, he takes out a paisley bandana from his pocket. "Actually, you won't. Put this on. Lesson three. Where you're going you can't know. These guys, they're superstitious, have good reason to be. By the way, how'd ya drive here? Rental? Jesus."

She holds up her hand to decline the bandana. "No way. Fuck you. And I borrowed a car."

"From a friend?"

Catherine is about to say no, but thinks better of it. "Distant. Very distant."

He shakes his head, unimpressed. "Call yourself a cop? This is sloppy, Catherine."

"Relax. I haven't spoken to this individual in twenty years."

"Then how'd you get the fuckin' car?"

"I followed her home. Then stole it."

"You stole it? You said you borrowed it."

"I stole it. So we have no live connection. No trail."

"But you're driving a stolen car?"

"I changed the plates. Lesson number one. So there's no trail."

"There's always a trail. Always. Prisons are full of people who think they never left a trail. Put it on. Or no deal."

She waits till he shrugs and gives her a look that makes it plain there is no other way. Only then does she relent and tie the blindfold over her eyes.

"Tight," he instructs.

She tightens, then knots. All light is cut out.

"Good," she hears him say, in the sudden moment before she feels her two hands jerked back and lashed together by what she guesses is a zip tie, this move happening before she can stop him. Annoyed, she struggles to free herself. "No, no, no. No way. I need my hands. Let me go. What the fuck is this? George?"

"How's it feel? To get cuffed. "'Cept I was more gentle. You guys had me facedown on the road, with my kids watching, one boot on my back, with a gun to my temple. You remember that? You remember that, Catherine?"

"Take it easy, George. And cut these ties. Or we have no deal."

"In front of my children. I asked you to put me in the patrol car nice and easy for my kids' sake, and I'd go peacefully."

"What is this, George?"

"I did some research."

"George?"

"You bring *me* to the attention of the feds, after what I've done to turn my back on all that, would you? I have a daughter at Juilliard!"

"George. I'm offering you a million dollars."

"Forty K a day, right? Actually no, I worked it out, that would come to forty dollars a day . . . for every day I spent in the can and not with my kids. Not so much."

"George, stealing cars was your idea."

"Forty dollars a day, Catherine. So you can walk away with *two million*?"

Before she can try to rescue the deal, Catherine hears the sound of large vehicles approaching and slowing.

"You were never gonna make it," he tells her. "You lack the criminal mind, if I may be so bold. This shit is not your thing. And for the record, I don't get outta bed for a million dollars anymore."

"You ratted me out?"

"No. They saw this coming. They called me before you did. Said some algo-rhythm *predicted* this. Fuck knows. And there you were, thinking I'd be the *last* person on the list they'd think of? Well, that isn't good enough anymore, clearly. These days you can't be on the list *at all*. But I was glad actually, nice to finally meet you, face to face. Seven years, long time."

Catherine hears knocks at the door now, voices.

"You look great, by the way," he adds. "Boy, it's been good to catch up."

24 DAYS, 5 HOURS

MOOSE RIVER PLAINS, NEW YORK

THE NIGHT IS COLDER, DARKER, than anything she's ever experienced, and she's seen some doozies. At some point she wakes, parched and disorientated, in the dawn. Do-or-die time. She breathes deeply, lets the bubble of panic in her chest burst and disappear. The phone is still up there, but it must have no signal or someone would have appeared by now, so she's back to square one.

Empties out her pockets. Has her notebook, money, a honey-and-oat bar, and a survival bracelet. The bracelet had been a last-minute purchase. She'd seen a pile of them all in fluorescent colors in a box by the register when she was getting the camping gear and added it to her heap of purchases with no more than a nanosecond of thought. Ten dollars. She hadn't even read the pamphlet about it, just stuck it in her pocket at Go Zero, then forgot.

She pulls it apart. A length of colored rope; a fishing wire and hooks in a steel envelope the size of a postage stamp; a stubby little key thing, which she reckons is for starting fires if you don't have the nice box of waterproof matches sitting in a lockbox; a small sheet of polythene, rolled and twisted through the core of the rope wrap; and a razor-sharp scraper. She sits back and thinks. The rope is too cheap and short to get her out of here. The fish hook too small for grappling. The razor blade? Well, that's one way out. But first, water.

She follows the walls, looking for damp places, then turns miner, digging into the earth with the scraper until she finds a spot where the water starts pooling in the dirt. She fashions a channel through the muck, directs the drips into a pool built of the fallen bricks, and lines it with the plastic sheet.

As the water starts to collect, she can't look at anything else. When it's an inch deep, she bends down and drinks. It tastes of compost. It tastes of surviving another day. Tastes of a thwarted life. Once she's done watching, waiting, and drinking three times, she realizes she can think again of things outside this hole. Thinks of Warren. The fate of untold suffering millions. The woes of the world that usually embroil Kaitlyn Day. Boston spinster. Librarian and super-intelligent nutcase. These worries have shrunk and, following the laws of perspective, fallen into line, to be obscured behind the imperatives of water, air, food, of drawing another breath, outlasting the day. She eats half the oat bar. Thinks back on the trail she walked to the river. Those tire tracks. The makers of those tracks. Screaming hasn't worked. Listening for any human sound hasn't worked. The phone didn't work. She doesn't have a carrier pigeon or a talking drum. Smoke signals?

Perhaps not such a crazy idea. In absence of a better one, she saws off roots with the razor blade, uses pages from the notebook as kindling. After two hours and shaking with exhaustion, she has a first low flame. The smoke comes off in great bursts, making her cough and retch, but she can see the smoke doing what she cannot: helixing upward, going where she cannot go. This is her job now, for as long as she can do it, to keep this fire going. I am woman. Keeper of the flame. She drinks more. Eats the rest of the bar.

MORNING. DAY 7. THREE OF them spent here. In hell. Shaking with cold, with dehydration, hunger. She has scratched, prisoner-like, the mark of these days onto a stone. A record and diary for when they find her, *if* they find her

There's a whine in her ears. She struggles to decipher it. Is it just the noise of the next part of her shutting down? No. As it comes closer, she remembers the thing that makes such a sound—the first industrial sound she's heard since she fell down here, *dirt bikes*—and so stands, shouts for help, shouts for all she's worth. Loud as she can. If it's her hunters, that's okay, too, she thinks. She pauses, listens, hears one, then two off-road bikes roar shrilly through the forest and pass near the entrance to the well. Then gone. The whine falls to a simper, trails into silence. This departure is crushing.

But then a third engine grows in volume, a straggler, even louder than the others this time. Comes close and, instead of passing by, the engine coughs and then assumes an idle.

Kaitlyn shouts, "Help!"

Finally, a teenage head over the rim of the well, a helmeted youth: "The fuck?"

22 DAYS, 5 HOURS

CARTHAGE, NEW YORK

"HI? CAN YOU HEAR ME? Can you tell me your name, dear?"

Half opens her eyes. She is in a small hospital room with a concerned-looking woman in her fifties. It all comes back: the man with the harness descending like a God (she doesn't remember mumbling "You're nicer than a fox" before collapsing against him); topside, remembering to turn off the phone, take out the battery, thank God no signal up there, either; then riding in the ambulance to Carthage, people asking her name. She neglected to provide it, like she'd lost her tongue, like a cat got it.

"Where am I?"

"You're in the hospital, honey."

"Where?"

"In Carthage. Now my turn. Need a name."

"How long have I been here?"

"All night. We want to move you up to a ward as soon as we can. Just need to sort out the paperwork."

The woman talking to her is wearing flowered scrubs and carrying an iPad, or something like it. Kaitlyn only now sees that she is hooked up to an IV. Saline, glucose. She's sore, but she's not in the hole. Spies her clothes hanging over the chair.

"Hurts."

"You dinged up your ankle, got some cuts and bruises, but nothing's broken."

"Yeah. Feels like . . ." She tries to move it, finds, with a wince, she can. "Like . . . the ATF."

"ATF?"

"Anterior talofibular ligament."

"Huh," says the nurse. "Well, we've been giving you fluids, cleaning you up. Your bits and pieces are in the locker. That's a lot of cash to be carrying, isn't it?"

"For a camper van I want." That was a line she came up with a long time ago.

"Uh-huh. But you'll tell me if I should call some other services."

"No."

"You need help with something, honey?"

"No."

"Sure about that now?"

"Uh-huh. They . . . they need to seal up those old shafts, though."

The nurse's finger hovers over the pad. "So, about that name?"

Her bones feel loose, like marzipan. Her eyes are heavy and her thoughts fall slowly. It's like watching the water drip from the earth walls again.

"Not from around here, are you?"

"On vacation."

Nurse nods. Waits. Beyond patient.

It's on the tip of her tongue: Kaitlyn Day. Just say it. You can be back in the apartment in Boston before bedtime. "O . . . K."

"Okay what?"

"O-apostrophe-K-E-E-F-F-E. O'Keeffe."

"O'Keeffe. That's your last name?"

"Right."

"What's your first name?"

Kaitlyn's eyes are on two crutches resting against the wall.

22 DAYS, 4 HOURS

FUSION CENTRAL, WASHINGTON, DC

A WEEK COMPOSED OF THE broken rhythms of this beta testing phase, tempests and doldrums, successes and frustrations, is taxing Cy's nerves. Perhaps it's simply the level of sustained engagement required, his own deep excitement at seeing all his tech finally deployed in a real-world scenario, like being enmeshed in a movie thriller of seven days' duration that just doesn't let up: car chase following artful evasion following sweet human moment following dashing spectacle then car chase again—until, finally, even the kicks are exhausting.

He's used to periods of intense work—to days or weeks of little or no sleep, screens and energy drinks until the code suddenly resolves itself into something as beautiful as the geometry of an arachnid's web—but more recently he's used to working hard to close a deal and then lying victorious on a private beach: caffeine-free cocktails with sliced-fruit trims; personal chef providing gluten-free, meat-free meals; yoga; only occasional calls from ecstatic investors.

And Zero 10, now having gone completely dark, nothing new on her *for days* . . . As impressed as he remains, it's getting a bit much, isn't it? A librarian?

At least he is able to share this overall experience with Erika. Fusion is even more her baby than it is his. After what happened to Michael, how could it *not* be?

Cy first met Erika when Michael, his freshman roommate, invited him to the Coogans' home during a break at college. Was introduced to the family as Michael's new coding buddy. Cy was eighteen—awkward, pimple-dashed—Erika twenty-two. The three of them, thick as thieves after that, spent a ton of time as a unit, the boys just rude kids, she their protector and defender. In fact, she'd been covering for her little brother since he was four, when he broke their grandfather's CD player taking it apart to see how it worked. Seemed natural that she would look after these two digital dorks as they, in their rapacious desire to forge worlds out of nothing but numbers, forgot to eat or stressed out over flame wars in obscure chat rooms. Later, as it became clear they were actually creating valuable assets, her role was to make sure they understood copyright and intellectual property law. Together, in this way, the trio laid down the early beginnings of WorldShare. Unable to afford champagne, they opened beer on the occasion of a launch of their first website. Bottles clinked. Michael lit a joint. Each spoke of this just being the beginning. Erika cried with pride.

Then, at twenty-six, Michael was killed in a mass shooting in Flagstaff, Arizona—an event so horrific it fixed on the American mind like a barb for three weeks on account of the footage captured on people's phones. Not that you can see it online anymore: Cy made sure it got taken down and scrubbed. He remains vigilant about this still, has a search-and-erase code on constant patrol, so that Erika will never again (except in her nightmares) have to watch her fallen brother be resurrected, then die anew, and anew, and anew . . .

After the *first* killing in Flagstaff that day, twenty-three minutes went by before Michael was slain. Twenty-three full minutes—more than enough time for the rampage to have been cut short. His murderer had even documented his spree as he went, killing, posting, killing, posting. It took thirty minutes for the police to arrive at the scene and engage the shooter. Eleven lives were lost in that half hour, time in which, if the police had had better detection and anticipation capabilities, Michael might have been spared.

Under Fusion, Cy promised Erika, that kind of thing would be impossible. In the future that they'd build *together* that shooter would never be permitted a semiautomatic because he had an outstanding warrant for domestic abuse and even the gun laws on the books should have stopped him. His every move and purchase ought to have been tracked so that the illegal purchase set off alarm bells at once, as would his awful posts in the days before the shooting. Had Fusion existed, it could have saved Michael's life—Cy is certain of that—as well as those of the others. After that, Fusion became a passion for Erika. She helped Cy conceive of it, kept Cy faithful to it, pushed Cy to prioritize it—in fact, her passion possibly now exceeds his.

"CY?" ERIKA'S VOICE IN HIS earpiece. "We have something."

"What is it?" Cy sits up, rousing from a catnap. Rubs eyes.

"A woman was picked up after a hiking accident in the Moose River Plains recreation area, New York. Gave her name as Georgia O'Keeffe. We think . . ."

Cy doesn't get it, and he hates it when he doesn't get it.

He lifts his head as images appear on his glass desk: they are the fat red flowers from the poster in Kaitlyn Day's apartment.

"The poster on Zero 10's wall," Erika says. "The artist's name . . ."

"Georgia O'Keeffe." Sounds a bit familiar, actually. "Well, look at you," he says as the image on his desk changes. "And this is?"

"A copy of the accident report from the local fire department, and now a livestream of two kids with dirt bikes talking about how they rescued a hiker who'd fallen into an old mine in the woods."

"And you think . . . ?"

"Just watch," Erika says.

As he looks down at his own desk, keywords pop up—*camping, woods, woman on her own*—highlighted and refined into watchwords—*solo, female, isolated area*. The screen then shows a location, seventy miles from the place they presume Zero 10 got off her bus. Cy watches the real-time efforts of Fusion, both staff and machines, put all this together. Then they receive a live link to the hospital CCTV.

Erika says, "Capture Team approaching the hospital now."

And with that, they are inside the same hospital that holds Kaitlyn Day.

22 DAYS, 3 HOURS

CARTHAGE, NEW YORK

THE NURSE, NAME OF TABITHA, leads the two Capture Team agents toward the closed curtain at a trot. She knew this poor woman was in some kinda trouble, just knew it. Tabitha, wearing new sneakers that squeak embarrassingly on the linoleum floor, clutches her tablet to her chest. A woman like that should have had insurance, she tells these strangers. Her clothes were good quality, and though her hair was unwashed and mussed up and smelled of woodsmoke, Tabitha still knew a salon cut and dye job when she saw it. She had just been discussing with the on-call resident nurse the possibility that O'Keeffe, Georgia, was on the run from an abusive partner when the agents turned up. She checks the electronic chart again. Dr. Travers had splinted the ankle (nasty sprain), ordered an overnight stay to monitor the patient for internal injury or concussion, and made sure she was properly rehydrated. Tabitha also noticed that she had turned down pain meds.

"I do hope she hasn't done anything wrong," Tabitha says, which doesn't get a rise out of them. She then leads the agents, slowly, to the patient's room. "She has been very polite. Just a little withdrawn."

Tabitha grips the edge of the privacy curtain, suddenly feeling anxious. Will Georgia scream, weep, embrace the agents as saviors? She pulls the cloth aside with the gusto of a stage magician.

The bed is empty. A hospital gown lies on top of the rumpled sheets and the IV line swings from the rehydration bag. Tabitha stares, then checks the personal locker next to the bed. The smoke-soaked clothes are gone. One of the agents flinches as if someone just yelled at him. The other starts issuing orders into his wrist mic. Tabitha hears words like *lockdown* and *full sweep*.

She calls to the other nurses: "Guys! Anyone seen my patient?"

They look up from their phones and screens. Shake their heads.

She turns to the lead agent. "I have to call security."

He looks at her like she's an idiot, then speaks to his colleague. "Team A will work out in a radial formation from the hospital. Dispatch Team B to the forest accident site and find her campsite."

He moves past Tabitha, not rudely, just acting like she isn't there, and holds his phone up to the water glass perched on the locker. The phone casts a pale green light over the plastic cup. It shines oddly, making Tabitha blink. When it clicks off, the agent studies the screen for a second, then speaks into his wrist again.

"Fingerprint is a match."

21 DAYS, 18 HOURS

VOLTA PLACE NW, GEORGETOWN, WASHINGTON, DC

AT ERIKA'S SUGGESTION, CY AGREES to leave Fusion for a few hours to "refresh and refocus." (When she uses her no-nonsense voice, he usually does as he's told.) He's too engaged, she instructs him, needs to dial it back a little, can't possibly keep this up for thirty days. She reminds him, also, that *he's* not one of the hunted, on the run. It's only they (and Fusion itself) who must never sleep. And one other thing: She wants him to know that she loves seeing this level of excitement in him. Really. It's been a while—quite a while in fact—since he's shown this much passion and focus, and it means a great deal to her that it should be this monument to Michael that has elicited it.

Moved, he finds he can only say, "Don't mention it." Squeezes her hand.

When he gets home, he plays tennis. Alone. Facing the *fut-fut* of the machine spitting out balls imbued with spin, he rips his returns to nobody. This is how everyone should play tennis: not giving a fuck if your ball is in or out, throwing every ounce of your pent-up energy at the fluffy yellow orbs and sending them ricocheting off the netting or the back fence like high-velocity rounds.

Forehand! Four Zeros down, six to go.

Backhand! Zero 10. What is it about this woman that fascinates me? The sheer improbability of her?

Forehand! Librarian 30, Fusion love.

Backhand! Two hours. The time it took for my brain trust to scour every security camera for images of the librarian in Carthage using her gait analysis from Boston before some bright spark realized, hey, maybe the fact she's just injured her ankle and stolen a crutch might make that approach just a touch unreliable.

Smash! Ninety minutes for the Capture Team to find Zero 10's campsite and log the area for data. And all they found was a well-stocked backpack, a couple of magazines, evidence she'd eaten some de-hy mac and cheese, and proof that Kaitlyn was pretty shit at putting up tents. Well, *that* was ten billion well spent.

Forehand! Three and a half minutes. The amount of time it took me to explain to all the teams, at volume and at speed, they were no longer to underestimate the remaining civilian candidate, Kaitlyn Day, who was demonstrating exceptional resilience and resourcefulness. Mistakes were to be expected but must now be eliminated. He wanted better, more, faster. No one's position, including his, was permanent if the paymasters' expectations weren't met.

Backhand! Immeasurably short—the time between finishing this tirade and Erika telling me, with a resigned kiss on my cheek, to take a break, go home, and "refresh and refocus."

It is getting dark when Cy steps aside and lets the next half dozen balls bounce and stutter to a stop, unstruck. *Fut. Fut. Fut.* When he walks off and the court lights flicker on automatically, the machine continues its work alone, until it runs out of balls then sulks in the cool evening air.

21 DAYS, 16 HOURS

WRIGHT'S LANDING MARINA, LAKE STREET, OSWEGO, NEW YORK

AN OLD MAN IS FINISHING up his rituals at the dock as the last light fades. Coils ropes neatly on the deck of his wooden ketch and clicks the padlock into place on the hatch, resting his hand for a moment on the cabin roof before picking up his fuel canister and stepping onto the planked pontoon. His ketch, built in a shipyard on the shores of Lake Michigan in 1954, looks like a museum piece next to this year's speedboats and fiberglass yachts berthed alongside it, but he knows every true sailor who comes along pauses to drool over the varnished deck, the brass fittings, the lost craftsmanship.

He heads back toward the shed, his base of operations, where he hires boats of all kinds to weekend sailors and day trippers out of Syracuse. The summer is picking up, which means longer days, warmer weather. Tomorrow is Wednesday, and he should spend the day getting ready for the weekend boaters, but if it's a day like today—with a bright sun and a steady breeze—he might play hooky again, head out for scallops himself, drift on the tide, open some Chablis. A stroke of fortune like today's should be celebrated. He chuckles.

He is so lost in his plans that he doesn't notice the two men in black windbreakers and combat trousers till they are almost upon him. It's dusk now, porch lights coming on West Third Street, the sky pink and purple and gold, and the evening star sending out her first glimmers.

"Mr. Steinsvik? Lasse Steinsvik?" one says.

"Maybe."

The guy flashes a badge at Lasse; he catches a brief glimpse of a government insignia.

"Are you, or are you not, Lasse Steinsvik?"

Lasse sets down his fuel can. "What can I do for you?"

The man pulls a phone from his pocket and shows him a picture of a woman. She's smiling. Plain white background.

"Do you know this woman?"

Lasse rubs the side of his nose. Well, shit. "The paperwork on that boat is all in order. Back in my shop. Law says it needs to be filed within five working days. My wife does that, and she's at our daughter's till tomorrow evening. Anything else I can do for ya?"

21 DAYS, 14 HOURS

FUSION CENTRAL, WASHINGTON, DC

CY NOTICES THE SIDEWAYS GLANCES as he strides into Fusion Central, takes his Captain Kirk chair, puts on the headset, clocks the image up on the big screen.

"Fill me in," he says.

"Team spoke with this gentleman two hours ago," yet another of one of these young guys in chinos excitedly replies. "So we put eyes over Lake Ontario, with support from U.S. Coast Guard Section 9."

"And how did you find *him*?" Cy asks, looking at the picture on his screen of a frowning Lasse Steinsvik. "Those are some eyebrows."

The smart rookie, Sonia—the top-of-her-class gal who found out that Kaitlyn had been using a card in the name of Cy Baxter on the Boston subway—fields this one. "In the *Outside* magazine that the Capture Team found at Zero 10's campsite. A preponderance of fingerprints were on one page in the classifieds. We surmised that what drew her repeated interest on this page might figure in her forward plans. So we sent agents to all the businesses advertising there."

Cy nods, approvingly. "Good work. Well done." Then, as little starbursts of dopamine are released across this team as a result of some Cy encouragement, he asks: "So what now?"

The not-as-smart-as-Sonia-is chinos dude pipes up. "We have located a craft making for Canada and giving off no signature—no tracking, phones, or active devices, none. So our thermal imaging drone is staying with it.

The boat is going to cross the border and out of our ground force jurisdiction in seven minutes, sir. Do we need to loop in someone on Canada?"

No, Cy's look says. "Stay on her. We share airspace with Canada. How long till the drone makes contact?"

Chinos guy stutters. "B-but, Cy, um, clearances for our ground teams to get up there? Permissions?"

Cy bites his tongue and gives his best help-me-to-help-you look. "Did we tell the Pakistanis before we got bin Laden?"

"Uh . . ."

Cy pinches the bridge of his nose. "Look . . . What's your name?"

"Brad."

"Borders are over, Brad. Of the top one hundred richest financial entities in the world, forty-nine are nations and fifty-one are multinational corporations. Crossing a border is not only within the rules of this beta but is also a great test for real-world scenarios. Where Zeros go, we go. Get on it."

Three minutes later, the night-vision images start to come in from a pursuit helicopter crossing Lake Michigan from Buffalo. At the same time a ground team reaches the Canadian border. With Zero 10 now three minutes from the border, Cy's leg is already bouncing up and down.

"Ground team?"

"Coming up to the border right now," Sonia reports, weaving her way through the desks, tablet in hand. "Requests to pursue fugitive pre-issued to border posts."

Cy, tightening with tension, watches the blip of the boat nudging closer to the shore, while the helicopter closes up the distance between them and the Capture Team crosses into Canada and moves toward the probable landing site.

Cy's thoughts go to Kaitlyn Day. Admires her immensely. This woman fell down a *mineshaft* and kept going! Nearly in Canada, probably imagining herself the future winner of the prize money, a rich woman, she's still out there. And with all the mental health issues she's facing? On paper she ought to have been the first to be caught. Just goes to show: never judge a book lender by her cover. He almost wishes—were it possible—for both of them to win, both Kaitlyn and himself.

"Estimate Capture Team twenty-five minutes from predicted landing site," Sonia says. "Helicopter pursuit team, twelve minutes. Thermal imaging from the drone out of Langley, sir, online now. Image up."

And there she is. Her thermal image, a warm smudge in the dark between the cooling land and the cold water. All those in the room watch as she makes shore and secures the boat to a jetty. They note the awkwardness of her gait as she starts up the track, that sprained ankle. They feel her pain.

"Night vision," Cy orders. "Where is she going? Prediction map."

Leaving the thermal world, the screens fill with the world as seen by cats, images intensify, dim starlight suffices as the dawn light illuminates a figure moving through the dark toward the bright light of four structures.

"Likely making for one of those houses."

Images and facts pop up in the corners of the screens, the identities of the Canadian householders, their photos, everything about them. The hard border poses no problem as Fusion's database races now to find a Canadian connection to Kaitlyn Day.

But as the data cycles, without success, the subject's path veers away from the houses, reaches a bridge, crosses train tracks, heading north. It's obvious how slow she's going, how difficult movement is. The pulse on the map then also shows the helicopter and ground team, closing on her steadily, making predictions obsolete. The drama is intense, as in a nature documentary where a fawn grazes ignorantly while unseen wolves converge.

When the night vision loses Zero 10 under a tree line, thermal imaging takes over again. A broad section of woodland is crisscrossed with logging trails.

"Ground team on final approach," Sonia chirps as Cy's eye catches a blur.

"What's that?"

"What?" Sonia asks.

"On the road, look at the night vision. Half a mile up the track ahead of her." Cy points at the main screen. "Zoom in and resolve that image."

The picture on the main screen shatters and blurs, then refocuses. Shades of green. A vehicle. A car.

"Make and model," Sonia instructs, all the happy tones gone from her voice. "Get an angle on the registration plate."

"Mini Cooper 2005. Waiting on registration."

Zero 10 is hobbling closer to the car, but they can see the effort it's requiring, the slow, dragging struggle. It's even possible to pick out the glimmer of a metal crutch, an oversized medical boot clamping the right foot. Jesus. Two hundred yards.

"Tighten on that car and acquire it," Cy shouts. "Get into its onboard. Remote shutdown."

"Model is too old," Sonia reports. "There's no onboard system. No GPS. No LoJack. Car is off-grid."

Another team member: "Capture Team seven minutes from intercept."

All watch as the figure on the road pauses, turns (perhaps to listen), seems to hear something, then increases her pace to what must be an agonizing half jog. Flash, flash, flash of crutches.

On another screen, a partial of the license plate emerges.

Sonia: "Extrapolate the missing characters!"

And with this, like a padlock, characters on-screen spin through all the myriad possibilities until a single combination is found. Sonia: "Car is registered to Briony Parker of Boston, Massachusetts. Looks like she lives in Beacon Hill. Probable connection . . . Boston Public Library, regular user."

"Regular user," repeats Cy. "Good for her. Any overdue books?"

"And she visited Canada for a forty-eight-hour period three weeks ago."

All eyes watch as Zero 10 reaches this car, ducks down over a back wheel, presumably locates the hidden key, opens the door. Inside. Thermal shows the exhaust coughing heat.

"Three minutes to intercept."

"Don't lose her," Cy now shouts like a sports fan in double overtime. "What type of drone has Langley put up?"

"A Predator, sir."

"So it's armed?" When two dozen heads turn sharply to look at him, he adds, holding up a hand, "Just asking."

Erika enters the Void at that moment. Probably for the best she didn't hear that one.

"What else is on the Predator?"

"Laser."

The Mini bursts out of frame and under trees. The drone's camera reorients just in time to see it swerve at speed onto another side trail. Seconds later, the first Capture Team vehicle misses the same turn.

"Laser-tag her car," Cy barks. "Get real-time coordinates to the team. And tell them to learn to fucking drive."

Two minutes pass. Then three, then five minutes . . .

The drone's night vision is having to widen and widen its gaze to take in both the Mini and the pursuit vehicles as the car heads eastward on tracks the mapping software can't even see, before it bumps onto a gravel road heading north. The first ground team's SUV stops dead in the woods.

"What's happening?" Cy yells.

"Track too narrow for the vehicle."

"Predator locked on target."

"Cy, Zero 10 now only a mile, max, from Ontario 401," Sonia informs him. "Approaching the Highway of Heroes, 401."

"How . . . how busy is the 401?"

"Busiest highway in North America."

"So . . ."

She guesses where Cy is going with this thought: "Any kind of drone intervention will become impossible as her car is absorbed into intense traffic."

All jokes aside, Cy in this instant can imagine the thrill the military drone pilots must feel when, on a foreign mission, they are empowered to launch a rocket that will, from out of nowhere, streak through the air and erase, in a puff of onscreen smoke, an unsuspecting target, a threat, many lives. What a terrible power, godlike in the swiftness of its justice.

Cy's stern looks from the gantry are not encrypted and need no decoding to his staff as, on-screen, Kaitlyn's jalopy reaches the highway and joins the stream of lights.

Sonia: "Sir? Canadian Air Traffic Control. Seek reason for entering their controlled airspace."

Erika: "Cy?"

All eyes on Cy.

"Continue drone pursuit," he finally says.

More startled looks.

Sonia: "Deputy Director Walker on the line, also. Sir? Urgent."

"I'll call him back."

21 DAYS, 13 HOURS

HIGHWAY 401, ONTARIO, CANADA

HER DAMN HEART JUST WON'T slow down. From the moment she heard the approach of multiple vehicles, the idea has been hammering in her brain that she has failed, that she doesn't have either the strength or the strategy to go on. The orthopedic boot encasing her ankle kept her pain to a low throb as she trekked toward the car, but after her pathetic dash to reach it, her agony is threatening to make her black out.

Kaitlyn, she tells herself in an effort to distract from the pain, you are very, very lucky with your friends. Briony from the library was happy to lend her Mini Cooper for a month. Then, when asked if she would drive it to another country and leave it at these exact coordinates in the middle of absolutely nowhere, Briony said yes again. Keys hidden on the driver-side back wheel? Okay, Briony said, she'd make a weekend of it, driving up in convoy with her husband, then leaving the car and going off to do some sightseeing around Kawartha Lakes in his convertible. It's true that Kaitlyn had also just handed Briony an envelope of many crisp one-hundred-dollar bills. The total was more than the car was worth, plus enough to cover the hotel and the two bottles of good white wine Briony and her husband enjoyed over dinner at the Riverside Inn but still, Kaitlyn was indeed lucky in her friends.

Reaching the highway she loosens her grip on the wheel just a little and lets her muscle memory take over, frees her brain to analyze just how close her escape had been. Whatever technology is now under Fusion's control is frightening in its speed and reach. Personal information just too easy to get nowadays. Facebook and WorldShare and Google had enough of it. But facial recognition at the hospital? Had the nurse taken a picture of her to pin to her electronic medical record? Not that she could remember. The boat? There was nothing in Kaitlyn's apartment to make them think she was confident on the water. She concludes that the magazine, with its old-fashioned ad, must have been her mistake, leaving that magazine behind. Her plan all along had been to burn it. Now it might be her downfall.

She is tired, losing focus, and in pain. Human error is creeping in. And as she weakens, her rival stays strong, and perhaps—as it gathers information—grows stronger. The scales are tipping evermore in their favor. And yet three times, if you count the tease in Boston, she has outfoxed them, and that must be giving them second thoughts as well. The solution is clear: To compensate for her declining physical reserves, she must increase her resolve. The scarier it gets, the harder it gets, the more she has to believe she's doing the right thing. That way she still has a chance.

Her thoughts are scattered now by the dull beat of helicopter blades. She doesn't hesitate to conclude that the pilot is tracking her. She tightens her grip on the wheel. The *thwup-thwup-thwup* of the blades gets louder. Much louder. Then the spotlight hits her. She swerves, blinded for a moment by the glare, regains control. You cannot outrun a helicopter in a Mini Cooper. Fortunately, she has a plan. It's less than ten miles up 401 to the airport, according to the sign she's just passed. Fifteen miles. She presses down on the accelerator, and the Mini leaps forward like a puppy let off the leash. Okay, pup. Let's see what we can do, shall we?

Half a mile from the junction in Pelmo Park, disappearing beneath an underpass, Kaitlyn hits the brakes. She then swings across three lanes and into the hard shoulder, falling in tight beside a passenger bus in the slow lane. As bus and Mini and two other lanes of traffic emerge from the other side of the now-gridlocked underpass, she cleaves to the side of the bus, uses it to block the aerial view of her. Sees the helicopter, several hundred meters ahead of her farther down the road, its lights searching for her racing Mini. The hard shoulder is narrow. Fine for a Mini, not so fine for anything else. Roars up it, exits via the first off-ramp. Can hear the chopper still, but can't see it anymore.

FUSION CENTRAL, WASHINGTON, DC

Cy and the team watched on-screen, with mounting anguish, as Zero 10 made a fool of the Detroit helicopter team. Their drone, however, has no problem finding and tracking the Mini; it is now feeding the car's current whereabouts to the chopper's pilots, who, minutes later, train their searchlight on it as it approaches the destination that Fusion's predictive tools has deemed most likely: the airport.

So intent is everyone on the screen that few notice the quiet arrival into the operations room of Justin Amari, special assistant to Deputy Director Walker, peeling a stick of gum, leaning against a doorway, folding his arms.

"But why is she going to the airport?" Erika asks anyone who might have the answer, staring at the litany of lights and alarms and images. "Does she really think we're gonna let her just *get on a plane*?"

The answer is not long in coming, as the chopper pilot is ordered by his own commanders to abort the pursuit at the perimeter of the airport's no-fly zone, a violation of which would imperil commercial aircraft. The same rule also applies to Fusion's drone.

"Ah, smart," says Erika. "We can't follow her near a commercial airport."

"Drone team, stay with her," Cy orders, his excited eyes on the drone imagery, enmeshed in the chase. "Follow her, drone only."

"Cy," Erika protests. "We can't." She has always liked him at his most invested, but this is going way too far.

"It's fine. Drone only."

"Cy! That's impossible. There are planes landing and taking off."

His voice jumps in volume. "My call. *My* call. Follow her with the drone."

Jerking off her headset, Erika marches over to address him privately. At a lower volume, but with increased intensity, she tells him, "We *cannot* do that."

But before he can reply, the images supplied by the drone begin to flicker and falter. Seconds later, the drone locator ceases to recognize its presence. The craft has vanished.

"Drone down," someone announces.

"What happened?" Cy calls, frustrated.

Sonia has the answer: "Canadian air traffic control most likely took it down with anti-drone tech. They jammed us, cut its engine."

Cy, taking his eyes off the screen and looking around him, only now realizes that the entire population of the Void is staring at him, reading a great deal into his every gesture.

They expect him to speak.

"Fine. Tell them to . . . to hold. Tell them to hold."

Only then does he turn to see, with some alarm, the gum-chewing Justin Amari. The two men lock eyes. No smiles exchanged. No friendly gestures.

Eyes still on Justin, he instructs: "Respect airport aviation rules. But. But send in the . . . the ground Capture Teams to sweep the airport. And, guys, monitor every passenger on *every* plane."

Cy, as he exits the control center, passes Erika. She noticed Justin, too.

"Fuck," he whispers softly, having muted his headset as he passed her. He then unmutes it to declare, as he climbs the stairs to the gantry, "Zero 10 is *not* to leave that airport."

When he's gone up to his office, Erika finally nods at Justin, who, after a deliberate moment, gives the type of nod that indicates there is probably going to be a conversation to be had, and soonish, about what has just gone down.

21 DAYS, 4 HOURS

FUSION CENTRAL, WASHINGTON, DC

OVER THE YEARS ERIKA HAS endured some hellishly long days at work alongside Cy. She has seen him misbehave and cross the line in myriad small ways but only when he is under enormous strain, brought about by his baseline fear that he might let them both down, squander everything they've worked so hard for. When he gets tangled in such a state, starts imagining doomsday scenarios, gets unreasonable or impolite or impetuous, that's when Erika plays her most important business role, that of recalibrating her partner. She doesn't judge him at such moments, even when he loses his temper and blurts out something reprehensible. Allowances have to be made for such special characters. You can't take a genius of that order and then complain if at times they don't behave like everyone else.

Still, even in view of all this, his order to fly a drone into the airspace of a busy commercial airport—in a foreign country—was something new, and she knew it was new. It was just, well, weird, completely out of the box, even for someone as insatiable and bent on winning as Cy. She stepped in, of course, handled it, cleaned up, as she always has, calmed the representatives from Transport Canada Civil Aviation who were seriously pissed about the drone, then appeased Burt Walker (better to go right to him than let Justin Amari get to him first), told some half-truths, fudged other details—pretty much the same approach she used about the CD player—but her real challenge now might be to work out what happened here to her partner, her oldest and only true friend, so that she can make sure it doesn't happen again.

Erika consults her tablet in the open-air foyer as she sips her morning coffee. It reports that Cy is still at their rented mansion, probably sleeping. She allows herself to sit for a minute on a bench by the floor-to-ceiling LED video screen showing a digital silver birch growing at an accelerated rate in the atrium, winters of ninety seconds, springs to match, the lives of leaves and butterflies and birds abbreviated but briefly glorious. Next she watches the people coming and going between the juice and coffee bars, starting their long, solar day. Bright kids. Erika has helped Cy make many, many millions of dollars out of spotting and nurturing young talent. She sees one, a girl, too thin, hair dyed blue, who stops when she notices Erika looking at her.

"You okay?" Erika calls.

The girl approaches, cautiously. Hoodie. Jeans. Allbirds sneakers.

"Yeah, thanks." She pushes her hand through her hair. "So . . ."

"Go on."

"I think I might have found a way to get better tracking data on individual users, if they're using burner phones."

She looks like she has more to say but then stares down at her sneakers.

Erika gives an encouraging nod. "That's great. Good job."

"But, is it okay . . . is it right? I mean, to track them if they've never given their consent?"

Erika takes a beat, as if she's thinking. But she doesn't have to. Has confronted these issues a gazillion times. She stares up into the spotlighted shivering leaves of the fast-growing digital tree (rate: one day per second) and then at the glass roof of the atrium, the black night beyond. Smooth answer first. "If other users in the network have given their consent, terms and conditions apply, all the rest of that, then yes, we are acting within the law. But . . . what's your name?"

"Josie."

Erika feels like she can see this girl growing up at as rapidly as the digital silver birch, with a head full of twice as much as a head this young should hold, wrestling with the ancient mindfuckery of right and wrong in an accelerated world, the greater good, individual freedom versus the security of the whole. Hell, three thousand years ago, they made Socrates drink hemlock for asking too many of these questions.

"There is nothing either good or bad, but thinking makes it so," Erika quotes.

The girl shifts her weight from one foot to the other, totally mystified by this. "I'm sorry, I don't understand what you mean."

"Sorry, Josie. Come, sit for a second."

The girl obliges.

When they are seated: "You probably know a lot of this stuff is personal for me?"

Ping. A text from Cy comes in on the iPad, three words: *Sorry for today.* Erika puts down the tablet.

"Yes, I'm so sorry about your brother," Josie says. "I . . . I can't imagine."

"Thank you. That's when we decided to try to use technology to stop things like that from happening, or at least mitigate them. And if we can make Fusion as powerful as we think it can be, as it *needs* to be, if Cy can make what he sees in his mind's eye a reality, then the next shooter won't even get out of his fucking driveway."

Erika, for the millionth time, replays the counterfactual in her mind, of Michael still being alive, a father by now, Erika spending weekends spoiling her nephews and nieces. Can almost see their faces, glimmers from some multiverse so distant yet so imaginable, the almost-life.

"I lost someone, too," Josie says.

"You did?"

"A cousin of mine. School shooting."

"Then you get it?"

"Why I wanted to work here."

"Good for you." Time to set Josie free. "But this is really complicated stuff. And our concern for privacy is real. If you see something you don't like, bring it up. Always. We need dissenting voices here, too. Now, go see Aidan. He heads up the ethics committee. Tell him I sent you. Never be afraid to stand up. That's who we are."

Josie rises, grateful. "Thanks, Erika."

Heads off to whichever tiny cubicle she's occupying in the vast building, new resolve straightening her back.

It's worth it, thinks Erika, all the work, even the mistakes Fusion will make, all worth it given the potential goal.

With Josie gone, checks her watch. 8:25 a.m. Oh my God. Suddenly wants to go home, be with Cy when he wakes. Even make up with him. But instead, goes back inside, into the Void so busy with espionage and, after a glance at the big clock and then at the portraits of the still-missing Zeros, heads to her office.

20 DAYS, 22 HOURS

DALLAS, TEXAS

FOR JAMES KENNER, TWENTY-SIX, ZERO 2, the three-million-dollar prize is irrelevant. Chump change. He's already worth far more than that anyway. No, what convinced this senior privacy designer to say yes when asked to join the specialist portion of this program was the chance to beat the best and thereby prove to himself and his investors the efficacy of his brand-new masking technology, which lets you make online aliases—or masks—so that you can operate online while never, ever revealing who you are: a ghost in the machine. Cloaked in your alias and a masked credit card, a masked phone, and a masked mail account, you can sally forth into what they used to call the World Wide Web, sure that you remain unknown to all who seek knowledge of you, shifting the power back to you.

In short: If Cy Baxter and his ilk can make money from swindling people of their private data, he aims to make a fucking fortune from its protection.

Introducing: MaskIt.

In development eight years—using AES-256 with row-level salt for extra-sensitive data, info minimization, and host-proof hosting (so not even the MaskIt engineers could find out your passwords and real identity)—this fuck-you repudiation of WorldShare and Google and Facebook and Twitter's shameless harvesting of intimacies is ready to be tested. And what better test (and business opportunity) than to go up against the government's own state-of-the-art beta test?

Cy Baxter, be afraid.

Yes, sure, Fusion—and its beta and everything about it—is to be kept out of the news when they're done, his participation forever an NDA-enshrined secret, but he intends to break this promise. Sue me; just more attention for MaskIt. When he's won this little contest, when thirty days have expired, he'll emerge from hiding and share his story with Wall Street and VCs.

And so far, so good.

Day 1 of his vanishment had been exciting. A total thrill to get the Go Zero order and use that two-hour window to move to his little sepulcher, an industrial storage unit paid for with his MaskIt credit card and under one of his MaskIt aliases. Inside the unit? Everything you could need. Small bathroom with basin and toilet. Bed. One well-stocked fridge, plus much canned food, in case of an emergency or power outage. But mainly he orders fresh and with confidence on Grubhub and clicks on "Leave at Door" just like anyone else would. Entertainment? A TV subscription under the name (couldn't resist this childishness) "E. Jack Ulayte." Evenings his computer streams favorite songs and movies as he cracks open a celebratory bottle of champagne. No need to curb luxuries, not with MaskIt. The point is to prove that one can live entirely normally online and remain untraceable.

To stay fit, James bought a Peloton bike (under the name 'Mike Litoris.') He wants to emerge after this month in the best shape of his life so that he's ready to become a protean figure in American life, its white knight, driving back the territorial gains of Big Tech and making Big Tech-sized money in the process.

For sure, Fusion will be doubly motivated to crack his encryption technology and so destroy him as a threat to its hegemony, but what's groundbreaking about MaskIt is that the program creates random new encryptions with each use, a modern-day Enigma machine cyclically generating new permutations of code so that you'd need something like 20^{600} code breakers to even locate an email's sender or recipient.

Thus, with each passing day, each slipping hour, he grows in confidence. Sure of his concealment, it's just a waiting game. He's basically won already.

20 DAYS, 6 HOURS

FUSION CENTRAL, WASHINGTON, DC

THE NEXT MORNING STARTS OFF much better for Cy.

When he gets in, it's good-morning high fives all round in the Void. In his eyes everyone is shiny and forgiven. Zero 4, who'd been a tough nut, is down. And the way they got him—digitally reconstructing spaces in his house, the analytics guys flagging the energy use, the VR laser work capturing the room's dimensions, the clincher being the use of ground-penetrating radar (as deployed by Israel to locate Hamas terror tunnels), the total no-stone-left-unturned aspect of it all—was fancy enough to impress even the CIA fussbudgets.

Once more proud of his team and confident in their virgin systems, Cy looks up at the big screen. Less than ten days in, and five of the Zeros bagged already, including one pro, the girl from Hong Kong. Just James Kenner, Brad Williams, Jenn May, and Don White still out there—all security professionals, but they were never going to be easy gets—and also, of course, this wild-card librarian. He is sure now he can behave himself for another couple of weeks, keep himself in check, be the good boy Erika insists on him being, secure the government funding he needs. Then, and only then, can he let his hair down and get back to California and his real life.

Passing around the floor of the Void, he smiles at his staff, pats a few on the back, even gives that chino guy's trapezoids a rapid squeeze. "Keep going," he says encouragingly, then wheels and heads up the glass stairs to his high office. There, looking down upon all these talented young folk, so much schooling and hard work represented, he marvels that they are ready to give their all, to prove their individual worth and do so to him, to Cy Baxter, the same guy who was once picked last whenever playground teams were selected. By his own hard work has he elevated himself, and if he stands above the rest now, he does so in a spirit of service, not of vanity or belated playground revenge. He has no scores to settle with the past, only with the future. Standing in his way are five people only, with names as mundane as

James,
Brad,
Jen,
Don,
Kaitlyn.

19 DAYS, 23 HOURS

RENFREW, ONTARIO, CANADA

INTRODUCES HERSELF TO THE LANDLADY as Jemima Reynolds. Tucked into the back of her cash belt she has a driver's license in that name, which she took from her library's lost and found.

The landlady, a nice-looking woman in her sixties—European accent, a loose blouse patterned with exotic birds—squints at the license through her reading glasses, then writes down the details in her leather-bound visitors' journal.

The bed-and-breakfast is proudly old-fashioned, with its wooden VA-CANCIES / NO VACANCIES sign hooked under the bigger sign reading THE BOWER. But what really caught Kaitlyn's eye—and caught it when she'd researched the area online before Go Zero—was the one on the door that said SORRY, NO WI-FI SO DON'T ASK. She climbed out of a VW Golf full of three beautiful twenty-something-guys-just-off-to-white-water-raft-at-dawn, who, being Canadian, were happy to give her a ride from the airport's parking building, where, off-camera and unfollowable by the chopper due to it being restricted airspace above, she'd ditched the Mini and slid into the Golf. Then, in the middle of this town, and once the stores were open, she got herself a new backpack, a set of clean clothes, another water bottle and compass, another survival bracelet (never going without one of those again, *ever*), and went to see if the Wi-Fi-less B&B had a spare room.

Having negotiated her way through the small talk—landlady loves hiking, husband don't care for it—Kaitlyn hides out in her room till dinner: a stew, served with home-baked bread and salad, which she eats sitting on her own in a little conservatory area. Then she starts back up to her room.

"You have everything you need?" the landlady asks as she sticks her head out of the family room. "You have tea and coffee in your room, and I put some of my cookies up there, too. Just made this afternoon, fresh."

The idea of a homemade cookie makes her kind of weepy and sick at the same time.

"Thank you."

"And you'll be going in the morning, now?"

"I haven't decided yet, ma'am. It's so lovely here."

At this the woman looks shy and proud.

"Can I let you know tomorrow?"

"Sure, absolutely, for sure, of course."

Kaitlyn climbs the stairs, bone tired, thinking that maybe she will just stay here, lie low, and take her chances. The hotel is private. Disconnected. As long as she keeps to herself, eats alone, reads all the books on the hotel shelves, how could they possibly find her here? Even Fusion needs clues.

But of course this is not her plan. Can't be her plan. If she was just trying to win the three million dollars, maybe it could be.

Her room is tiny and decorated in half a dozen clashing chintzes. Reminds her of her grandma's place. Although not even Grandma had so many pictures of Jesus. She lies on the bed and eats a cookie, then takes out her notebook, feels in the back flap, and pulls out the picture of Warren. She can allow herself this. Her reward for the airport escape. She wants to tell Warren all about it. Maybe it was Warren who told her about restricted air spaces in the first place. He knew all about that kind of thing, of course. Encyclopedic on security measures. Much more his field than hers. But he couldn't have known that this factoid would keep her alive at some point down the road or, less dramatically, keep alive her chances (and his, if you think about it), allowing her to abandon the Mini in that underground parking garage, unobserved, then bum a ride out of the airport area courtesy of three decent young men.

"Hey, honey," she says to the photograph, simultaneously sleepy and sugar-rushing and scared but also very, very comfortable. Warren grins back at her. Cheerful summer clothes. Good-looking. Not in a square-jawed all-American way, no—much better than that. He's slim, wiry. Thick black hair and just enough of his Algerian mother in him that the TSA used to frisk him every time. He looks like what he is. Wicked smart, devilishly funny, loving. Hers.

Now, in her mind, they are lying on the pontoon out in the lake under the stars. Their second anniversary. The week before he headed out. But back on that pontoon in front of the cabin, when their champagne is waiting in an ice box with a couple of plastic flutes, is still a happy time. Mostly . . .

"I have a bad feeling, is all," she said to him, staring up at the Big Dipper.

"You had a bad feeling on my last trip," he replied. His accent is somewhere between Upper East Side and French. His heritage, an occasional rolling *r*, a trick of word order handed down from his mother.

"And I was right, wasn't I?"

She was right. His last assignment had been tracking payments between the Gulf States and Syria. Got a real bad time at a checkpoint. Warren had been on the Syrian border, Moroccan passport in hand, second in line behind an old pickup truck whose driver was arguing with the border guard—over a bribe, Warren guessed—when a kid with the AK-47 and a uniform walked up and shot the pickup driver in the head. It was the perfunctory brutality of it that unmoored him, he told her later. Boredom, alarm, bang. Gone. The thought: What am I doing here?

But he was still going back out there. Warren puts himself in danger. Gets something out of it. Says the money is good and, anyway, he's a patriot. Wants to believe his government needs his help and is worthy of it. She gets it. She believes in him, but hates that it has to be so secret, tells him over and over she can't ever get used to that part, insists he take every precaution and also think seriously about not doing it anymore.

He was looking up at the stars, too, didn't look at her, but she felt his fingers twist around hers. Warren's gone out of his way to make his own life difficult. Taught in inner-city schools for two years after grad school. Learned Farsi. Got his PhD and tenure, then offered his services to the U.S. government rather than hedge funds or private equity . . . Married her.

"Stop thinking about worst-case scenarios," he told her.

She just sighed.

Now her own voice intrudes. I have to think about worst-case scenarios, they are the only scenarios that are going to help us.

He had changed the subject, got up on one shoulder, looked at her. "I don't want to talk about this on our anniversary, babe. I want to talk about just how beautiful you look, like a blue jay in the moonlight."

"And why would you want to talk about that exactly?"

She can still hear the wolfish grin in his voice. "I want to talk about *best*-case scenarios."

"Put this in your scenario and smoke it," she said as she curled her legs and rocked to her feet. She then launched into the lake in a flash. "Nothing for you if you can't beat me to the beach."

She dived, felt the dark waters encase her. As she surfaced and pushed forward in a swift crawl toward the beach, the champagne in her blood, Warren, a stronger swimmer, drew alongside, the two of them plowing the water under the stars, until they reached the beach and fell on their wool rug, rolled into each other, he on top, she on top, he on top.

But when she wakes in the middle of the night, the dream is distant and thick, and Warren is nowhere to be found, lost to her again, hardly real anymore, a dim flicker, a memory that she sometimes feels she has made up. As for her, she exists in the world of worst-case scenarios. No stars now, or sex or champagne.

She gets up in the morning light and puts the notebook back into the pocket of her walking pants, checks out of the little B&B, and heads off on the trail on foot.

17 DAYS, 20 HOURS

FUSION CENTRAL, WASHINGTON, DC

BURT WALKER AND SANDRA CLIFFE, on an unscheduled visit, are accompanied by the ever-watchful Justin Amari.

It's the first time Erika's seen the delegation since the Canada incident, and she has prepared herself mentally for agency pushback and calls for more oversight of Cy. Fortunately, as Walker quietly tells her, both the CIA and Ottawa are prepared to pretend it didn't happen, and all appreciate the importance of keeping news of Go Zero out of the news.

"Is Cy going to join us?" Walker asks with just a hint of an undertone.

"I've just messaged him. He had another meeting." Erika raises her phone in confirmation. "On his way."

Happily, talk then turns into a brag-fest about how Fusion caught the Zeros they've captured already.

From lunch the delegation moves to the Void conference room for a preview of the toys they are going to use to catch the final five. The frosted glass table digitally displays the five captured Zeros plus portraits of the remaining five still at large.

"As we know, people don't stop being themselves on the run. Under pressure, they get more like themselves." With this, Erika hands things over to Lakshmi Patel, a small young woman full of yoga-instilled vim, black hair tightly drawn back, large, attentive eyes as brown as onion soup.

She talks these CIA reps through two very special programs they're trialing here: Clear-Voyant and Weeping Angel. Both are super-cool, according to Lakshmi, and are really going to make a difference in catching the four tech-savvy Zeros. She makes a point of not mentioning the librarian.

"Two hours after Go Zero," she informs them, "we accessed malware remotely in every device owned by every participant, turning these devices into tools that we can control."

Justin Amari has a question: "So you're deploying measures that would be illegal in a real-world scenario? Secretly installing malware, that's a breach of data privacy laws."

This guy again, thinks Erika.

"Not quite. But good question. *Mindful* of privacy laws, all we did was tap into the malware that people already have on their phones, rather than installing anything new, because we all carry hostile artifacts in our devices like your gut carries bacteria, but three Zeros—Brad Williams, Jenn May, and Don White—all explicitly used their precious two-hour window, between Go Zero and our pursuit, to geo-block their devices, basically prevent us from accessing them. Which means they intended to take these devices with them, despite the risks involved. They clearly consider them necessary to their plans."

"How can these devices be necessary if they can never use them?"

"Great question. They all, we predict, know that any minor slipup in an area with high 5G capacity could lead to exposure, even with their devices blocked and disabled. So we predict they have likely moved to—if you can pull up the map now, please—low 5G coverage areas, shown in gray."

The conference table has done its trick and turned into a map of the US variously highlighted. Most of the delegates can't help looking impressed, even Justin seems momentarily mesmerized at these startling transmutations.

"That's what our prediction models tell us. So, when we talk about being off-radar these days, these areas in gray are what we're really talking about." Lakshmi is enjoying this. "They have a few things in common. They're mostly rural, wooded, or mountainous. In rare cases, they're in deprived urban pockets. 5G has made microtracking in cities and towns child's play, but the signal has its problems. It doesn't like walls. Or trees. Or rain. In the cities, that means it needs a fine mesh of relay stations and signal boosters. Fine. Anywhere human beings go to spend money, that mesh is already tight. Out of town, though, the blind spots start growing and the data has to squeeze through old pipelines. It still comes, but it drips rather than floods."

Burt Walker looks confused. "I have a technical question. If you can't access their devices, and they play it smart and just decide to lie low somewhere in one of these gray zones, what other tools are at your disposal to catch them?"

"Okay, that's where our Clear-Voyant and Weeping Angel programs come in." Here Lakshmi hands it off to her boss. "Erika, maybe you'd . . ."

"Sure. Happy to." It's time now for Erika to reveal something that not even her CIA partners know exists yet. "We have two additional programs we've been developing independently that we've just decided to bring online and make available to Fusion as well, so I'm pleased to tell you about them because we think they're pretty awesome. First is Clear-Voyant. This involves, basically, crunching massive amounts of personal data to provide psychological insights. Gleaning a person's psychology from a complete analysis of their online and offline histories, SAT scores, preferred communication strategies, and written and spoken words. From the psychological profile that emerges, we then generate predictive scenarios with very precise likelihood estimates that use post-processing and fine-tuned search heuristics as their epistemological base."

"With what success?" Sandra Cliffe asks.

"For instance, we know that anyone under thirty-five living in the United States has a high psychological reliance on access to screen time. Despite this, in the case of Zero 7, Brad Williams, thirty-five, a security expert, by using Clear-Voyant, we've determined a high chance that he'll successfully deny himself use of all devices with Wi-Fi capabilities. However, we've further predicted, from his habits and other sources, that he will likely spend some of these difficult days on the run stimulating himself by watching normal, regular broadcast TV. Boy's gotta have it. And looking at his psychological profile, we believe that he will have taken a companion with him. Boy also needs girl."

Sandra Cliffe interrupts. "Surely a man with his training will realize that taking a companion doubles his risk?"

"Again, we become more ourselves under pressure, not less. He knows the risk, but we believe he won't be able to help himself. Brad grew up in a big family. He has the money to set up his own household, but he still shares a house with two college friends. He needs someone around." Erika summons across the table the image of a slim, high-cheekboned woman in a plunging evening dress. "This woman mentioned him in her social feeds recently but has gone quiet since the beginning of the beta testing despite typically being a heavy social media user. Before that it was lots of heart emojis back and forth, and even messages of 'I will miss you,' which we believe are a ploy."

"So where does that get us?" Burt asks.

"It gets us to Weeping Angel," Lakshmi replies.

"I hate to think how you came up with that name," Sandra Cliffe says dryly.

Lakshmi explains that the term was coined when they looked through the lurid material all the candidates actually watched on their screens. "Erika, wasn't it actually you who said it was enough to make the angels weep? Anyway, it stuck."

Erika figures it's a moment to offer more coffee. The two CIA PhDs pass.

"So looking at the model, we think Brad and his companion are sitting in front of a TV somewhere in a gray zone," Erika continues. "This is a perfect time to employ Weeping Angel. We use gray-zone TV sets to tell us about who is in their vicinity."

"Explain that, please?" Burt asks.

Erika then turns to the deputy director. "Here's how it works. By infiltrating the broadcast frequencies, we can gain access to a targeted TV. Once we have control, we switch it into what we call 'fake off-mode,' so that the owner thinks the TV is off when it is in fact still on. It just looks off. The TV now operates as a bug, enabling us to capture external sound and send the data back to us. Our software automatically sieves it for buzzwords, or the target's own name or names of loved ones or friends and so forth. And that's only one function of Weeping Angel. It's actually capable of taking control of almost anything with a silicon chip."

"So," Justin Amari asks, slowly finding his voice, "you are . . . you're listening to the . . . to the private conversations of millions of Americans . . . spying on them . . . through their TV sets . . . in order to locate a single individual?"

Burt steps in. He gets it. "Easy there, Justin. I think they're saying they are using them as filters only to *eliminate* suspects. And it's only Fusion's computers, correct, who are getting this information? It's not as if your human teams have access to all this private data?"

"That's correct," Erika replies. "The system does all the sifting automatically, and only when the system identifies a likelihood of a least eighty-five percent that the party might be our target does an actual human analyst become involved. As all our staff are bound by strict confidentiality agreements, you can think of this as complete privacy protection."

"Eighty-five percent, is it?" Dr. Cliffe asks. "And how did you arrive at that percentage?"

"Well," Erika says, "that's roughly the number at which our models say you need a human eye on the data. Human intelligence. To provide the final analysis. Ultimately, though, the public's secrets are safe."

"Safe with *you*," Amari adds.

Sandra Cliffe looks very uncomfortable in her chair.

"So, just to be clear," Justin continues "you *can* eavesdrop in any room with a TV set in it, whether it's on or off, in real time, by executing a few lines of code? By pressing a button at any workstation down there in the Void you can induce fake off-mode?"

Erika: "Correct."

"And you can record and retain this information?"

"Correct."

"And you could then, feasibly, if you chose, go back and search those conversations for *any* buzzwords you later happen to wonder about?"

"In theory."

"Well then, in that case, it is starting to look a whole lot like you are bugging all Americans, without their knowledge, or permission."

"Are we in danger," Erika replies, "of forgetting what we're doing here?"

The agency triumvirate stares at her. While Walker seems untroubled, saying, "Not at all," concern is evident on the faces of Dr. Cliffe and Justin

Amari.

"The whole point of this project," Erika says forcefully, "is to come up with new tools to keep us safe."

Justin: "Still, for the record, because the agency has not been made aware of these programs till this minute, it would be good to know how long this program has been active, and how many TV sets you have so far accessed. A number?"

When Erika hesitates to reply, Dr. Cliffe adds her voice: "We'd all appreciate an answer, I think."

"Not widely active. Still testing it, but this beta, of course, is part of our testing."

Through the glass walls of the conference room, Erika's guests all see Cy approaching.

"The cavalry," quips Justin Amari.

Entering, Cy looks a little stressed but manages a smile.

"Hi, everybody. What have I missed? Where are we? Apologies."

"Perfect timing actually," Dr. Cliffe replies. "We were just hearing about your trials of these new programs, Weeping Angel and Clear-Voyant, and I had a question that Erika was about to answer, about how many TV sets across America have been accessed."

"How many? Televisons? Oh. Millions," Cy replies, without hesitation. Sitting, he checks Erika's expression. "Is there a problem? This is a trial program, developed and owned by WorldShare under our agreement with your agency. You don't have to use it. But we also didn't want to hold it back when it has obvious utility here."

"And just how many millions, would you say?" asks Justin.

"If we're just talking about TVs? Oh, I'd say, basically every TV in the country produced after 2018 has been in fake off-mode for the past six months.'

"Really?" A small silence ensues, before Justin continues. "And all that audio information you've harvested? You have it?"

"That is correct."

"Where?"

"At one of our data farms. A super secure storage site."

"So it's being collected passively, and continually?'

"Correct." Cy surveys the room, surprised to see looks of concern. "There a problem here?"

Justin says, "I think some people would think so, were they to learn of it."

"Really?" Cy counters. "With all due respect, you're the CIA." Cy weighed the faces of the agency's three representatives. "You of all people have a history of doing what is necessary; that's why we were so eager to partner with you." He let this last sentence resonate before proceeding. "And you're famously limited in what you're able to do domestically, under your charter, but not *entirely*. Correct me if I'm wrong, but till now your domestic division, the National Resources Division, I think it's called, has been permitted to conduct operations on U.S. soil only against foreign targets. Our value to you, we presume, is that, through us, you can passively expand your intelligence capabilities on home soil, should your charter be, shall we say, reviewed. If I'm wrong about any of this, be good to know, because we at Fusion have put everything on the line here. And I mean *everything*. Both on the line, and at your service. If that's unwelcome . . ." He lets this last sentence hang.

Burt Walker for one is really listening. He clearly has grand plans. "Noted. But we still have to be able to sell the justification for such information gathering."

"Well," Cy goes on, "the information is used only to protect Americans. I personally have no problem justifying it, and I suspect a couple hundred million Americans won't, either. You wanted America's security to go up to the next level? This is what it looks like. Welcome to the next level. For progress to take place, I submit to you that we must be super-aggressive. That's the ethos we developed at WorldShare, brought to Fusion, and now offer to you."

Justin Amari was never going to be sold on this, and his face shows just how unpersuaded he is. "Unrestricted evolution of surveillance at the cost of citizens' rights will not fly. That's just problem number one."

Sandra Cliffe hedges. "I would simply question whether this particular technology, which we are only *just now* learning about from you, should be used for the purposes of this trial. Such a level of surveillance is without precedent in this country and would be unlikely to ever be authorized for domestic use. So why use a technology now that, going forward, will not be at Fusion's disposal? Also, beyond this beta test, Dr. Walker will need to sell this project to the director and then to Capitol Hill and ultimately the president. Each will review the procedures, convene advisory groups, have to approve the use of each technology and, with it, *maybe*, the covert expansion of the CIA's operations on home soil for the first time. So, to use Justin's word, yes, *problem*."

Burt Walker's own wheels are now spinning fast. "Look, we all want to make slow, steady advances here without drawing undue public attention. Grandma's footsteps, if you will. Nice and easy. And from long experience, the agency knows better than anyone that any hint of a 'surveillance society' will spook the public terribly, be viewed as un-American, and awaken resistance that will, in the long run, constrain our reach. So we have to make subtle advances, and these two programs of yours, well, as much as I might admire them scientifically, no one would call them subtle."

Sandra Cliffe adds: "If anything smacks of the Russian or Chinese model, we need to be very careful. You're preaching to the more or less converted in this room, but Weeping Angel, in particular . . . feels very Chinese."

Burt takes over: "I think that's a good point. For instance, fifteen thousand licensed taxicabs in Chongqing, China, have cameras with facial recognition. Imagine that in America. Who would ever take a cab if everything you say or do was being recorded by the government? As a domestic policy, that's un-American. *Internationally*, okay, intel gathering is our forte. We have enormous latitude there. I'm sure we'd find great support, in both the agency and on the Hill, for a plan to install fake off-mode in TVs in Moscow, Beijing, Tehran, Pyongyang . . . just not at home. Not yet anyway."

"So you're asking us to do what, exactly, because I'm confused?" Cy asks.

Walker: "For now, stand down Weeping Angel."

"Stand it down?"

"I think we're looking for balance here," Cliffe summarizes, turning to look at Justin for what appears to be approval, as if she is now delivering a script penned by him.

Something about this quick look, from a senior official to a junior one, inflames Cy. "Is that what we're doing here?"

"Going forward," Cliffe adds. "Yes we are. A balance between what the Chinese call *the public good*, which legitimizes a police state, and what we here in America call civil liberties and freedom.'

Hearing such tired, tedious, regressive arguments, Cy can't suppress a loud sigh as his eyes meet those of, in turn, the annoyingly too-silent Erika, the misguided Sandra Cliffe, the wimpy Burt Walker, and last and most certainly least, the stubbornly self-righteous and grotesquely over-influential Justin Amari, bringing about a lengthy silence that is strangely appropriate to a roomful of wary occupants who know that, under each other's close surveillance, the next utterance might prove very damaging indeed.

16 DAYS, 23 HOURS

BLUE RIDGE MOUNTAINS, DILLARD, GEORGIA

BRAD WILLIAMS, ZERO 7, IQ of 169, (by this measure actually a genius) is very much regretting the subgenius decision to bring his girlfriend along. They're a new thing, he and Kimmy, and when he first got the letter saying he'd made it into the Going Zero program, he was in the first flush of lust. She featured so heavily in his erotic dreams, the ones about what to do with three million clams, that an invitation became pretty much pro fucking forma. And not all the daydreams were even sexy. He imagined her, in joint victory, at the new house he would buy with the winnings, in that yellow dress of hers with no back to it, no panties underneath, welcoming his really high-end business clients at his enormous front door with her gorgeous smile. Or Kimmy at the clubhouse waiting for him along with the other wives and girlfriends when he comes in from a narrowly over-par round with the CEO. Or else Kimmy, if he were ever to pop the question, with their picture-perfect children on the family Christmas card: "Our family, ready to protect yours." Brad understood that this trial was top secret but still imagined there were ways to let it be known that in victory he had heroically and single-handedly outsmarted the combined intelligence forces of the United States and shown it where it needed to do better. A medal would be nice. But the cash will suffice.

Brad Williams: ex-military, now a high-end, online RRS: reputation repair specialist. Day job, serving Fortune 500 companies and Hollywood A-listers. Knows how upsetting it is when all your years of hard toil are discredited just because of a little negative coverage online; how frustrating if you've made a teeny mistake in the past that you wish to erase and rectify but can't, and now have a fabulous business that won't pass a simple credibility check. Even at nineteen he saw a market here. Wrote his first code, and developed technology to rapidly repair damaged reputations, inoculate that vulnerability, and allow a damaged figure or brand to do even better than before. Called his company SecondChanceSaloon. For a fat fee, he sends men and women and companies back to their spouses and employers and constituents and shareholders freshly laundered, reputationally rescued. And thus far, touch wood, business is good—no shortage of candidates needing such help, their frailities expunged—but he's plateauing badly, too many other competitors have now entered this space, so a big and much-publicized win over Fusion would really bump him up to a whole new level and set him apart from his rivals. With new premises and marketing, the right PR (the ideal wife) he'd be dominant in the sector and beating off those VC billionaires with a stick.

But Kimmy, well, she just isn't working out. Under her smooth, smiling surface, the girl has Certain Ideas, plus a will of pig iron. Also has a talent, which amazes him, of being able to completely ignore shit she doesn't want to hear. He caught her on day 2 almost paying for clothes in the cutest little boutique ever outside Savannah with her own credit card, and then, after they'd driven through the night to put a big distance between them and what she felt was a "totally necessary" purchase, had to stop her using the damn thing *again* for a bunch of junk from a Native American gift shop she'd taken an inordinate shine to.

It should be so easy. He has been keeping up on the latest surveillance and data mining techniques for years. This stuff is his business or, more precisely, adjacent business. He geo-blocked both their phones and laptops at the outset. Playfully body-checked Kimmy for any little digital traitors that might have found their way onto her person, which in the end proved sexy. In room 18 of a cheap motel outside Atlanta she rode him like a bronco, banshee-yelping when she came. That set the stage for the days that followed: they plotted, they fucked, plotted, fucked. But it stopped being fun around the time he found, then angrily mailed back home, her Fitbit and calorie counter, which she'd promised not to bring. Jesus H.

That's when the arguments truly kicked in. She said he didn't really stand a chance of winning this and so should calm the hell down. He said this was typical of her, to have no faith in him, and asked her henceforth not to fuck with his dreams.

It also turns out that when Kimmy isn't narrating her latest petty gossip on Instagram, or giggling at cat videos on WorldShare, she doesn't have much to say.

No matter how extensive their precautions—avoiding cities, moving from gray zone to gray zone (zero cell phone beacons or facial recognition)—traveling any farther would simply kick up too much digi-dust. So that's how they wind up here, under false names in a small hotel in the middle of the Little Tennessee Valley. Paid in cash for two weeks in advance. The place is way out in the woods in one of the best 5G gray zones he identified beforehand, built for solipsistic retreats away from it all and the like. The spa was to keep Kimmy happy (complimentary bathrobes, slippers, twenty-four-hour room service, lymph-drainage massages), but she's still bitching.

Apart from his in-depth knowledge of America's surveillance vulnerabilities—those areas of the country where statistically no harming information of a digital nature has ever surfaced—being Black gives him a surprising advantage, one that requires no use of his special genius. Little-known fact: Facial recognition algorithms, designed by white engineers, have ended up thinking all Black people—surprise, surprise—look the same more or less, which means Fusion's system *should* get flooded with false positives when it searches for him—a legion of Brad Williams look-alikes popping up, armies of dead ringers, sending Fusion off on wild-goose chases of gigantic proportions all across the country.

"I'm so bored, I read a whole damn book today," Kimmy complains as she opens the door into the room.

Brad watches her paddle on bare feet between him and the television. The bikini is tiny, but she wears it well. He is staring at her ass too hard to notice the book in question sailing in his direction. It hits him square in the crotch.

When the echo of his cry subsides, and much later the pain, and after her apology is accepted, he sees that her expression is unchanged.

"Can we go out tonight, baby?" she asks. "I'm so bored. Let's drive into town and find somewhere to dance. I'm going pinball-crazy here."

He flicks off the TV on which he'd been watching a crime series with a genius enforcer Brad sort of modeled his look on. Picks up the book. A brick of a thing with silver foil and sweeping lettering on the front. *Desire.* Whatever.

"No. I told you a million times already, we are not going into town. They have cameras on every damn streetlight. No point pushing it. Those machines learned fast."

"Can't you wear a disguise or something?"

"No! They can see through disguises. Don't you get it? The next-gen stuff can see right through an N95 mask. Jesus, why is it so hard for you just to sit by a pool for a couple of weeks and tan your motherfucking ass? Or read another goddamn book."

"This is the worst vacation I've ever been on! Period. And I can't even call my friends and tell them about it."

"It's not a vacation! It's not a—"

"Well, you can say that again, *Bradley*!"

She picks up some scrap of green fabric scrunched up in the corner of her suitcase. She pulls the dress on over her itsy-bitsy, cleavage-and-crack bikini, then slumps next to him on the sofa, oozing fleshy luxuries. She smells like chlorine.

"We are on the run," he reminds her, rubbing his hand on her left boob, encountering no resistance.

"But you didn't do anything wrong, did you?" She bites the side of her thumb like a kid.

"No. It's a test. I told you. These Fusion people are making sure their shit works. I was specially selected to help them figure out where they still need to patch the net. That's me, the best of the motherfucking best. They told me to Go Zero, and that's what we're doing. Going *Zero*. So that means no cell phones, no computers, no credit cards, no Fitbits. And we stick to the gray zones."

"Gray zones," she moans.

"Yeah, gray zones. And in two more weeks the test will be over. Brad one, U.S. government zero. Christ, Kimmy, you know all this shit."

"Cy Baxter is kinda cute. Does he have a girlfriend?"

"I'll introduce him to you, right after the motherfucker hands me three million dollars."

"Us," she says. "Hands *us* three million dollars. *Us,* baby."

Brad is genuinely surprised. "What do you mean us?"

"Us!"

"I'm the one they recruited. I'm doing all the work and paying all the expenses. What is your ass doing?"

"You think this is easy for me?" Kimmy asks. "Cut off from everything? Half that reward is mine, motherfucker. Otherwise, I'm turning you in right now."

"You don't get one and a half million dollars for sitting in a spa and reading a book, moron. Let's get that clear, right here, right now."

Turns out Kimmy has plenty to say after all and she fires a choice selection of these words at him as if they are rounds from, oh say an M16 assault rifle, rat-a-tat-tat-tat, all of them on target and hailed in close proximity to the Sony Bravia OLED TV sitting dark and innocent on a table against the wall, a small red standby light the only indication of its secret inner life.

WHEN THE FUSION CAPTURE TEAM arrives at six the following morning, Brad is almost pleased to see them.

14 DAYS, 22 HOURS

U.S.–CANADA BORDER

HER ANKLE IS HOLDING UP pretty well. Ibuprofen helps. After a few days she was even able to ditch the orthopedic boot. And the last week, bumming rides from town to town and staying in the chintzy rooms of elderly bed-and-breakfast owners who do their shopping at farmers' markets and write each other postcards *still*, has done her a world of good. She is calmer. Has slept finally. Allowed herself to think, really think, about Warren and about what she's doing.

What she's doing adds up. It's worth it. Yes, it's been far harder than she thought—the nightmare in the mineshaft, her injuries, the escape from the hospital, stress levels regularly off the charts, all of that—but her plan to push north, cross the border by boat, kill some time safely in Canada as she'd planned, it actually pretty much worked so far, didn't it? A word of encouragement, then, would be nice, she mentally entreats Warren. A phantom hug?

Buying a copy of the *Washington Post*, she reads the classifieds. Nothing. Jesus. Where are you?

Finds a room for the night near the border in Hamilton, Ontario. Decides on schedule to leave Canada tomorrow to get closer to where she needs to be. The latest landlady feeds her home-fried chicken, chatters about her grandchildren.

13 DAYS, 21 HOURS

BRYCE CANYON, UTAH

JENN MAY, ZERO 8, HAS a pretty simple philosophy in life: Don't get involved. She was bought up in a huge Catholic family in New York City. Eighteen years of continual domestic drama gave her all the human contact she needs for a lifetime.

She first encountered computers at the local library, was instantly drawn in by their logic. They were never moody or cruel. A binary system, yes and no, clear choices, fanning out like a delta. Yep, Jenn and computers got along just fine.

At college it turned out that her ever-improving skill set was more than good enough to keep up with the frat boys who played video games for three days before a test, and in this climate she made smooth progress through every challenge their professors threw in her way, while these guys scrapped and fought and scrabbled noisily around her. She pretended they weren't there. They couldn't take their eyes off her.

After graduation cybersecurity beckoned. A great firm offered her a stable and healthy income and the opportunity to work from home. She took it, along with a minimalist apartment in Sacramento. A regular at the yoga studio down the road, she has the occasional discreet dalliance while traveling for business. When one of these guys recently declared his love, she was slightly disgusted. Seeing a therapist about this, she tried to put her finger on what prompted such a reaction. Her siblings do not even have her address or her cell number, and she likes it this way.

It was one of her government contacts who asked her to put herself forward for the Fusion Initiative beta test. They needed someone who could really challenge the system. So she agreed, prepared, and received the Go Zero alert with the same icy calm she greets every challenge. Geo-blocked all her devices. Has no social media presence anyway. Set her business email account to inform prospects she is away for one month. Gave her current clients the numbers of three excellent technicians who knew her and her work and could handle any immediate problems.

She has a Bitcoin account, and so it wasn't much trouble to use the dark web to buy a decent fake driver's license and credit card. With that, she left town.

13 DAYS, 18 HOURS

U.S.–CANADA BORDER

AT FIRST LIGHT, A LONE hiker on an overgrown side trail near the border stops before a simple sign bolted to a steel post.

WARNING:

US. BOUNDARY.

THIS IS AN UNLAWFUL PEDESTRIAN CROSSING.

VIOLATORS ARE SUBJECT TO ARREST, FINES

AND OR FORFEITURE OF PROPERTY.

U.S. CUSTOMS AND BORDER PROTECTION.

PLEASE REPORT SUSPICIOUS ACTIVITY TO 1-800-218-9788.

She stops, drinks water from a bottle. *God bless America, land that I love.* Oh why oh why have you forsaken me?

But reenter she must. That was her original plan—Canada, but then double back; she is expected stateside. Has a rendezvous she must make.

She screws the lid back on the bottle and stows it. Touches the sign for good luck, then walks on, pushing through the foliage, finding, losing, re-finding the seldom-taken path.

12 DAYS, 21 HOURS

FUSION CENTRAL, WASHINGTON, DC

SONIA DUVALL, REASSIGNED—AT HER REQUEST—ONTO Jenn May's Capture Team, has always liked this Zero's chances and relishes playing her own part in catching her. If anyone can escape detection and capture, she figures it's Jenn, and Sonia's the type who actually likes having her work cut out for her.

After diving into Jenn's private life looking for clues, Sonia identified strongly with what she found, for she, too, has struggled with relationships, is bored by the men she can have, longs for those she can't. Add to this many other strong links—only child, father died early—and it's no wonder that Sonia feels she is hunting for a version of herself.

Days have gone by. Nothing concrete. It was when she went into the logs of every car rental Jenn had selected in the last five years that she identified a pattern not even the machines had seen. Next, her team went through facial recognition using traffic cams—focusing on gray zones, the kind of wide-open landscapes Jenn seemed to go for when traveling for leisure, then crossed this with her preferred vehicle types. She went over traffic cam footage for every make of car Jenn had ever driven, teaching the algorithms to memorize her driving style, to look out for how she slowed at lights, not wanting to stop, how she'd park nose-first by putting the front wheel up on the curb, how she always put on her blinkers super early before making a turn, how her eyes struggled at night and so after dark she opted for the slow lane and drove well under the speed limit. Twelve days in, they had eighteen thousand possible matches. The cameras on toll roads, trained to read license plates, strained to look out for her face. The algorithms twitched and tweaked, peering through windshields.

Sonia guesses Jenn will probably avoid the toll roads altogether, but they have to check them. Subtracting all the male drivers, left seven thousand candidates. With the facial recognition software sifting out most of the rest, the list soon shrank to eighty-four folks whose faces were either Jenn-like or too faintly visible behind grimy glass to be ruled out altogether. When each of the visible faces was rejected—nose too long, eyes too closely set, lips too full—deep dives by these analysts into the unobservable second group left Sonia, by Day 17, with the registration plate of a car found to be owned by a second cousin twice removed of one Jenn May.

Finding the car itself wasn't hard after that.

12 DAYS, 20 HOURS

BRYCE CANYON, UTAH

THE AIR IS THIN AND clear here. Jenn May's not a person to be awestruck by nature, even these thin red needles of rock that create such an alien landscape, but she looks at it for a while as the dipping sun throws sundial shadows over the land. Her yoga routine completed, she gets into her car ready to spend the rest of the day on the road, a nine-hour haul to Jackson Hole, where apparently there is an excellent off-grid retreat that she can stay at.

Two hours into the journey along Route 89 the car radio stops playing a Bach cantata and launches into a hardstyle composition with a chorus that, four times, repeats the words *Die bitch*. Jenn frowns. Reselects Bach. Twenty seconds later "Die Bitch" again. Something weird is happening to her sound system. It's auto-defaulting for some reason. She turns it off. Enjoys the silence for a few seconds before the thing turns itself back on again! What the hell?

Jenn raises an eyebrow and starts to look ahead for a turn that will take her off the freeway and to some convenient one-horse town where she can stop and disable the system somehow, even if it means taking a rock to it. But then the car begins to speed up. She pumps the breaks. Nothing. Steering is still hers, though. She manages to keep control, weaving through the sparse traffic, but she can feel her palms growing sweaty, her blood beginning to thump. Ten years of serious mediation practice means she just about manages to hold it together. Just. But then she loses the steering as well. The car brakes, speeds up again, then plays a terrifying game of chicken with bleary-eyed families in camper vans and beaten-up pickup trucks. She screams repeatedly, as the radio blasts "Die Bitch." No matter how she turns the wheel, the connection to the wheelbase is gone. For eight terrifying minutes she is as powerless as if she were on a roller coaster, the ghost driver a madman weaving her in and out of the traffic, undertaking on the hard shoulder, tailgating semies with her warning lights flashing, her horn blaring, all to the torture of "Die Bitch" on repeat.

Then it stops. The car lurches forward one more time, then slows. "Die Bitch" is replaced by Bach again. The AC comes on, gently wafting air over her, as she is driven, smoothly now and conscientiously at the legal speed limit, to a parking lot outside Holden where the car is parked in the shade expertly, by forces unknown, as she sits there and watches, hands on the ineffectual wheel. In a spot with a view of the mountains she tries the door. Still locked. Undoing her seat belt she lunges over, tries the passenger door. Same thing. Tries then to lower the electric windows, waggles the button. Nothing. Finally another car approaches. She waves. Waves like crazy. Shouts up a storm. Even presses the horn, but the horn makes no sound. Her waving is unseen or else ignored. The car passes out of sight. For half an hour she cries, imprisoned there. Occasionally, rage erupts, and she tries in vain to break the windows. Unbreakable though, at least by her. Gives up finally. This ghost car, possessed of evil, owns her.

The Capture Team takes two hours to reach Jenn May. She is handed a tablet. The team stands at a distance while she leans on her car and signs the capture paperwork and then plugs in the earpiece, as instructed, to be connected to Sonia Duvall. The iPad screen carries the image of Sonia, hair scraped back, wearing a gray jacket and a blood-red blouse. Strangely, she seems to be sitting in a forest of sequoia.

"Do you remember a George Phillipson from college?" Sonia asks her.

Jenn remembers him, vaguely: a pair of eyes, a shudder and hunch of a man, clever in flashes, thundering with pent-up resentment the rest of the time.

"Yes, he asked me out once. I said no."

"Pure coincidence, but he was employed here. We have a lot of really good coders," Sonia says. "Anyway, we noticed his connection to you, of course, as soon as we had your college transcripts and then he confirmed he knew you, which strictly speaking isn't against the rules. He managed to convince us that was an advantage and that there was no personal animosity between you. I'm sorry to have been proven wrong."

Sonia maintains eye contact and Jenn feels read by this distant woman, but doesn't resent it.

"So that explains 'Die Bitch'?"

"Yes."

"Can I assume he does not work for you any longer?"

"You may assume that, yes."

"Douchebag."

"We would not disagree with that assessment."

11 DAYS, 13 HOURS

COUNTY ROUTE 17, NORTH OF MOIRA, NEW YORK

SHE DOES SOMETHING POTENTIALLY QUITE stupid. Everybody does, from time to time, and they do it more often when exhausted or when factors like pain intrude, or they're emotionally at the end of their rope or just when hunger or thirst are added to the mix.

At this point, on a quiet road in the amber end of a darkening day, three hours into her walk, half of which is borne by a wounded foot, she is mentally all over the place. One moment she's thinking of Warren, the next of lyrics from a childhood song to keep her flagging spirits up: *If you like Ukulele Lady, Ukulele Lady like a'you. If you like to linger where it's shady, Ukulele Lady linger too.* . . . And then she finds herself wondering where exactly on the map she is right now. It's getting cold, too, with no B&B in sight. A stiff wind buffets her face. She needs to get off this road and find shelter. Imagines wolves in the woods left and right, spiders crossing her sleeping face were she to take a bed in the moist undergrowth. Might never wake up from such an evening! Like alternating timpani—*clomp, flap, clomp, flap, clomp, flap*— her rocker-bottomed plastic boot and her original leather Timberland ring and clap on the asphalt. *Maybe she'll sigh . . . do-da-do-da-do . . . Maybe she'll cry.* . . . Headlights rise in the distance. In this moment, rather than hide, she starts to wave. The vehicle grows closer. She shields her eyes against the lights, waves even harder, and mercifully the driver slows.

Thus far on her adventure, in bumming rides she's been super, super careful to select women drivers (with the exception of the four beautiful Canadian boys), flagging away the men, but nothing about this moment is normal, and anyway the pickup truck is stopped beside her before she notices it's an older lone male.

She assesses the risks, decides she can probably handle this guy. The guy is in his fifties, leaning over the steering wheel, checking her out, no doubt pretty surprised to see a woman way out here, alone. He looks okay to her. Checked shirt. Wiry build. No open beer cans on the dash. A bit of rust showing here and there on the paneling, suggesting this man knows a thing or two about hard times himself.

His features lit by the glow of his own headlights, he looks hard at her. Tuft of back hair rising above the collar. Asks: "You okay?"

"Could use a ride."

"Hop in, then. Throw your stuff in the back."

After slinging her backpack in bed of the truck, she climbs in the passenger seat, pulls the car door closed. A great relief to be out of all that cold air.

"What the heck you doing out on an old road like this anyhow?" He checks the mirror, shifts into gear, pulls out onto the silent tarmac.

She invents a story about being a big hiker, just heading home.

Changing gear, he looks askance at her. "Sure you're not in a bit a' trouble?"

"No. Why?"

"Those cuts on your face, bruises. Look like you got pretty banged up out there. What, you run into a bear?"

Smiles. "No bears," she says. "I'm good."

"You say so."

As uncomfortable as she is, what with her lies seeming thin, and with him glancing at her a little too often for comfort, which makes her think for the first time she's made a real mistake in getting into this truck, all this argues with the counterfacts that her ankle is pounding like hell, the six painkillers she gulped aren't doing anything other than making her head swim, and the night was getting too damn cold for sleeping out anyway. As she struggles to order her ibuprofen-infused thoughts, the image arrives of a hot bath, vivid and steamy. Ah, just the thought: to sink, to soak! Some of these B&Bs have little bottles of bath bubbles. Warren once drew her a fancy bath after she had a shitty day at work. Candles, wine, bubbles. She slid in, moved the flotillas of foam around with her hands, and slooshed them over herself, but she got bored in ten minutes. Padded down to the kitchen complaining to him the stuff made her hair sticky and now there was melted wax on the tiling. "Over to you, Prince Charming." He'd laughed at her. She can see him now. His face turning serious suddenly, as if sensing a danger.

Wake up, babe. Now!

She focuses again. Sees a road sign: MOIRA, 12 MILES. Remembers the drill Warren had taught her and, before the old driver can object, reaches up and turns on the cabin light.

"Do you mind?"

Then, when he's not looking, she raises her phone quickly to her ear, concealing the screen so that when he next glances at her she is already attentive to her handset.

His next sidelong glance at her invites Kaitlyn to inform the man, "Calling my husband, Warren." Then she says into the phone, "Honey? Yeah. Oh, I'm okay now. So lucky, I got a ride with . . ." Turns to the driver again. "With? Sorry, your name, sir?"

"Bill," the driver reluctantly supplies.

"Bill," she relays into the phone. "Oh, we're exactly twelve miles north of Moira, New York. . . . On County Route 17. Yes, 17. Oh no. Don't worry. I'm perfectly fine. . . . Yes, I always write the plates down. . . ." Smiles at Bill. "Old red Ford pickup, license plate PJL69243. . . . New York plates, yeah. Like you told me. You're such a worrier! I'm fine. And Bill is so nice to pick me up. He's gonna drive me as far as . . ." To Bill: "As far as where? How far you going, sir?"

Bill, grumpy now: "Potsdam."

"As far as Potsdam, honey. . . . No don't do that. I'm fine now. You sure? Okay. Love you." Quickly she ends the performance and slides the phone back into her pocket, screen unseen.

"Warren's so grateful to you for this. Says to say thanks."

"Uh-huh."

Bill, perhaps offended by what he just overheard—She took down my fucking plates? Who does she think I am?—doesn't say "sweet young thing" or anything else until they get to Moira, boring Bill becoming merely the first of several silent, slightly piqued male drivers who will uneventfully thereafter drive cunning Kaitlyn some 163 miles in the next day and a half.

10 DAYS, 5 HOURS

FUSION CENTRAL, WASHINGTON, DC

BURT WALKER THINKS FUSION CENTRAL looks way too much like a theme park. The greeters aren't dressed up as anthropomorphized rodents, but they might as well be. From the power smiles of the receptionists to the high-def trickery of the indoor arboretum to the Void staff bopping around like problem-solving Oompa Loompas in a tech version of *Willy Wonka & the Chocolate Factory*, everything is designed to make you engaged, safe, happy, make this venture seem like fun. It all makes his blood sluice backward. His halls, the halls at Langley, are austere, cold, spare, and practical. The CIA has an actual dress code; it's a place for serious people to do serious work, and these people know one thing: that stability is fragile and may be shattered like a teacup on a tile floor with the smallest tremor of God's thumbs. Fun? When you're faced with a Ukraine-level crisis, with the world plunged from peace into a Code Red in a single morning, with foreign skies filling with bombers heavy with ordnance, with hell falling on democracies and their innocents forced, in their millions, to go on the move, and with the selfish Western world required in response to regain its small claims to nobility, what place for T-shirts with pictures of Mickey Mouse, for high fives, for free candies in giant bowls, for pinball in the hall, for "fun"?

Burt, in the back seat of a town car on final approach to Cy's magic kingdom, briefcase open on the seat beside him, ignores the reports it contains. Frets instead about Cy's new toys, such as the fake off-mode program and Weeping Angel, both arguably valuable but arguably disastrous, and either way he is complicit now in their future impact. By providing the money and support for their deployment, he may as well have invented these himself! As a scientist, he can predict what new threats these weapons pose, though not in the damage they will do to personal privacy. That debate, a quaint twentieth-century one, is just ignorant background noise: the right to privacy is gone, lost already, or at least so compromised it's really worthless. No, the real present and future threat is *manipulation*, the inculcation of prescribed attitudes and modes of behavior into unwitting citizenry, the unseen shift from *monitoring* to *control*, the last chapter of the long tale of democracy, free will deformed into willing compliance.

On this epochal issue, and as a scientist, he is secretly with the civil liberties types, has always been, even as he represents the CIA. I am not your enemy. He is even trying, in his heart, with good conscience and with all his wits right now, to think of a sweet spot between what this technology gives and what it destroys, between creation and destruction, between a moral and an immoral universe, finding only that he can't. It looks right now, as his car stops at the front entrance, where Erika Coogan is waiting for him, like a clear-cut choice, between one thing or the other.

He steps out into the late May sunshine. She goes for the friendly touch on the arm as well as the handshake.

"Burt, thanks for making time for us today."

"No problem."

"I thought, first, a walk with me in the grounds, so we could talk?"

"Sure."

Side by side they slow-walk across the tessellated forecourt. They veer off on a path beside a fake stream. Burt has heard that the sounds of running water are supposed to be good for creative thinkers. He'd like to add a caveat: Not for the ones over sixty. Just makes them nervous about where the restrooms are.

He interrupts her travelogue: "Erika, I don't mind telling you, as impressed as I am, as excited by the huge potential of this technology as I am, and as excited about the trial as I am, this . . . the Weeping Angel and Clear-Voyant stuff has . . . It's made us wonder what else you've got that we don't know about. I'm not sure our relationship has room for surprises. This partnership . . . We need to know what you've got, what you're deploying, and, moreover, what you're *collecting*."

Erika takes a beat. "I can understand that. But much of what we are doing here is simply sorting through data that is already being collected as a matter of course, here or elsewhere. But I do think, with your help, we can reassure everyone on both sides that the security protections in place at Fusion are both state-of-the-art and boilerplate.'

"So let me put it this way, Erika. The math on this is simple. We will both need to be able to defend *all* of what we do here with the minimum amount of fuss." He is a scientist, but one deeply immersed in politics, making high-level calculations of a different kind. "From our point of view, for us to feel comfortable, the balance of this partnership cannot swing in your favor. Cannot happen. We will not become a back-seat partner here."

"Of course not."

"With this partnership, Fusion enjoys partial access to colossal amounts of classified data that is central to this country's security. On every level, from private to governmental."

"Fully understood, we—"

"So going forward, we, and I include Cy here, must understand each other, fully."

"Hundred percent."

"All right. Enough said. How *is* Cy?"

"Fine. He's—well, it's a lot for all of us right now. But it's tremendously exciting."

Her slight hesitation on the subject of Cy is enough to delay the reassuring smile she wants to give Burt, and he, alert to this unspoken uneasiness, studies her face for further clues.

"The agency is, of necessity, placing a very light foot on U.S. soil here," he says. "For the first time. It's historic. Let's not F-star-star-star that up."

"You have my word."

"Okay. Waffles?"

"Sorry?"

"I heard you do waffles here, in the cafeteria. Sweet tooth."

9 DAYS, 19 HOURS

KANSAS CITY, KANSAS

DON WHITE, ZERO 9, HAS been a modern-day bounty hunter long enough to know that the homeless are among the few left who are invisible. The poor may always be with us, but people step over them. People swerve round their outstretched hands without pausing in their own conversations, or press their feet on the accelerator and keep their eyes forward and windows hard up when they find themselves passing through a tent city or being accosted at a traffic light by some poor soul.

You want to get off the grid? Then bed down with the lowlifes, the junkies and winos, the bottom tier of vagrants, the crazies not even the asylums can handle anymore, the murderers who got reduced sentences for reduced mental capacity, the military veterans who, robbed of a future, prefer the comradery to be found in this urban no-man's-land, under the railway bridges, in tent cities, in those narrow tracts far enough away from civility that they're allowed to exist, undisturbed, for years.

Don keeps himself to himself. He's hidden money in a couple of stashes on the edge of town, let his beard grow, gotten used to sleeping in filthy clothes. He's strong and fit enough to defend himself; no one dares come near. In quick time he has made the crazies think he's crazy. Talks gibberish, swigs water from a vodka bottle, can't seem to remember who he is or where he's from, raises his fists, punches fellow denizens hard when he needs to. Of course, he has a burner phone in his pocket. Bought it on the street. The only person who has the number for this phone is a neighbor of his mom.

His pattern: sleep all day, walk all night. That's it. Eat shitty food. Stay away from the cops. The disgust is hard to manage. The boredom is intense. He even gave away a bottle of vodka (a real one) to some stringy fucked-up kid just so he could watch a ball game on the kid's scratchy cell. Forget the three million dollars. Three more weeks of this, and he swears to God he'll never take his old life for granted again. He'll live in praise of a clean bed, sing hallelujahs for a full fridge, and bend in prayer before his morning shower.

He's under no illusions: the next nine days and nineteen hours are going to be the toughest. You don't get used to this kind of living. And the closer the prize gets, the more his heart bangs in his chest and the more he starts to second- and triple-guess himself, thinks there's something very flawed in his whole plan. One nosy cop, it all unravels. Maybe he should just get out of town, but then, just when he has definitely, absolutely decided to shift location, he remembers—being a professional himself—how risky it is to scent a fresh new trail, and so he commits once again to his occupation of three layers of sooty cardboard under a bridge among the needles and empty bottles and forsaken lives.

Thinking about this, he walks to the gas station where guys like the new him do their shopping for noodles and cookies and cheap wine. Keeps his head down. Knows they have cameras trained on the parking lots, on the aisles, suspects every SUV is a Fusion vehicle, every idiot with a bicycle helmet an agent of the state. He has begun, a little, to understand what it must feel like to be crazy. The paranoid are sure they're always under constant surveillance, convinced they're being watched and watched and watched, and the great joke now is, *they are*. We all are! A few nights ago, when he heard one of his neighbors whispering prayers and apologies to aliens who'd gained access to his inner thoughts, Don registered a twang of fellow feeling. It bothers him, this new kinship with the doomed.

So maybe tonight, he thinks, he'll treat himself. Nothing much. He'll just pick some things from the gas station he actually *wants* to eat: Oreo cookies, a couple of cold bottles of Prairie Weekend. He reaches the station, adjusts his cap to hide his face from the camera at the counter, picks up a pack of the cookies, then heads for the beer. The bottles are frosted.

He can hear the sigh they are going to make as he eases off the cap. Can see that tiny curl of vapor that makes his throat ache with longing.

We are our habits. He remembers Billy Graham saying this over and over again—not the evangelist, no, but a really good ex-detective who had kinda mentored him in bounty hunting when he first got out of the marines. *And we cannot break those habits.* Every time they were looking for some guy who had skipped, Billy would go and interview the family, nose out who got on with the guy best (usually Mom), and then just sit outside her house and wait. If there was no mom anymore? No family? Hang around outside the guy's favorite bar. *We are our habits.* Billy always got his man, knew we lived by patterns and always, *must*, return to them, if we are to remain who we are.

Don puts his hand on the door of the chiller. He is paying cash. Even if Fusion knows his habits, his weakness for Prairie Weekend and Oreos, they can't trace a cash purchase, can they? Fuck it. Who knows what they can do? Maybe they would start looking harder in places where those two things were bought together. It isn't worth the risk.

He moves to the cabinet next door and picks out a Corona. Returns his Oreos to the display. He grabs a bag of Doritos. Shuffles back, miserable but righteous, to the cash register.

9 DAYS, 19 HOURS

FUSION CENTRAL, WASHINGTON, DC

"LADIES AND GENTLEMEN! ZERO 9 is down! We have him."

Thank Christ. Only two to go. Kaitlyn Day and James Kenner, Zeros 10 and 2, and that will make ten. All ten. They will be over the line, and with nine days and change to spare.

Cy goes down onto the floor of the Void, where he offers slaps on the back and handshakes all around: "You guys! Nerves of steel!" Ushers their Zero 9 team leader, nametag of Terry, up onto the dais, before spying, in the corner, Burt standing with Erika. Good moment then to prove again to this gloomy government stooge just how lucky he is to be in business with cool folk like this. "Come on, Terry. Tell the other kids how you did it."

Laughter. Relief around the entire facility, people coming out of their lairs, where, penned in and pent up, they have played their parts in this operation for three long weeks now.

Terry can't be more than twenty-five. Acne vulgaris still. Face like a seeded bun. Physique of a pencil. Voice starts with a nervous squeal, and then he gets into it.

"It's Clear-Voyant mostly. We decided that Don White *is* Kansas City, to his core. He was a marine, we found, then a bounty hunter. Then his knee, trouble with his knee, so . . . he definitely knows how to hide, but he hardly ever leaves K.C. Not a camper or a hiker. So we made the model, tested the model, and then worked the model."

"Words to live by," Cy says.

A nervous laugh from Terry. "Um, anyway, the model predicted he would hide in a, well, a homeless community. We thought he'd have a cell for emergencies, his mother is pretty elderly, but we had no way to pick him out in the greater Kansas City area. Not if he kept to the same patterns. So we focused on convenience stores near known tent cities and rooming houses. We knew already his tastes in things like beer and snacks. Then we slaved the beacons."

Time now, with Burt watchful in the corner, for Cy to be both boss and educator.

"Let me just jump in here for a second, Terry. Thanks for that. *Beacons*, remember that word. So . . . what do we know? We know GPS is nice if we want to track a smartphone to an address, see if someone is in their own home, but it's poor for detail work." He's turning this debriefing into a TED Talk, speaking into a headset microphone, his amplified voice filling the Void. "It gives at best a sixty-foot accuracy region. But in a large city, that means I don't know if you are in Starbucks or the Dunkin' Donuts next door. But I *want* to know that. And I want to know *more* than that. Sure, we can look at your credit card receipts, your loyalty cards to find out in retrospect. Easy. But I want to know in real time, not just where you are exactly, but if you're buying wholegrain rice instead of your normal white variety . . . *and* I want to know if you bought this whole-grain rice only after spending thirty seconds staring at the pizza options. Because then I *know* you were tempted by pizza for sixteen seconds. This knowledge lets any chump sell ads more effectively, if they can get to you *at that instant . . . reach you . . .* Then, when you're on your way home getting ready to prepare your meal for your family and they hit you with a discount voucher for the new pizza place down the road complete with a simple 'Click to accept' message that will expire in the next forty minutes, chances are you're going to leave that healthy shit in your fridge and order pizza. At Fusion? At Fusion, this knowledge is devastating in terms of helping us catch the bad guy. Thanks to the prevalence of CCTV, and to our friends at Verizon and AT&T, their amazing work in augmenting good old monolithic cell towers with a bunch of little beacons placed throughout every building and city in the land, beacons galore, beacons, beacons, beacons, Fusion has a complete mesh network to work with, which lets us record detail with that granular level of accuracy *in real time*. You own a normal phone and pause in an aisle before your favorite beer, helps us catch you. Terry, what's this guy's favorite beer?"

"Prairie Weekend."

Laughter. What glorious fun.

"A few seconds later," Cy continues, "the guy stops a couple of feet away at his preferred snack food and we know it—Terry, what's this guy's preferred snack food?"

"Oreos."

Laughter.

"So you tracked him with his phone?" Cy asks. "How?"

"He was too careful. Didn't turn on his burner phone. In this case, neighborhood CCTV mining gave us a possible male of the right age and height and gait, entering a store. We slaved the store's internal cameras and watched the guy, wearing a hood and everything, spend quite a while considering which beer to buy, but when we pinged the checkout scanner he actually bought six Coronas. But the next item was ..."

"Just couldn't help himself."

More laughter.

"Screwed by some Oreos. Case closed," Cy crows, for the benefit of the crowd in general but for Burt in particular. "And so, with all these beacons, 5G, and soon 6G and 7G, means we can now read anyone like a book, play 'em like a puppet. New world, people. New world."

Over collegial comments of "Amazing!" and "Awesome!" Cy gives his best film-star grin. "And what did you have waiting for him in the back of the capture vehicle?"

The team leader touches his pad and a huge image of Don White, miserable and unshaven in the back of the SUV appears across the wall of the Void. An agent on each side, one with a box of Oreos, one with a six-pack of Prairie Weekend, both grinning at the camera and thrusting their gifts into Don White's chest. He looks like he's going to throw up.

Cy leads the applause, then points to the big board, where only the images of Zero 2 (James Kenner, tech entrepreneur) and Zero 10 (Kaitlyn Day, librarian) remain undimmed.

8 DAYS, 17 HOURS

SARATOGA SPRINGS, NEW YORK

THE STREETS HAVE CAMERAS. EVEN the plastic garden gazebo in which she shelters for the night has cameras. They are everywhere. I am Kaitlyn Day, she thinks as she tries to walk like someone not herself, consistently. I am taking part in a government experiment to test its latest mass surveillance capacity. This part makes her laugh. When the truth sounds like a paranoid delusion, then what the hell do you do?

In her pants pocket, scrunched up, change from her last hundred-dollar bill. She flattens out the notes. Two twenties, a ten, four singles, two quarters, a dime, a penny. For the bus ticket to where she's heading, she needs forty dollars. That cannot be spent. She rolls up the twenties, hides them in her shoe. The rest—fourteen bucks and change—will have to cover two to four days of food. Well, lots of folks must be living on that. Shit, three quarters of the human population would be grateful to have that much. Live cheap, then. Available in bookstores now: *America on Seven Dollars a Day*, by . . . By? Good question. Who exactly is she? Reminds herself over and over as she ghosts around the edges of town, cleaving to the disregarded areas. At times she thinks her watch has stopped. She stares at it, waits for the jerk of the minute hand, but the progress seems irregular. Slow, slow, fast, fast, slow. Is it the watch, or is it her? Time is not playing tricks; she is. Not good. Not good. Losing it.

Warren, I'm hanging on by my fingernails here.

Do you want to go home, babe?

God yes, but I don't want to give up, either. I can't.

She listens for his voice. Holds herself together, whispers in rhythm with her steps, half of which are painful again. Hold it together, girl. Keep walking.

IN THE MIDDLE OF THE second night, staggering with sleeplessness, she hops over the fence into a city park and manages a couple of hours of semi-unconsciousness under a mass of decorative shrubbery. Buys a coffee and a muffin from a street cart and then—it must be done—a newspaper (so expensive!) from the vendor opposite as soon as he rolls up his shutters. Eats on the bench of a different park. Opens the *Washington Post* to the back pages. Sees:

LONELY GIRL. WELL DONE. ON YOUR OWN NOW. TIME TO SHINE. IT'S TIME!

She wants to cry, scream. To Warren she says, Honey, I'm still here.

In the park now, she wipes her eyes, then looks down at her booted foot. Decides, time for this thing to go. Removes it, feels the cold air flood her skin, rotates her untested ankle slowly and finds movement there. Painful still, but it will have to do. A dense shrub receives the now-unneeded boot. Rest in peace.

Nearing the bus station, she bribes a down-and-out-looking kid with five dollars to buy her a ticket from the depot ticket window. Staggers aboard, head lowered. Sleeps.

It's all so close now, she thinks as the bus rocks and rolls. She has only nine more days to survive. No matter how many other Zeros they have caught, they still have one random and damned determined librarian to track down, and not long left to do it. Advantage me, she tells Warren. Advantage me, baby.

8 DAYS, 6 HOURS

DALLAS, TEXAS

VOICES.

He must've dozed off. Hadn't heard a vehicle pull up. But now two men are talking outside the door to his storage unit, and the voices are close:

"This one?"

"This is it."

"Sure?"

"This is it."

And then . . . then . . . a knock on the door.

A goddamn knock on the door. He stares at it. Waits. And then . . . a louder knock.

For James Kenner—Zero 4, privacy expert, software developer—the thing he didn't plan for was a knock on the door.

Holds his breath, puts his computer to sleep. Kicks off his shoes. Moves on sock feet. Lights off.

"Mr. Kenner?"

Ah shit.

"Mr. Kenner. We know you're in there."

A second voice: "Fusion Capture Team, Mr. Kenner."

James, in the dark, hopes, ridiculously, that if he says and does nothing in this critical moment they might just go away.

"Do you want to open up, Mr. Kenner?"

Only a few minutes later—an eternity in Kenner-time—the wooden door shatters at the first attempt, popping a rectangle of light into the black cement box, into which steps a large male silhouette wielding a sledgehammer.

"Zero 4? James Kenner?"

LATER, LEANING ON A BLACK SUV after signing his release form on a tablet computer, James, humbled, demands to know how they found him.

He is told: "Your playlist helped."

"My *playlist*? I streamed everything under an uncrackable alias. You cracked my alias?"

"No. Pretty good masking software ya got there."

"Then I don't get it. My *playlist*?"

"Well, you were a tough nut to crack. We started with a full-scale attempt to decrypt MaskIt's engineering, certain you'd be employing it, but so far it's still resisting our efforts, so props to you there. So then we went through your life. And then your house. Ransacked both. Every detail. Human lives—every action, every purchase, it spawns a myriad of wavelets like a pebble dropped in a pond. But you know this. Then we followed all the leads. All went nowhere. Until we found a T-shirt, in your bottom drawer. Breakthroughs can come from anywhere."

"T-shirt?"

"How we found you."

"But—"

"We look at everything, obviously, so as part of that we looked at every piece of your clothing."

"T-shirt? You said a T-shirt? You found me from a T-shirt?"

"The one that reads SURELY NOT EVERYBODY WAS KUNG FU FIGHTING? Not a Top 40 hit these days, 'Kung Fu Fighting,' so it stood to reason that you might like this song, that it might be a favorite on your playlist, so we started to monitor U.S.-based streams of that particular song on all the major world websites, eliminated everybody who *couldn't* be you, and ended up with a pretty short list of Kung Fu Fight lovers, if you will. Only like ten thousand a day. But still a lot of numbers to crunch and triangulate but that's Fusion for you. Which led us to the account of a certain E. Jack

Ulayte, which led us to track the other songs this character was stream-ing. This playlist, so they guys figured out, were all songs James Kenner listens to a lot. So from that point we had E. Jack Ulayte as possibly you. And pretty soon, after hacking several websites for their private data, we saw Mr Ulayte popping up regularly, and even one or two food deliveries in his name to this address. So then all of Mr. Ulayte's internet traffic was ours, and from that we located the actual computer in question that was using this alias to stream those songs. The addresses for both the stream, and oh, the deliveries of penne all'arrabbiata, bingo, right here."

"Bingo," James mutters, unshaven, stiff, unwashed, shaking his head, "T-shirt . . ."

"But as I say, you pulled a lot of our resources out of us, so congratula-tions on that. And I'll say this, too: You posed the *right* question."

"Oh yeah? And what question would that be?"

The agent shrugs. "Surely not *everybody* was kung fu fighting?"

7 DAYS, 18 HOURS

SPROUL STATE FOREST, PENNSYLVANIA

DAY. EVENING. NIGHT. DAWN. FIVE hours on the bus, six hitchhiking, then three hours actual hiking. Ankle afflicts every step. Finally, she emerges from the thick woodland and stops on the edge of a ridge, looking down on a small cabin in an isolated clearing fringed with black oaks and maples. Smoke puffs gently from the chimney, and a light is on inside. She could cry.

As she staggers down the trail, she can see someone moving inside. She'd break into a run but her legs aren't up to it. So tired. Stopping twenty feet from the front door, she gets a clear view of the person inside. A familiar figure. She bends, picks up a pebble. Throws it so it pings off the glass. The figure inside looks up. The two women lock eyes on each other.

Seconds later, the front door opens. The woman who steps out onto the porch wears yoga pants, a sweater knitted in rainbow colors. Around the same age. Hair cut in a black bob, large round glasses. Lifts her hand in greeting.

"Honey, you look like shit."

This gets a smile, but a weary one. "Hi ya, babe."

"You made it."

"After a fashion."

They fall into each other's arms.

The woman in the rainbow sweater whispers, "You're in luck. I made soup."

They turn and go in together. The door shuts.

7 DAYS, 9 HOURS

FUSION CENTRAL, WASHINGTON, DC

STARTING HIS MORNING VERY EARLY, Cy stares at the big screen—nine out of ten portraits are dimmed, including every one of the five professionals. I'm *this* close to getting back to Palo Alto, he thinks before his eyes shift to the last undimmed portrait and then at the backward-running clock. Okay, where are you Kaitlyn Day? Enough of this.

His early admiration for her has faded—steeply, in fact—in the last two days, replaced by annoyance and a certain mystification. Yes, she is testing Fusion's capabilities handsomely, but there's something seriously *not right* about this whole thing, and it bugs him now, bugs him like hell. Just look at it: a librarian, with no expertise in this field, on her own, trammeled by mental health issues, even needed an orthopedic boot for her sprained ankle, and still she leads the best surveillance facility in the world on a terrific dance. Just doesn't add up. Several times he has gone through her case notes, her biography, and nothing would suggest that this lame duck could be performing this well. At this rate, she is going to win it all, and perhaps fatally wound Fusion's claim to find anyone, anytime, anywhere. More hours than he wishes have been spent trying to predict her next move. Her slipping off to Canada was an excellent gambit; it caused them to run interference with the Canadians every damn day, which cost Fusion time and tracking opportunities and left the Zero 10 team struggling to have any sense of her current location or movement. If her challenge was to stay off the radar, she's winning: not a single blip popping up. Almost ridiculously, Fusion, for all its tremendous powers, is being found wanting in the case of Kaitlyn Day.

Sonia Duval materializes, as ordered.

Without looking at her: "I'm making a change, Sonia. I want you back on the Zero 10 Team. Take over from Zack. You're in charge now. You good with that?"

This young woman glows like a screensaver of a sunny day. "Absolutely."

He then asks, "Why can't we find her?"

Sonia takes a moment, joining Cy in looking at an unspoiled digital map of the United States and Canada that highlights not a single point of interest.

"Maybe because she doesn't act like herself?"

7 DAYS, 6 HOURS

SPROUL STATE FOREST, PENNSYLVANIA

FROM THE BATHROOM, WHERE SHE is busily dyeing her hair blond, she can smell the soup on the stove. It's Kaitlyn's mother's recipe. Delicious. The two women eat it together, catching up on what's happened over the last three weeks, a recitation of the whole odyssey, blow by blow and unpacking the wisdom and effectiveness of her having enacted a wild master plan to both draw attention to herself and to evade detection at the same time.

After this, sleeps as deep as a dived submarine. Mad dreams. Waking, somewhat restored, as the sun begins to swoop down and as night draws in, she connects again with her friend at the dining table. In the middle of the table sits a cell phone. Beside it, its battery.

"Thank you for doing this. You're incredible."

"Honey, you're so welcome. Just as long as you stick it to them and make 'em pay."

"I'm trying."

"I can see." A gentle smile. "Okay, then, shall we do this?"

"Let's."

"Do you want to, or shall I?"

"You do it."

"All right. Let's blow this thing wide open."

Two hands, smelling of chopped onions and fresh thyme, remove the back of the phone and insert the battery. *Click*. A thumb then presses the power button, and a few seconds later the screen lights up. In the top right-hand corner, two bars, a good enough signal.

7 DAYS, 6 HOURS

FUSION CENTRAL, WASHINGTON, DC

"CY!" IT'S SONIA DUVAL, BACK already.

"Mmm?"

"We have a phone! We think belongs to Zero 10. It has switched on again."

Her voice, loud in his ear, is quivering with excitement.

At his desk he wonders: Is it another decoy, another yank on his diamond chain from this damn woman?

"How do we know it's her, and not another of her misdirects?"

"Well, yes, it's the last untracked handset she bought in Boston, but it's using a new SIM card, so it's clear this is the first time an effort's been made to conceal the identity of one of them. We've been pinging the handset via its IMEI, and we . . . Cy, we have a location. The missing burner phone is live."

"Where?"

"A hundred miles west of Scranton, Pennsylvania. Middle of the woods somewhere. Signal's only just getting through."

A knock on his door. It's Erika. They stare at each other.

"You heard?" she asks.

Cy can feel it in his bones that this time it's Kaitlyn Day. "I want to be there,' he announced, surprising Erika. After all, it's the last capture, and it can be a celebration of the billions in Federal funds that will now flow Fusion's way and, also, some part of him wants to meet this particular Zero, face to face, see if he can get some answers to the nagging mystery of the librarian's unexpected longevity.

To Sonia: "Where's the nearest Capture Team?"

"New York."

"I want to get there first."

His eyes then turn to his partner, his best friend, his lover: He sees excitement in Erika's face also. This is her triumph, perhaps even more than his.

"Let's get out of here," he says. "Come with me."

6 DAYS, 23 HOURS

SPROUL STATE FOREST, PENNSYLVANIA

THE HELICOPTER SETS THEM DOWN on a steep flank of meadow. Cy, in his Cybermonk outfit and clutching his gray laptop bag, is escorted across the frozen earth—not easy in Allbirds—and into a Pennsylvania Department of Conservation & Natural Resources SUV. Erika is hustled in beside him. Doors clap. Neither speaks. Two hundred miles, the distance between Cy and this Zero when they found her phone, has become two miles of dirt track. Two miles then becomes one hundred yards.

When he steps out of the vehicle, the driver holds out a polyester puffer coat, which he shrugs on awkwardly. A member of the Capture Team from the second backup chopper barks something about perimeters and covering exit routes, but Cy goes straight up the front path to the cabin. The siren call of the red pulse of the phone is irresistible. Erika follows close behind.

Then Cy is up on the veranda. Knocks and hears, instead of a commotion, "Come on in."

Inside: one main room, a comfortable open-plan kitchen/dining room/sitting area done in American Arts and Crafts style. Stepping inside, he registers bad paintings and a lot of quilting, an open fire, and, on the settee before it, a woman, knitting, smiling generously at him.

But this is not Kaitlyn Day. Close. Same hair, same glasses, same age. But not her face. And there is a gap between the front teeth.

"Hello, I'm looking for Kaitlyn Day."

"Well I'm pretty sure that you're looking at her."

"Kaitlyn Elizabeth Day?" Cy adds.

"Kaitlyn Elizabeth Day," the woman repeats, "last time I checked."

The rest of the Capture Team is pouring in behind Cy now, filling up the room with windbreakers and baseballs caps.

"Of 89 Marlborough Street, Boston, Massachusetts, apartment 7?" Erika says from behind him while Cy just stares at this passable likeness.

"Modest, but it suits me."

Cy's eyes fall on the cell phone lying on the table.

The woman follows Cy's gaze and smiles.

"That's Kaitlyn's," he insists. "We know that."

"Now, *that* is correct . . . That phone *does* belong to Kaitlyn Day. You're right about that, oh you bet."

Cy raises his voice. "Who are you?"

Erika pulls out a photo, walks toward the woman. Shows her the still from the initial Going Zero interview session. "Do you know this woman?"

The woman takes the picture, studies it, then hands it back. "Yes. Of course, I know her."

"Who is she?"

"You haven't figured that out yet?"

6 DAYS, 20 HOURS

SPROUL STATE FOREST, PENNSYLVANIA

SHE MET WARREN AT A house party in Georgetown when he was finishing his PhD and she was working at Inova Fairfax Hospital in Falls Church. She thought his eyes had sort of skated over her at first. Maybe he wasn't on the prowl, or he'd spotted someone else, but after they were introduced, and as they'd talked, she could sense him coming closer to her. Some guy had made a quip about women drivers, and she'd given him the benefit of the insights she had gleaned working since the age of seven for her dad, who'd pit-crewed for many NASCAR teams. Warren's attention settled on her after that. She liked it. They talked about DC hangouts. Families. Her work. What she liked to read when things were quiet. She knew as he pulled her over to where people were dancing that he was into her.

"What's your name?"

She could smell from his whiskey breath that he was enjoying himself, and enjoying her.

"I told you already and you forgot. Once is all you get."

The atmosphere was loud and sweaty; the air smelled of cigarette smoke and beer and the whiff of end-of-semester grad-school abandon. He fitted his hand into the small of her back; it felt good there. Always did after that.

When he pulled her a little closer, saying "Come on," she pushed him away a little, spun around under his arm, let herself be caught again. He dipped her, which surprised and delighted her. She laughed out loud, a thick throaty laugh, and his face lit up hearing it.

As the music ended with a blast, he spun and caught her one more time. Someone was arguing with the self-appointed DJ. Catcalls and shouts for competing tunes broke out around them. But they were already a little bubble, just the two of them. He had good eyes, high cheekbones, a tiny mole just by his left ear. Side by side on the stairs, where they could hear each other, she gave it to him straight.

"They say you learn almost everything you essentially need to know about another person in the first fifteen minutes."

"We're fast running out of time, then."

"It's how you can make very accurate assessments with a frugality of information," she told him in her best fancy accent. "It's called thin-slicing, apparently."

"A frugality of information? Nice. So, cool, what's a thin slice of *you* taste like?"

She rolled her eyes. "Seriously?"

He made a rueful face. "Okay, so, as we just clocked our first fifteen minutes, tell me about *me*, then. What've you detected, Sherlock? Now you've just thin-sliced *me*?"

"Wanna know?"

"I'll regret it, but yes. Hit me."

"So. You're a smart guy, obviously, but you need a few drinks to have the confidence that you'd like to have naturally. Smart but shy, and compensating."

"Ouch. Anything else?"

"Also, in trying to be this cool dude, in *reaching* for that, you're missing a lot of the fundamentals that you're only gonna find out later that you're really gonna need."

"Wow. Missing the fundamentals? Such as?"

He was holding her hand then.

"Such as my name."

He laughed and shook his head. "Fair enough. Then take pity on me. For another chance, I'll buy you dinner tomorrow night at any reasonably priced restaurant in DC you choose. So tell me. What *is* your name?"

She looked up at him. He wasn't like the other entitled, book-smart guys she'd met recently. She sensed something else in him calling out, and something similar in her calling back. A cosmic echo. And then she wondered how a person can feel comfortable, safe, and on familiar ground, and also excited, at risk, and on the brink of a whole new world all at the very same time.

"Samantha. My name is Samantha."

6 DAYS, 20 HOURS

SPROUL STATE FOREST, PENNSYLVANIA

"SAMANTHA," KAITLYN DAY SAYS. "MY friend Sam. Tough gal. Good luck finding her."

Cy is still buffering: "Samantha?"

"Samantha Crewe. She does kinda look like me. But she doesn't wear glasses. Not in *reality*. If *this* is reality. Any of this. Did I mention the soup?" Her gaze settles on Cy. "You, sir, look like you could do with some soup."

6 DAYS, 19 HOURS

SPROUL STATE FOREST, PENNSYLVANIA

SAMANTHA CREWE, NÉE WARHURST, ER nurse practitioner, thirty-one, natural blonde, vision 20/20, beer drinker (no K. Day'ish gap between her teeth), is right now watching through binoculars from a wooded ridge half a mile away from the cabin as Cy Baxter himself (wow!) and a woman she figures must be Erika Coogan (double wow!) come out onto the porch. Sam knows she should be farther away than this, but she also wants some sign that her pal Kaitlyn is okay. As she watches, she sees Cy pull off the puffer jacket he is wearing, throw it to the ground. A full-on temper tantrum it looks like. And Erika Coogan, waiting until Cy's done kicking the grounded coat before touching him on the arm, leaning toward him like she's saying something comforting, kind, whereupon Baxter's shoulders slump. He's listening. Appears capable of it. He finally nods, allows himself to be led back inside.

Sam waits another two minutes, until she hears the rising *thud-thud-thud-thud* of a helicopter. An aerial sweep of the forest will begin now, and God knows what other toys they can employ. She stows the binoculars in her clean new backpack, checks to ensure she has her notebook, her water bottle, her survival bracelet. So far, so good for phase 2 of her plan. At lease she has their undivided attention now, just as she wanted: Baxter and Coogan's travel to this site proves that. And not only the attention of Baxter and the Fusion Initiative, she hopes, but the full attention of each and every security service in the United States. From this moment, she's going to make full use of it.

PHASE TWO

6 DAYS, 19 HOURS

SPROUL STATE FOREST, PENNSYLVANIA

INSIDE THE CABIN, CY, IN a sagging armchair opposite the benignly smiling Kaitlyn Day, continues his interrogation of this maddening mad woman. But instead of looking intimidated, the interrogee looks delighted, like she doesn't want this to end.

"You need to tell us everything you know."

"Sure. That's the plan."

"The plan?"

"She *wants* me to tell you almost everything. As much as I know of it. Full disclosure."

Cy and Erika share a look.

"Was she here?"

"Yes indeedee."

"When did she leave?"

"Next question."

"You said *everything*."

"I said *almost*."

"Where is she going now?"

"No idea. I didn't ask. Next question."

"You seem to be enjoying this."

"Sue me."

"Why did she come here to see you?"

"To tell me it was time to turn on the phone."

"We need to go back to the start. Tell me about Samantha's plan."

Kaitlyn flicks an imaginary scrap of dust from her jeans as she revisits the beginning.

"Ah, let's see . . . so Sam came to me with the application forms and some other stuff downloaded from the internet and said she wanted to be part of this trial thing, and how would I like to really screw with the government and the surveillance capitalists over their invasion of public privacy and their covert influence in grooming public opinion. All of that. If you knew me, you'd know this was a rhetorical question. That kind of thing is something of a bête noire for me, actually, so I said, 'Would I ever,' because I love my country, I mean I *actually* love my country, Mr. Baxter, what it *could* and *should* be, I mean, not what it currently is and is heading *toward* being. The idea of this country. But the government does such terrible and idiotic things, such brain-dead stupid lame shit, against which, in the course of my entire adult life, I've protested or tried to do so and written letters and letters, but they didn't change one damn thing."

She draws a breath here, having forgotten to do so for a while.

"And don't get me started on WorldShare and you two bozos. So anyway, I said yes, and we made the plan and that was that. It was very exciting because of course I had to do all the buying of the phones and so on, and ask my friends to carry them and borrow things like cars and"—she waves her hands around her pleasant surrounding—"cabins. Of course, Sam gave me all the money and we'd talk it all through every day until she quit her job as a nurse and moved into my apartment and dyed her hair and I took all my vacation days from the library and came up here on the bus incognito and Sam arranged for there to be lots of food and books and things waiting for me. I've had a lovely time of it actually, because it's preferable to be alone with the world as it is. Just finished reading *Fifty Shades of Grey* and *Das Kapital* back-to-back. We're all enslaved—that was basically the message of both books." Her laughter here is prolonged.

When this new Kaitlyn's mirth subsides, Erika leans forward, only half as irritated as Cy is.

"Kaitlyn, I'd like to think I could help convince you of how important the work we're doing is."

Kaitlyn shrugs. "I actually thought it was *important* to oppose any organization that wants to collect information about everything on everybody and hold on to it forever. That's your MO, right? Over at the good old C to the I to the A? I'm quoting your own Gus Hunt, by the way, in his speech of 2013. It's on YouTube. Excuse me, but urrghhh."

Erika finds herself fascinated by this eccentric live wire, humming with grievances big and small, another would-be legislator but with no power to legislate.

"And I'm afraid I can't approve of a private company that profits from algorithmic amplification, dissemination and microtargeting of corrupt information, much of it produced by coordinated schemes of *dis*information that splinter our shared reality, poison social discourse, and paralyze democratic politics," Kaitlyn adds. "And to what end, folks? What end? To create a killing field for truth and so instigate violence and death on the way to finally sacrificing democracy itself to private surveillance capitalism and nudging us all toward Armageddon? No, ma'am. I guess I don't approve. Did you know that's a real place by the way? Armageddon. It's in northern Israel. I assume house prices remain low there. Oh, and what we did up here—the cabin, Sam and I, everything—was all entirely legal, just in case you're wondering. We read the agreements you sent. I signed the papers saying you could look into my data, so I'm in the clear and so is she. I guess what I'm basically saying is go fuck yourselves."

Cy doesn't look like he wants to say anything so Erika steps up again:

"So I'm getting an understanding of your principles, Kaitlyn. It's helpful, thank you. But can you tell us more about Samantha? I assume she feels like you do about . . . what we're doing here?"

Kaitlyn ignores this question, her mind already elsewhere. "I learned the periodic table as well, while I've been up here. Had *so* much time. Always been on my to-do list since my best friend in first grade learned the whole thing by rote. Wanna hear it? Hydrogen, helium, lithium, beryllium, boron, carbon, nitrogen, oxygen, fluorine, neon, sodium, magnesium, aluminum—though the British call it alumin*ium*—silicon, phosphorus—"

Erika tries to interrupt.

"Sulfur, chlorine, argon—"

"Ms. Day, EXCUSE ME!!!"

The added volume does it. With her flow arrested, Kaitlyn looks at

Erika, seeming to prefer this to looking at Cy. "*Ms.* Day? No one's called me that in a while. I am unmarried, but silly me, you know all about that, I guess. Never found my soul mate. Now? No chance. I've lost all my looks and I never had much to start with. Never found love, not like Sam and Warren did. But where was I? Oh yeah . . . Potassium, calcium, scandium, titanium, vanadium . . . Been so awful for Sam since he, you know, . . . *terrible* . . . Chromium, manganese, iron, cobalt, nickel, copper, zinc, gallium, germanium . . . Disappeared'n'all. What's after germanium? Oh, it's vanished. Gone. Relax, I'm just playing with ya. I'm fine. Mentally stable—"

"That's enough!" Cy shouts. "You were asked a question. You need to answer. And by the way, I can tell you right now you're not seeing a dime of the prize money. You are—I mean, your friend is disqualified. The beta test is over."

Erika sees that Cy's churlish, little-boy, I'm-taking-my-ball-back-home streak is now on full and unattractive display. He's really undone by all this.

"Why's it over?" Kaitlyn asks, baiting him further. "You haven't caught her yet. And she's the one you have to catch, right? Surely not me."

"She misrepresented herself," he replies. "Misled us."

"Oh. I thought this was a test to see if you could outsmart terrorists and enemies of the state and so forth? If you're calling time, kinda looks like she won."

He draws breath, calming himself. "So you're saying that Samantha thinks we're still going to keep hunting her for fun? What's the angle?"

"Aren't you going to? Keep hunting?"

"We caught Kaitlyn Day."

"But you were looking for Samantha Crewe; you just didn't know it."

It hits him: like being turned over on the beach by a freak wave, rolled over and over, stinging sand and salt water, because he *gets it* now: the nagging enigma of this woman, why someone with the smarts to lay false trails across the data-verse could have done something so stupid as to use an ATM on a busy street, offering her face for its camera and so linking—all for Fusion's benefit—Sam's face to the name *Kaitlyn Day*, but not before, *not* before Sam had presumably gotten her face onto Kaitlyn's driver's license and passport, which he now guesses were both recently renewed!

If she hadn't done all that, Fusion would've concentrated more resources on archive photos, probably discovered this cute little switcheroo days earlier.

"How did you communicate?" he asks.

"Come again?"

"I said, how did you communicate? Do you have another burner phone?"

"Oh, this will strike *you* as funny: We communicated in person. I *know*. Face-to-face. Usually at the library, when she came in, or on hikes we took together. She doesn't much like hiking, but it was training for being out in the woods. Poor Sam. She was so lonely. So betrayed. Nobody believed her. Not even her family. Anyway, where was I? Oh yes. We talked in person. I don't trust devices—one of the benefits of being clinically paranoid. So. Anyway. Hiking. So I met Sue, who owns this cabin, through our little hiking club. Oh, and the personals, how we communicate. We place ads in the personal columns. If anything went wrong I was to leave a classified ad in the *Washington Post*—physical paper, mind you—addressed to Lonely Girl. But nothing went wrong, so I never had to leave anything. Now, are you people sure you don't want any soup? It's pea and ham. My mother's recipe. She's dead. We didn't get along, but what can you do? The bitch could cook."

"I don't want soup," Cy says.

"No soup. Oh. How about this, then?" Kaitlyn remembers something, reaches into her pocket, pulls out a thumb drive, passes it to Cy. "You might be interested in this."

"What is it?"

"A message from Sam. I've told you *my* why . . . why *I* did this. This is *her* why, why she did it."

Cy knows there's not much else to glean here. He takes the thumb drive, stands quickly, tucking his laptop under his arm, and makes for the door.

"You'll need the password to open it," Kaitlyn tells him.

At the door, Cy grits his teeth. "And that would be . . . ?"

"Just plain text. Capital T, lowercase o-m-y-r-i-s. Tomyris."

Cy and Erika both jot this down on their phones, but Kaitlyn is still talking. "You know Tomyris, right? The queen who destroyed Cyrus the Great. Cyrus was a great leader, two and half thousand years ago. So, it was looking like Cyrus was going to take over the whole world, but then he fucked with the wrong lady. She killed him, in the end, had his corpse beheaded and crucified, and then shoved his head into a wineskin filled with human blood." With this she turns to Cy: "He's buried in Iran. Most of him, anyway."

It feels to Cy like this madwoman has just reached into his chest and yanked out a lung. She can't be allowed to have the last word here. Not today. With the thumb drive tight in his fist, he pulls down the door handle but only opens the door a crack before turning again. "You're dead wrong, by the way. What you said earlier about privacy. People don't want privacy, not anymore. Privacy is passé. Privacy is a prison. People can't *wait* to give it away, if you really want to know the truth. The fact is, they're so damn lonely—which maybe, just maybe, you know a little something about—that they barter away their privacy *with relief,* first chance they get. Because, why? I'll tell you. Because what they crave is to be *known*, not unknown . . . to be *transparent, watched*, as if they matter, as proof they matter, all their secrets laid out there in public view, their sins proclaimed, heck, even *advertised*! Nothing hidden. They want it that way. And why? Wanna know why? *Ms.* Day? Because being watched . . . it feels a little like being loved."

Click of latch. Door closed. He's gone.

6 DAYS, 18 HOURS

SPROUL STATE FOREST, PENNSYLVANIA

ERIKA CATCHES UP WITH CY before he reaches the SUV. "Cy. . . . Cy, wait. Are we still chasing her?"

"Oh yeah. Yes. We. Are."

In the back of the vehicle, after indicating to Erika he needs a moment alone, Cy slides in the thumb drive, hunches over the laptop, taps in the password, *tok, tok, tok, tok, tok, tok, tok. Tomyris*? Fucking bitch.

Only one video file on the thumb drive. Called "Play Me." Cute. The virus detection software kicks up a TRUST THIS? window. *Click.* And, finally, there she is, in vivid color and poor quality, public enemy number 1, Zero 10, the person who *is supposed to be* Kaitlyn Day, now established as Samantha Crewe, looking back at him. No glasses on her nose. Blond now. She's filmed herself in the cabin, sitting in the same fucking chair Cy was just seated in talking to Bizarro Kaitlyn. Samantha Crewe waits a beat, then begins.

"Well, I guess I don't need to introduce myself. You already know everything about everyone?—where anyone is at any given time?—almost everything we've ever done? At least I hope you do. Because I need you to use you now. To find my husband. See, that's why I decided to take part in your ten-billion-dollar whatever—lotta money by the way—you must be really trying not to blow it. I wanted to motivate you. Did I? My husband is missing, and I want him back. I need him back. You're inside all the government databases now, Mr. Baxter. I know that as part of your deal they gave you the keys to the kingdom. So I want you to find him, because they know where he is. Find him, then you'll get me. His name is Warren.

Warren Crewe. Former economics professor at Harvard. He went missing doing covert work for the CIA, somewhere in the Middle East, we think. A servant of this country. The cops, the State Department, and even the White House have all denied any knowledge of him working for them, and claim to have no knowledge of his whereabouts. I have been told that it is more likely that he just left me. Walked out. Has gone intentionally missing, is probably on some beach in Cambodia. Problem with all that is, I know him. I know my husband. And now I want you to know him. I know he was working for elements within the U.S. government, and that my own government is lying to me when they say they don't know where he is. I believe they know very well. I believe there are reasons, which they can't disclose, that prevent them from telling me what they know. I'm offering you a deal. Find my husband, and in return you get me. You get me, you save your project, and, as a bonus, I don't tell anyone about what dark shit you've really been doing down there at WorldShare. I know things, Cy. And I have evidence you won't want me to share. Like. . . . Virginia Global Technologies. So that's the deal. Me for Warren Crewe. I'm waiting. And I'm watching. Oh . . . and Kaitlyn knows how to reach me when you find the answers I'm looking for."

Cy proceeds to watch the clip a dozen times. It would be so easy to characterize it as a left-behind-wife's hysterics, drag it in his mind to the trash can, hit "empty trash," *skrnnschh*, but her reference to Virginia Global Technologies—that one name—elevates the threat level she poses to *existential*. Also, no one who is as smart as this woman evidently is— who takes the audacious life-risking trouble she has taken, inveigling her way into this project (by means he has yet to fathom), and then intimates she has damaging information on his company—is kidding around. Nope, that dog won't hunt. Whatever happened to her husband, she has to be taken—if not at her own word—then *seriously*.

At some point Erika knocks on the car window. Time to go. Through the lowered glass, Cy takes a last look at Kaitlyn Day on the porch as the team departs in their SUVs. Kaitlyn, as if to a friend, waves. Part of him wants this madwoman to get the world she desires, if only so she can see what a catastrophe it is. For some reason, he waves back.

Soon they are in the helicopter once more, high over Pennsylvania farmland, whirling south.

6 DAYS, 1 HOUR

FUSION CENTRAL, WASHINGTON, DC

THE MOOD IS SOMBER, THE celebration canceled, the figurative champagne very much not on ice.

Urgently, Cy calls the brightest and the best of his people to his office where the figure of the unmasked Samantha supplants the sequoia forest imagery. Cy dictates that the hunt for Zero 10 will continue and intensify, that the contest is not over, and that whether or not the Kaitlyn/Sam deception is within the bounds of the original rules, the bad guys don't play by the rules and so they must adjust and carry on. With this announcement, confidence in the room evaporates and in its place a new desperation made physical by the large backward-counting digital clock, visible below in the Void, which continues to illustrate just how precipitously time is running out before this mission ends in total failure.

"Okay. So the good news: We, *all* of us, can now focus all our resources, all of them, on finding this last remaining Zero. And we have a whole week to do it. The bad news: This is . . . this is no longer an ordinary situation. As has become clear."

Leaving unsaid much of what *he* knows, about what Samantha *might* know—in fact, hiding from everyone the very existence of her thumb drive with its demands and disclosures, even from Erika—Cy calls on Sonia Duvall to lead the private briefing.

"Samantha Crewe. Thirty-one. Maiden name, Warhurst. Mother was a housewife, father ran engineer, worked on some NASCAR teams. Sam learned to get her hands dirty. Tomboy. Solid student but unspectacular. Contemplated being a doctor then her dad gets sick and she can't face the debt. Goes into nursing instead. Three brothers, all in the auto industry. Used to be close to them, less so since she married. Way less so recently. Now it gets interesting. Marries Warren Crewe, whom she met here in DC while he was doing postdoctoral research into global mechanisms of income disparity. He then teaches economics at Harvard, on the tenure track, but jumps off to pursue direct action in the real world. Samantha has publicly claimed, since Warren's disappearance—more on this in a second—he was doing advanced mathematical work, believes it was for the CIA or its affiliates, for whom he was doing intelligence gathering. On his last trip abroad, Warren tells Samantha he's going out of the country, will be back in a week or so. Is always vague on where he goes, but she notices that he packs a Farsi language guide. This is the last anyone ever hears of him. This is three years ago. Samantha has been active since then, writing to officials here at home, newspapers, anyone who will listen, demanding answers, claiming somebody knows something. The CIA, for their part, uncovered and presented her with a flight log and CCTV footage of a man who clearly appears to be Warren Crewe, flying to Bangkok on the very day he was last heard from, and in the absence of any further information, presume him to be in Thailand still, an overstayer."

Lakshmi Patel has something. Cy recognizes her as the one they hired from the FBI, a bookish young woman, humorless, a rosebud that won't open.

"Samantha refuted this evidence, however; she claimed in emails we've recovered and posts to relevant chat groups that this is all part of an elaborate cover-up, that Warren is in Iran, or why else take a book of Farsi? She has managed to get some publicity, too. . . . a couple of articles in regional papers, one article in the *New York Times*, appearing with her parents, appealing to the U.S. government to investigate, repeating her claim that Warren was in the employ of the CIA."

Sonia finishes: "When the CIA denies this was ever the case, Samantha starts an online petition for direct U.S. government intervention, fifteen thousand signatures, but so far no action has been taken. There's more background coming in by the minute, but that's a primer."

Sonia closes her file. Looks around the room. Clicks shut a redundant pen.

"So," Cy says. "While we intensify our search for the wife, let's also open up a small side investigation of the husband. We find the wife, end of story. Were we to, somehow, learn where the husband is, I suspect we get the wife. Two birds, one stone. What else? Sonia, you seem to hold all the cards today?"

"Actually," Sonia says. "for a behavioral analysis of Samantha, I'd like to hand off to Lakshmi." Sonia turns to her colleague, who takes over:

"So . . . from what we have seen so far of Samantha Crewe, and know of her past, this is a highly motivated person, with enormous commitment to her cause. She *believes* her claims, whether they're true or not. She *believes* the U.S. government is betraying her and is actively keeping her husband's whereabouts from her. She has developed a deep distrust of institutions, increasingly has cut herself off from the lineaments of normal life, and is drifting ever more into an extreme and antagonistic relationship with her country and now with this organization. I believe she is capable of a wide range of possible actions."

After a moment, Cy slowly, clearly says, "Perhaps, Lakshmi, you can tell us this: Exactly who the fuck are you fucking?"

"I-I'm sorry?" Lakshmi stutters.

"I asked, Who are you fucking? Because someone gave you access to this room full of people with an IQ average of one sixty-five, so it must be someone pretty important. So who you are fucking? Because if all that your FBI experience can give us is that Samantha Crewe is *capable of a wide range of possible actions*, there's no way in hell you got here on merit."

Lakshmi's face is scarlet, mouth open.

Erika hasn't seen him this bad in a while. "Cy—" she begins.

But Lakshmi chooses to defend herself: "With all due respect, Cy, I'm most concerned with how this entire project got fucked by Samantha Crewe, and how we are now going to unfuck ourselves."

The room is temporarily suspended in a lacuna of astonishment with an underlayer of self-loathing as Lakshmi closes her binder, rises as elegantly as possible, and prepares to depart.

Cy breathes deeply, taking himself down a notch. "Lakshmi, I'm sorry.

Stay where you are. Please. Let's keep going. This is tough stuff, but I'm sorry. You didn't deserve that."

Lakshmi, a moment spent considering her options, her future, sits back down, and Cy resumes.

"Anyone else? Who else has got something?"

Another silence.

"All right. So what have we decided? Anyone? Come on, I'm getting lonely here."

After a fear-filled moment, Sonia again, consulting her notes: "Double down on finding Samantha, and open a side channel on Warren Crewe—"

"But off the grid, for Warren. Keep it dark. Have the teams report *only to you*. If he *was* CIA, there will be classified issues there, and I don't want the agency up my ass any more than it is already. Not right now." Rising from his chair, he tucks his laptop under his arm. "Let's find *Samantha*. Our focus: one registered nurse, six and a half days. Get on it." On the way out he swipes the wall, like a dismissive act on a dating app, whereupon digital Samantha is replaced by a deserted beach, the wavelets unfolding, smooth as upholstery, a *ssshhh* of sea searching stones.

With Cy gone and the door closed, it's like a sudden change in cabin pressure.

The first to speak is Sonia. "So we're supposed to investigate the CIA now? Isn't that kinda fucked up?"

Erika, decompressing, mindful of her garden walk with Burt Walker and therefore the existential danger in keeping secrets from their principal patron, fills the Cy-sized vacancy in the room: "Let's just presume the CIA is telling the truth, that Warren Crewe wasn't working for the agency. But keep an open mind. Anything remains possible, and everything about him is of interest." To the rest of the room: "But let's not forget that our primary focus is Samantha. We should slave in the new ghost algorithms to the traffic cameras. We think she won't be in a late-model car. She seems to have anticipated a program like Weeping Angel and gone low tech to foil our efforts. But we may be able to pick up her driving mannerisms. And update her gait profile. That limp is real. As Sonya so pithily put it, that alone should allow us to un—"

And here the entire room provides the rest of the sentence: "—fuck ourselves."

5 DAYS, 16 HOURS

VOLTA PLACE NW, GEORGETOWN, WASHINGTON, DC

HE FORCES HIMSELF THROUGH A silent dinner with Erika. Civility is hard work at such times. Later, he swims laps in his indoor pool, alone, the still lilac surface smashed, his short, thick, quick arms churning, punching, dragging. Usually he swims twenty, but today fifty; needs to heart-pump the frustrations of this shitty day out into the remotest capillaries of his being and from there flush it out of his system *entirely*.

Drained, he sits naked in his steam room looking at his hands gemming slowly with sweat. In the thick atmosphere, his thoughts race as he puzzles the mystery, the deep mystery of Samantha Crewe. She's not so cute now, this figure selected as one of the five representatives of ordinary, uninformed credulous America. Beneath that easily underestimated form hid an evident genius. That was their first mistake, to write her off, then to condescend to her. All their predictive tools were calibrated to catch a sleepy citizen with only elementary understanding of the awesome powers now available to find anyone, know them, reveal them, influence them. From this core mistake all else has flowed.

Advantage Samantha Crew. But he has to win, and *will* do so. Five days and sixteen hours left. And tens of billions at stake. He runs through her case once more. What is he missing? Something. Something still doesn't add up. She has too many skills and some pretty damn good knowledge of Fusion's strategies. Take, as but one example, her choice of an old model car to drive, which effectively rendered Weeping Angel worthless. Is it possible someone in the general public knew that to drive an old timer would be necessary? Fusion hadn't even told the CIA about Weeping Angel when the beta began. Other things, too. Gait recognition: Via a splendid nexus of cameras across the land, Fusion had not once detected this woman traveling so often on foot. How could she know that too many irregularities of gait would send up an alert? No, someone else must be helping her, besides that angry nutjob, the real Kaitlyn Day. And it occurs to him, right on the heels of the first thought, that this someone must be an insider, working right now for Fusion, or the CIA, a mole with some deep desire to see this project fail. How everything would suddenly make sense! The math would now work. *Of course*, they underestimated her, because they were wrongly looking for a lone amateur, when in fact they should've been looking for someone with links to an expert who has the knowledge of Fusion's secrets and the tradecraft of a seasoned veteran in the surveillance space, one moreover with some kind of serious score to settle with the CIA, and perhaps some kind of alliance within the institution itself.

And so it's there, naked, in the steam room under a rented mansion, that Cy Baxter realizes that all his fortune, even his future, and also that of Erika, not to mention that of everyone else he cares about in this world, lies now in the hands of a demented woman and whoever the hell she's in cahoots with! Oh oh oh, just wait till I find these collaborators, these co-conspirators, he resolves. Just wait till I find them. Some very bad things are going to happen to them.

He charges from the steam room, into a vivifying world where everything is clear and cool and where he will now be clear and cool too. No more Mr. Nice Guy: no, Cy is shuttering that person. As he sheds his towel to jump into the plunge pool—small, deep, arctic-cold—he feels controlled, despite the coursing adrenaline, for he holds an advantage now, one he didn't hold a few minutes earlier: *He knows things*, things that his enemy doesn't yet know he knows, and in that, folks, lies real power. Advantage Cy Baxter, he declares to himself as he nakedly stands before the icy water, then drops, in a feet-first rush, and with no fear, into its shocking depths.

5 DAYS, 23 HOURS

GREEN RIDGE STATE FOREST, MARYLAND

WITH BLACKFLIES IN FULL SEASON, Sam pitches her new tent under trees to protect from both the noonday sun and eyes in the sky. So glad she took the time to redye her hair back at Kaitlyn's, return it to blond. Being Kaitlyn was wearing thin, and it's with relief that she's finally able to renew her acquaintance with being Samantha Crewe.

But is she the same Sam who began all this? For one thing, this crazy ride has taught her so many new things, and equipped her with all-new attributes every day, many of which are not only alarming and dangerous but also irresistible, such as sticking it to Cy Baxter with the video clip. Also, Warren haunts her more than he used to, his voice in her head much more often. But her mind is exploring amazing new ways of thinking, of responding, of reframing old attitudes, of summoning herself into atypical action. Who is she anymore? Her name is still Samantha Crewe, she is thirty-one years old, she is still a nurse with experience in a busy ER, but what's changed is that the U.S. government and its entire intelligence apparatus is now after her, and she is, thus far, beating them. She is beating them, goddammit, and the CIA, which is complicit in the disappearance of her husband, is losing.

Oh, Warren, she thinks as she struggles with the tent once more, with its sections and straps and pliant sticks and unpromising slack shape.

How angry she'd been at him the last time she saw him, she recalls, after his taxi had been summoned, all his bags packed by the door, leaving for a journey he was still on.

"Babe, I don't understand why you're so mad," he'd said to her. "Calm down."

Sam forced the plates into the dishwasher, then cursed at herself. She liked those plates. They were a wedding present. Count to ten.

"Because, Warren, I hate the fact you are making me into this stay-at-home woman asking her husband not to do dangerous shit."

He flinched. "You don't stay at home. You spend half your nights treating gunshot wounds in the ER."

She turned around, leaned against the sink. Wiped her hands on a dish towel. "But I don't go around looking to collect them."

"Well, for one thing, we need the money."

"We get by! We don't need the money."

She reached for her beer. She knew why he did it, and it wasn't money. It's because he thought it was the right thing to do. She wanted to strangle him. Instead, she hung up the dishcloth.

"You married me because I'm *smart*, honey," she reminded him.

"That, and you have a killer bod."

She drew a breath.

"Okay, sorry," he said. "Yes, I married you because you are the smartest person I know. And you are also a good person. So you kinda know I have to do this. Is that what's really bugging you? That underneath it all, as much as you don't like it, you understand?"

Probably. Dickhead.

"Then why can't they just hire you straight up? Make you an official employee? Legitimize you?"

He avoided her eye. "Maybe it's safer to be off the books these days."

"Safer for whom? You? Or them? Tell me what's going on? This one time."

But he held up his hands. "Even the walls have ears, remember. That's why I don't tell you what I'm doing. But trust me, it's important. It's the type of thing where, if we had kids, I'd say we're doing it for them, and for *their* children. As it is, I'm just doing it for you."

She couldn't take it when he looked like that. Noble and full of emotion, a valiant softy. She picked up her beer and went over to kiss the top of his head.

"I love you, Sam," he said.

"I know."

THE TENT IS UP. SHE stands away, looks at her handiwork. This spot has good cover. Cottonwoods overhead. They'll have drones combing the area, searching for movement through the tree canopy. But she's good, probably, for a couple days.

Inside the tent, in light filtered through canvas, she skims a couple of novels she grabbed from Kaitlyn's, then clambers into her sleeping bag and imagines all that tech and power at Fusion now hopefully working *for* her, working to find Warren. With any luck, she may soon have answers to all her sleep-murdering questions, enough to justify the past twenty-four days of running, of masquerading, of surviving—answers that will also quiet her occasional doubts, doubts about Warren, the crazy idea, injected like a virus by the CIA and multiplying inside her, that Warren went to Thailand and is there still, that he has betrayed her, and that her life with him has instead been a lie. On three occasions, in the course of her loyal campaign, she had met low-level CIA representatives in DC, and each time the implication had been the same: How well did she know her husband? Really? Because all the evidence, as they saw it, pointed to the fact that he may have *wished* to disappear, to vanish. But what evidence did they have for this? Warren had a private business: Did she know that? Did she know he was also going bankrupt at the time of his disappearance? Filed for Chapter 11? She shook her head. No, she did not know this. Kept a separate mailing address? She did not want a copy of the documents they produced to prove this, or those that showed him to be on that flight to Bangkok. Had he really told her *none* of this? they asked, again and again.

No, she replied. No. No. No.

She wouldn't be the first woman this has happened to: the seemingly perfect marriage atomized upon reading a husband's texts, a mistakenly opened credit card statement, a record of strange purchases, hotel rooms in the wrong cities, wrong days, the whole crystalline architecture of a life shattering in a breathless instant, the person you thought you knew, who shared your bed, your life, not being that person at all. Or at least not all of the time.

She has had to manage such creeping doubts as the months turned into years, to keep faith with the Warren she *experienced*, day in, day out. *That* man did just as he said. No snake oil. If he truly had a separate business and had not told her, then he had done so to protect her. Financial troubles? Were the government's documents even to be believed? No, she trusts her husband, not American power, and so clings to what she *does* believe: that he flew not to Bangkok, but to someplace in the Middle East and vanished there, and the CIA reps not only know way more than they're saying about what happened to him but are also actively engaged in trying to gaslight her, to deceive her, to make her think she's going mad, to make her doubt Warren and even, finally, herself.

She reminds herself of all the hard evidence supporting her own counternarrative. The Boston cab driver she spoke to who confirmed, yes, he'd taken Warren to Logan that day, saw him enter the terminal. She'd also been back through the bank statements on the joint account, found the shell company that sent the checks. A nice woman there, polite but sounding, you know, a bit busy, a bit caught in the middle of her day, told her, yes, they had paid Warren Crewe, but for half a dozen research papers for different clients on opportunities for investment in Eastern Europe. No travel involved. Just data analysis. No, of course they had nothing to do with the government. Sam called again a month later and got the same answers. Same again the next month and got the same story. Only thing was, she spoke to different people every time, and they all said *exactly* the same thing. Word for word, like they were reading a script. She even told the last one she thought it was strange it was always a different person who picked up. After that, she always got the first lady every time. Isn't this exactly the kind of thing you'd expect from a high-level cover-up?

So, until the truth arrives, until then, she will hang on to Warren's voice, whispering to her in the wind.

In the a.m. she gets out of the sleeping bag, checks her watch, her money. She's not actually just going to lie here for days. That's not the next stage of her plan.

4 DAYS, 7 HOURS

VOLTA PLACE NW, GEORGETOWN, WASHINGTON, DC

"YOU HAVE GUESTS," THE UNIFORMED Hungarian housekeeper who came with the place whispers to Cy as he follows his employer down the stairs with a new morning fluorescing through the windows. "In the drawing room."

The mansion is so large that the drawing room is a surprise. Cy can't remember even being in here before. And was he renting it, or had he bought the place as another tax write-off? His accountants have made it a challenge for even him to work out what he owns and what he merely controls. He doesn't really care either way, as long as they get WorldShare's tax bills down to zero.

The room is big and beige and white, like most of the environments he inhabits–but with huge modern art abstracts in red and yellow for "accent." Islands of sofas grouped around oak coffee tables, each with a discreet fan of current periodicals with an emphasis on tech and culture. Double-height windows give a view over a terrace and formal gardens, and as Cy enters, it's at these windows, taking in this view, that three men in their de rigueur dark suits, stand, waiting for him.

"Gentlemen. Morning."

Turning to face him, Burt Walker, Justin Amari, and a third heavyset man Cy doesn't recognize. Can he trust now any of them? Might *all* of them be working against him, with Cy just a dumb pawn perhaps in their elaborate chess game?

"Nice place," Burt begins.

"Mmmm. More than I need. So what can I do for you this bright morning? House calls now?"

"Can we sit?"

"Take a seat, please."

After they sit on matching couches (the stranger standing, some kind of bodyguard type?), Cy, with fingers laced, looks into the serious faces of his partners.

Burt goes first: "As you know, despite this new development, you've been looking for the wrong woman et cetera. We agree about the continuing need to track down this last Zero. We believe that failure to do so, within the beta test time frame, will open us all to, well, accusations that the beta isn't a success. I think we need to show that we captured all ten Zeros in the allotted thirty days. No messiness. But . . ." Here he pauses, looks seriously between serious faces. "We need you to stay away from Warren Crewe."

This takes Cy by surprise, but not too much surprise. Naturally, some human or digital informant has already betrayed him, revealing to these overseers Cy's command to broaden the search to include Warren. And, in response, he nods. Keeps his cool. "So Warren *is* with you guys?"

Burt offers him a new but clearly well-practiced poker face. "We just need you to stay away from Warren Crewe. Simple as that."

Cy tries to process all the multiplying implications of this demand, and the resulting mental data dump will take some sorting through but in the interim he quips: "Short meeting, I guess."

"With your agreement, very short. We can get out of your hair. Let you get back to work so that this poor, confused woman can get some help."

First question to emerge from his processing: "So you're tracking us, too, Burt?"

"You? Well. Let's just say that when your teams make a thousand failed attempts in a few hours to access our classified digital files, one would hope that we would notice, yes."

Cy decides to try something. "What if I need him? Scratch that, I need him . . . in order to find his wife. If he's why she's doing this, he's relevant to us."

It turns out all three of them own pretty good poker faces.

Extraordinary, Cy thinks, that Warren's whereabouts may even be known by these envoys and yet, from these faces, *nothing*: secrets, secrets everywhere, and none of them hackable if locked inside a human being.

"Just stay off Warren Crewe," Burt reiterates. "The director sends his regards, by the way."

"So that's a . . . whaddayacallit . . . an order?"

"Heavens, no. We're partners. Call it . . . a little friendly advice."

"And what if . . ."

"You really want to do a what-if right now?"

"What if, in the interests of making our partnership a successful one, I don't follow your advice?"

The look that this last comment generates on Burt's up-till-now-neutral face could reverse global warming.

Cy takes a breath, double-clicks a new strategy, and gives one of his Cy smiles, raises his hands. "I'm just saying, Burt, that we may blow the trial."

"We have more confidence in you than that."

"What's going on here, guys? Come on. Level with me. You come in here—"

Justin Amari for the first time finds his voice, and it contains more than a hint of animosity. "You know, Cy, we did a little digging of our own before the agency decided to partner with you. Not as high tech in our investigations as you're used to. A bit old-fashioned by your standards, I suspect. But we've been at it longer. Your work for foreign governments, lucrative sales of technology to China, Russia, increasing the cyberthreat those countries pose to the United States. It's not exactly a good look right now, is it?"

"Whoa, whoa, whoa, I never once breached a single trade ban or sanction as a consultant, nor have I engaged in any illegal transaction. And I doubt your agency would be trusting me now if that were the case, given the access to information I have."

"To *certain* information."

It was true that the vast classified files of the CIA, the FBI, and the NSA were not yet at Fusion's disposal; they were still hidden away, tucked behind firewalls of ferocious sturdiness.

Burt steps in again: "We've been prepared to look the other way, up to this point, because happily you sold much better technology to *your own* nation. And it's always advantageous to know what the other teams are working with."

"Are you calling me a threat to my country?"

"The CIA has a long history," Justin says. "After 1945, we even took in Nazi rocket scientists if we felt they were good partners."

This takes Cy's breath away. "So wait, you're calling me *a Nazi now*?!"

"Would that analogy upset you?" Justin replies.

Cy jumps to feet, as if to throw a punch.

Burt rises also, holds up his thick hands. "Step this back. This is real simple. Everyone calm down."

"And for the record," Cy protests, "this project is a national security priority. And *you* are jeopardizing it right now by not letting me do my work. Just so that's, y'know, *understood*."

Burt, much less friendly suddenly, responds, "We are leaving . . . with this message. The agency has supported our project conditionally, and we have looked the other way on some elements of your business, but, we have our own interests. *Higher* interests. And we will defend those interests. Should you fail to accede to this demand, the agency is putting you on notice that we're no longer prepared to look the other way. So to recap: Stay away from Warren Crewe. Focus on finding the wife."

4 DAYS, 5 HOURS

FUSION CENTRAL, WASHINGTON, DC

THE NEWS THAT THE WARREN Crewe side of the search is officially off is delivered in his office by Cy, first to Erika alone—who is of course of the opinion that they need to comply with CIA demands, and do so immediately—and then to the same team leaders he had previously assembled, at which a "What now?" mood descends upon the room, a palpable sense that the main hope of finding Zero 10 has just been taken away from those tasked with securing a last-minute breakthrough. And none need reminding that 2:00 p.m. will mark the twenty-seventh full day for the chasers. The closing of the capture window—noon on May 30—is therefore at hand.

When Cy and Erika are alone again, the silence is only faintly broken by the watery trickle of a slow-melting digital glacier on the screen.

"They're spying on us. You realize that?"

She shrugs. "They're the CIA."

Trickle, trickle, trickle. Megatons of ice dissolving.

"As soon as we started to look for Warren, they *knew*. We thought we were being quiet, leaving no footprint, but they heard us like the thunder of a thousand hooves."

"Well, at least, from all the data we managed to pull on Warren—a Farsi language class he secretly took in the months prior, phone calls in the days leading up to mobile phones in Iran—it looks like there's a ninety-five percent likelihood he's in Iran, being held by the Iranian government."

"If he's in Iran, love to know why."

"Not our job now."

She watches this man she loves, often despite herself, as he opens his laptop and begins to tap, tap, tap. "What are you doing?"

"Finding this fucking woman."

4 DAYS, 2 HOURS

FUSION CENTRAL, WASHINGTON, DC

ERIKA CANCELS ALL HER MEETINGS. Stalks the Void instead, hoping she can *will* into being a breakthrough but after several circumnavigations of the floor she gives up and retreats to her office to work, combing through the ever thickening file on Samantha Crewe herself.

Erika notes that Samantha, a digital novice, certainly did a commendable job scrubbing her social media. In response, Fusion's algorithms have had to go wide and deep looking for biographical breadcrumbs, to turn up traces, granular patterns, telltale tidbits that have survived her attempts at concealment.

Take Sam's hospital employment records, for instance: They contain complimentary notes from patients, approving reviews from senior staff. A single critical report accuses her of disrespecting authority, with a linked complaint from an attending doctor who claimed she'd ignored his treatment plan and went over his head to the chief of general surgery. She had, an investigation found, been right in the end.

Elsewhere, in the catacombs of extended-family memorabilia, her nieces had posted family photos, scans of old prints revealing her as a kid, holding a wrench as long as her arm while working on a car with her ma and pa in the Brookland neighborhood of DC Other photos, lifted by the teams that went through Sam's storage unit in a Boston suburb, cataloging in real time its contents. Photo albums, boxes of letters, all now digitized by Fusion to search for faces. Found, also, an old laptop. Into its stale contents they breathed new fire, reconstructing old search histories, emails. No signs of bleaching here. And yet nothing that serves as a map with a big *X* revealing a hidden treasure, only more pieces of a stubbornly incomplete picture.

For lunch, an assistant brings Erika a salad. Tasteless but for the dressing. The day then unrolls in an agony of inertia, one familiar to cops on a stakeout, and she can feel the frustration building, also, across the Void. Every hour is precious now, but Samantha is, as ever, giving nothing away.

Fruitlessly, expensively, Capture Teams have been sent out to bars where she used to hang out as a student. A vacation rental in the woods she once frequented. Her old high school is swept for cubbies once used by Sam for secret cigarettes. Nothing.

And yet, out of all of the noise and debris of a life, Erika starts to perceive a person. As if the blue dots in the VR suite are resolving into detail, Erika sees a woman materializing before her: one whose life got derailed when her loving husband disappeared into thin air. Warren is not seemingly a man who could, without compunction, betray her and make her life a living torture. The extant emails from Warren to Sam, and from Sam to Warren, paint a picture of a loving couple. The picture that Erika is developing is that Warren was working in some way for the government and did disappear while in its employ, leaving behind a wife who only later developed a rage against the country, or the government rather, that refuses to explore his mysterious disappearance. The Sam that Erika now perceives hangs on to her faith in Warren like the last candle in a gale, even as the supportive emails from friends dry up, even as she gets cast as a kook by all but her own stoic parents. Only then does Sam gets angry, with politicians, with her friends, those who one by one turn their back on her and her hopes. Then in rolls the Fusion Initiative.

The application form asked: *How did you hear about us?* Sam (under the name Kaitlyn Day) wrote: *Overheard conversation at the library.* But in all likelihood, given Warren's apparent role in the intelligence world, where early chatter about the contest was encouraged in order to find the best contestants, Erika assumes that Sam heard about it some other way. Erika imagines the light going on in Sam as she starts to plan, to view the beta test as a last chance. Exemplary, the sheer commitment involved! The

Fusion team thought they were chasing a woman who had simply wised up by reading a few detective novels, but the evidence before Erika now is that here is a woman who, even before the start whistle blew, had been researching how to frustrate surveillance at a very high level, going deep with her tactics, working out bluffs and double bluffs, feints and misdirects with chess-master rigor—almost as if she knew right from the get-go that she was going to be among the chosen. Well, what if she *had* known?

Before logging off, Erika scrolls back to the pictures of Sam and Warren and then stops on one of them with Sam's folks: John and Laurel Warhurst, stocky and thin in turn, both resolute, stable-looking; his base-ball cap tagged with race-team logos, a pack of cigarettes squaring the breast pocket of a short-sleeved shirt, smoke unfurling from a lit one in his mechanic's bulky fingers as they also enfold his wife's shoulder; and she, with blond-streaked hair, a fully orthodontic smile, bubbly-looking but formidable in her spandex workout suit, determined that she and her hubbie and get their fair share of life.

Erika crosses the floor to find Sonia. "Give me all we have on Zero 10's parents."

3 DAYS, 22 HOURS

BROOKLAND, WASHINGTON, D.C.

"MRS. WARHURST?"

"Uh-huh?"

"I'm a friend of Sam's," Erika announces. "Ruth Schoenberg? Do you remember me?"

A look of incomprehension crosses Laurel's face, now a dozen years older than in her photograph, as she holds open her front door and inspects the stranger on her threshold. "Sorry, did you say Ruth?" she asks.

"Went to college with Sam. On the soccer team with her. When we won the Westbrook Trophy."

"Oh. Yes! Ruth."

"Ruth Schoenberg."

"Oh. I think, yes."

"So good to see you again, Mrs. Warhurst. Sorry to stop by like this, but I was hoping you could help me speak with Sam."

"Sam? No, no. She doesn't live here."

"Oh, I know, but you see, she's not answering any of my calls, which is really unusual, and I've started to worry about her a bit, and I thought of you and wondered if you or Mr. Warhurst have heard anything from her recently?"

"Well, you know, it's complicated with Sam. . . ."

"I'm sorry . . . I know. I'm really worried. Even with all that's happened, she has always stayed in touch."

"Oh, Lord. Come in, come in."

"Do you mind?"

"Come in," Mrs. Warhurst repeats before calling up the stairs, "John! It's Ruth, Sam's college friend."

Later, coffee half drunk, Erika has given out stories from Samantha's college years, details only a true intimate could know, and learned enough in return—stories, newspaper clippings about Warren's disappearance—to know these two people truly know nothing of Sam's present whereabouts; their looks of real concern vouchsafe this, as do their own unanswered calls to Sam's cell phone.

"And when we realized that Warren might be gone for good, well, we did our best to support her, but what can you really do? It's the not knowing that gnaws, that eats," Mr. Warhurst tells Erika.

"So they never found where Warren went?" Erika asks, innocently.

"Nothing. Vanished. *Pfff.* Sam still thinks Middle East somewhere, that he's still alive, but I think . . . Well, Laurel knows what I think, that you gotta consider if he had some other kind of life we didn't know about."

"John," Mrs. Warhurst admonishes.

How often has she had to snuff out the flame of her husband's doubts? More and more as time has gone on, certainly.

"Well, stranger things have happened. Secret family or something, somewhere in the world. Seems he had some business he never declared, told nobody about. Financial trouble. So? And he was always out of the country. Wouldn't be the first time, all I'm saying."

Erika rises, goes to the mantelpiece, stocked with thick silver frames holding images taken over the years, the evidentiary record of a child through time: as infant, time-capsuled, in diapers on a rug; as toddler at play; as teen with hockey stick; as college student drinking orange soda, cheeks hollow above a straw; in graduation gown clutching scroll; in nurses' whites; and then, the climacteric of this anthology, a wedding photo, which Erika picks up.

"Oh," she sighs, affecting a fond and false tone with less effort than she'd have imagined. "She looked so beautiful on her wedding day. I was so sorry I couldn't be there."

In her hands a petrified scene: Samantha in bridal white, happy with her hour-old spouse at her side, his left hand a perch for her right. A brides-maid, then, to Sam's left. And to the right of Warren . . . a face that sends Erika's mental recognition systems scrolling through time and the inner database of her own past, arriving at a breathtaking match: a face only recently stored, grinning back at her.

She takes a moment to prepare herself before turning and, summoning as much ease as she can, asks the good couple: "Where is Justin now? I don't hear from him."

"Who?" Mr. Warhurst replies.

"Warren's friend Justin. I think he's in government now, last I heard. Some big-shot job."

"Is that the crazy liberal guy who talked my ear off?" Mr. Warhurst adds with a smile.

"John, stop. I don't think Erika wants to talk politics."

Erika very slowly sets the precious photo back on the mantelpiece.

3 DAYS, 20 HOURS

FUSION CENTRAL, WASHINGTON, DC

AT 6:00 P.M. ERIKA STRIDES up to the gantry level, her pulse galloping, her tablet in her hand with its dark screen hiding her cell-phone snapshot of the tell-all photo that makes sense of—well, if not everything—*almost* everything. On her tongue, ready to fall, is the shock news that, yes, Sam has partaken of help, assistance, advice, succor, training in specialist tradecraft, all this time—no wonder she's been a fiend to catch!—from one of their own pay-masters, Justin Amari.

Cy's assistant half gets up from her seat as if, in reflex, she wants to stop Erika, but it will take much more than a twenty-something in a pastel polo shirt to limit the unrestricted access that Erika, for years, has enjoyed—and certainly she will not be stopped today, not with the ground-opening news she carries in her hands.

"Is he in?"

With a dipped shoulder she pushes open the frosted glass door (only Cy has frosting in this place), eyes already down on the tablet as she awak-ens it so that she and Cy can go straight into damage control and counter-attack mode, but . . . when she looks up . . . it's not Cy's face that claims her eye. Rather, it's the upturned and startled face of Sonia, who is bending forward at the hip, shirt half open, showing a flash of pink bra scattered with roses, her palms planted with fingers starfished on the desktop for purchase, mouth open in a passionate *O*, with Cy behind her, hands on her hips, as if steering her, as if teaching her how to dance.

"Oh shit," Cy groans.

Erika just stands there, for a few breathless seconds, until emotion breaks over her like an ocean.

Pain.

She retreats, reaches as far as the ground floor before the flush-faced Cy catches up with her, his clothes still half undone, shirt outside his reinstated pants. Can't look at him. Just can't. Her eyelids are rimmed with salt water, and she almost breaks into a sprint when she hears his voice bidding her.

"Erika, stop, please."

He has hold of her arm now and takes her aside, whispering things, feverishly, words, apologies, platitudes, apologies again, but she isn't listening and is picturing that pretty bra, then that woman's face conveying pleasure, and then Erika's man behind, enjoined, moving, ramming, taking his own pleasure. She thinks, also, of all the years, working her guts out, building him up, cleaning up his messes, telling herself they were soul mates, yin and yang, in for the long haul, with a deep, intense attachment and love for each other, yes *love*, her half of which was just proven—distressing thought, this—in her pure physical reaction to the scene she'd just witnessed.

This kid, Sonia. *Really?* She sees again the face, the sexual abandon of an upstart's victory over her, and again, behind this victor, the walking, breathing nightmare that used to be the Cy she trusted.

She makes it to her office, Cy still right behind her.

"Erika! Stop! What's your problem?"

"What's my problem?" She drops the tablet on her desk. "You are really asking my what *my* problem is?"

He shuts the door. And she thinks: He doesn't care what I think of him, only wants to make sure none of his staff know what an asshole he is. Erika feels creeping disgust spread under her skin like an allergy, and not only with Cy but also with herself and with everything around them, this whole carefully constructed edifice. It's like all the pristine surfaces of the world have been sprayed with old cooking oil, everything tacky now, unclean to the touch.

But he is holding up his hands, head on one side, deploying the little-boy smile. *Really, Cy?* The look on his face pleads for mercy, and the smile gives way to tears, as if he knows already that the damage he has just done is irreparable. In this moment, he is as inarticulate as a trapped child denied all ability to lie further but still unwilling to accept the truth. How pathetic, she thinks. The tears should be mine, but in their stead she feels only rage. "That fucking girl? *Really?*"

"I know . . . it's . . . I've . . . I don't know. I don't what happened. I was so stressed about this whole—"

"So stressed you fuck an intern. Do you want to go down in flames, Cy?"

"I know. . . . You're right. I'm so fucking sorry, Erika."

"How many times?"

"What?"

"How many times, did you fuck her?"

"God. I didn't—"

"How dare you? How *dare* you?"

"You know me. I don't go looking for that sort of thing."

"What's happened to you? I'm serious. I don't see you anymore. You're such a child. I can't believe this. Everything we've put into this. That *I've* put into *you*."

The Cy she is looking at is so very different from yesterday's Cy. *This* Cy is now a man who is not to be believed, and whatever remains of her feelings for him after such a huge category shift—and it's way too early for her to tell what, if anything *at all*, will remain—she knows already that it will only be some unsatisfactory fraction of what had existed before. In the end, some things—air, avocados, railroad tracks, a note on a violin, silence, trust between lovers—need to be perfect.

Thoughts turn unavoidably to their lost past. "My brother loved you, always said you had something about you. You were going to do big things, such good big things. I believed in you, tied my dreams to yours, and all to see you . . . what? What the fuck are you doing, Cy?"

Hearing all this, this raw data (unprocessed) streaming at him (coarse, pain-filled, toxified with emotion) and with no defense open to him, he can only be stung by her attack, and stung again by the sheer accuracy of it. The best he can manage is to speak the nearest truth he can claim: "I don't feel anything for her. Nothing at all."

"I know. And the sad thing is, you think that makes it better."

"What can I do, Erika? I'll do anything!"

"You can get out of my office. And maybe out of my life. How 'bout that? I'm such an idiot."

"Don't give up on all this. Erika, listen to me. Can we just get through the beta test? Then we'll get out of here, out of DC, go home. I'll make this up to you. I can fix this, I *will* fix it. Remember what we're doing here, together. How important it is."

"Please leave. Please leave my office."

"I'm serious. I'll do anything."

"As I've just witnessed! Now, please, leave."

"At least think of Michael. Don't forget. This is all for *Mike*. We're doing things that have never been done before."

"I'll scream. Out!"

When Cy is gone, Erika remote-locks the door, then sits. Ten minutes go by, she doesn't move. He really thinks he's above the law, she now realizes. He thinks that, with such modern power, normal rules no longer apply to him. And how many tyrants have afforded themselves just this dispensation? Finally, she stands; fixes her makeup; thinks, Fuck him; and then calls one of the minnows in the outer shell of Fusion to find out where Sandra Cliffe's special aide is. Offsite today, they tell her. Still humming with anger and hurt, she picks up her phone. Hesitates. No, she decides. She picks up her tablet—still sleeping, with all it contains—and exits the Fusion complex.

Drives home, parks in the driveway, hails a cab on the street.

To the driver, she gives the home address of Justin Amari.

3 DAYS, 17 HOURS

JUSTIN AMARI'S RESIDENCE, WASHINGTON DC

JUSTIN IS JUST BACK FROM the office himself, tie removed but not dress shirt, as he lets his uninvited guest, Erika, walk past him into the living room. His apartment is classic divorced-guy-on-a-budget. Cheap bookshelves with nonfiction and old vinyl. A TV with a game console attached but both unplugged at the wall, Erika notices—he now knows about fake off-mode, after all. A laptop stands open, however, on a dining table.

"Drink?" he offers, showing no surprise at her presence.

She says nothing.

"Not here for a drink? Then I'm guessing it's to play *Call of Duty*. What level you at?"

"You know her."

"You mean Samantha, right?" He picks up a bottle of mescal and refills a tumbler in which an outsize ice cube is dwindling. Pauses a second, then keeps pouring. Says nothing right away.

Erika expected him to deny it or to bluster. Not this.

What *does* she know about Justin Amari?

His file says he devoted fifteen years to the agency, rising from the cybersecurity division, where he recruited hackers, to strategy and bigger advisory roles. Left to save his marriage, but it turned out his job wasn't the reason the marriage imploded. Divorced, childless, jobless, spent the next three years consulting around Washington, writing simple code for random companies, but didn't like his private bosses any better than his government ones. Money problems after the divorce, drank too much, commissioned tattoos all over his body—women, ships, snakes, Polynesian motifs—a company man who afterhours filled his ears with old Nirvana albums, smoked dope. No stranger to the THIRD AND FINAL NOTICE, he went deep in debt until Sandra Cliffe remembered him, gave him his present gig. In renewing his license to ask tough questions and to make trouble, he realized how much he'd missed it. More and more he found purpose again. Dialed back on the drinking, paid his bills, hit the gym, got his teeth veneered.

Smiles more now, whereas before he tended to scare women with his poker face and picket-fence grin. At forty-two, he's healthier and breezier than he was at twenty, but in Erika's eyes he's still a little off-kilter and used up: something of a struck match.

"You're her friend," she adds.

He screws the top back carefully on the mescal bottle. "Warren's, originally. Met at college. Helped get him his first gig with you-know-who, but then we sorta lost touch. How'd you find out?"

"Old photo. Her parent's mantelpiece. The three of you at their wedding. You look close."

"Close enough."

"You set this whole thing up for her? Got her into the program? Yes or no?"

"That would be yes."

He sounds calm about it. Like they're just meeting about interdepartmental communication strategies or more efficient ways to replenish the photocopier.

"And you've been helping her all along. That's why we haven't been able to catch her. Because you want Go Zero to fail. I guess the CIA doesn't like to share. Is your buddy Dr. Cliffe in on this?"

He sits down at the table. "You *can* take your coat off, you know."

She keeps it on.

"You give me too much credit," he says. "Sam's good. Done most of it herself. But yeah, I briefed her on the sorts of strategies you'd be using to trace her before she went Zero. Dr. Cliffe knows nothing. The agency knows nothing. But who else have *you* told about me? Cy? Burt?"

She declines to answer. "You know all about what Warren did for the CIA."

He shrugs, lifts the glass to his lips. "I know a little. But no specifics."

"Why didn't you yourself help her find out where he is?"

"You may have noticed that the CIA is not actually big on releasing information. Whatever they have on Warren is locked deep. Super classified. I looked. I tried. Nothing." He takes another sip, staring past her out the window and into the street. "When I asked, I got stonewalled. But they clearly didn't like me asking questions. The hostility was real. Just like when your boyfriend asked us the other day. For what it's worth, I don't think Burt knows anything, either. But he knows it's a big no-go. Someone told him so. Which means we know there's something there. Leaving Sam . . . where? For years not knowing what has happened to her husband. Yeah, that sucks."

No, thinks Erika, I will not reveal to this maverick, this unstable character, that Fusion now believes Warren, in all probability, to be in Iran. She looks around the apartment again, trying to get some higher sense of this guy, but it's like the opposite of real Kaitlyn's apartment, which was so crammed with personality. This place is blank, puritan in its simplicity. The decor equivalent of a white shirt and charcoal tie.

"What is this about, Justin? You're trying to sabotage the project?"

He twists his glass so the ice cube clanks. "Oh, I'd sure like to stop you guys, believe me—if only I could—because this is way, way too much power to be put in the hands of you and the CIA. It really should be stopped. And you do realize, don't you, that the CIA will always take more than they give? They've been looking for a legal way to bring their global game home for years. Fusion is it. They're using you. Even to the extent of turning a blind eye to your other activities."

"Other activities?"

He cocks his head. "How much *do* you know? How much does Cy tell *you*?"

"We share everything."

"Then you're as big a criminal as he is."

In flashes, unbidden images assail her: her lover screwing Sonia, the look on both their faces, Sonia's mouth an *O*, her fingers starfished on the desktop, an asshole and a bitch going at it, two cretins deserving of each other.

Monitoring her expression closely, he stops swilling the small glacier in his glass.

"I don't require your opinions on WorldShare, Justin."

His eyes widen. "*You don't know.* I guess you really don't. . . . I've always wondered."

"What are you talking about?"

"Give you a clue: Virginia Global Technologies. Your little shell company in the Caymans."

"I know all about that company."

"So you know what it's doing?"

"It's a small sub-office. It's a tax thing. Standard practice."

"Not . . . not if you're using it as a loophole to claim the tech you're selling to enemy states isn't made in America."

"Nonsense." She shakes her head.

"In return, buying up personal data? People's secrets? Worldwide?"

"You're making this up now. You're losing me." But in fact her heart rate has quickened.

"And at the agency," Justin continues, "some people *know* all this, know you're breaking U.S. law and defying international sanctions in delivering military-grade spyware and other stuff to Russia and China, and we work with you anyway! And why? Because we have to. *You have what we need.* We've always supported corrupt regimes abroad if they help us with our global ambitions, so now we're supporting corrupt regimes *within*. So I'm very sorry if I fucking object to this shit, Erika."

He pauses, waits, looking at her over the top of his glass.

"I don't think you do know about all this, actually," he concludes. "But it doesn't matter, because I think you're just as morally bankrupt as he is at the end of the day. One can know something is wrong without knowing the details, by ignoring the evidence. Either way, if you have a scintilla of courage left in you after being kicked from pillar to post by a grade one asshole for ten years, then do this: Help us find Warren Crewe. You have the tech and the access. Dig into the classified files on Warren that the CIA are concealing and give that information to a good citizen. Like me, for instance. Give it to me. Or Sam. But do the right thing. Use the power you still have to do something really worthwhile."

She ought to go, race home, phone Cy, alert him. But she doesn't move.

"Even . . . ," she says. "Even if I . . . if I wanted to . . . you know as well as

I do that we have no direct access to classified CIA files. We already tried to get the Warren Crewe file, and it led to your little threesome's house call."

He gives her a smile. "I can tell you how to do it."

She stares at him, this man who would betray his country. "What's stopping you from doing it yourself, then? You have more access than we do. *You're* the fucking CIA."

"I don't have the clearances to get through the outer walls. Guess who does? Fusion. Yeah. And your hacking teams there can do it *under the radar*, so that the CIA has no idea it happened. It's a win-win."

"I'm not listening to you."

"Oh, I think you are, Erika."

"You're insane. You're suggesting I personally order a hack of the national security database? For you?"

His porcelain veneers deliver a pretty good smile. "You have two guys, Milo and Dustin, in your cybersecurity maintenance team, they're good. Use them. You enjoy unique access to classified files already, so you can do it, breach the walls without spooking the whole henhouse. Literally no one will know. I can't do that, but you have the means. Use it. *Use it*, Erika. Extract this one file, one tiny file, it's not gonna hurt the country, learn where Warren is, that's it, then get the fuck out before anyone knows a thing. Redeem yourself. Then pass that information to me, I'll pass it to Sam, and she will accept whatever it tells her about her husband, and give herself up to you. Oh, and I won't send your boyfriend to prison for the rest of his life."

He lets this last threat hang in the air, radioactive, before adding: "And don't worry, Sam *will* come in and make it look like you caught her, so Fusion will appear to win your little beta test. *You'll* win. The congressional money will pour in. And quietly, very quietly, an American patriot can come home. And you will have done something that we call *the right thing*. Remember what that is?"

He's watching her, seeing it all go in, as she looks at the tabletop, at the false grain of the cheap imitation oak. She could easily just stand up and leave. Doesn't. Tellingly, crucially, doesn't.

"You haven't told anyone about me yet, have you?" he asks. "Not Burt, not Cy, no one." When Erika doesn't deny it, he adds: "Good. Then maybe we *can* work well together."

3 DAYS, 15 HOURS

700 BOYLSTON STREET, BOSTON, MASSACHUSETTS

KAITLYN DAY SCANS THE BAR code on three library books (all romances), wishes the borrower goodbye and many hours of happy reading–one of the great pleasures of life–only to see, next in line, someone she never expected to see in the Boston Public Library.

"Take a picture," she tells him.

"And why should I do that, Kaitlyn?" Cy Baxter replies, with a smile.

"See what an honest job looks like."

"Samantha said you can help me reach her."

"Did she now?"

"I want to help her."

3 DAYS, 7 HOURS

OUTSKIRTS OF BERKELEY SPRINGS, WEST VIRGINIA

THE OFF-ROAD MOTORBIKE IS PARKED in the alley waiting for her, as Kaitlyn had promised it would be, bequeathed surely by some distant activist friend of Kaitlyn's, no questions asked, none given, and delivered here on time. The power of sisterhood made manifest. A PIN opens a helmet box on the rear, which also holds the bike's key, so that Sam, donning the identity-concealing helmet and inserting the key, will now be able to move more rapidly and freely than ever before. As long as the impressively vague connection between the bike's owner and Sam goes undetected, then she, too, can remain undetected.

Her first errand? To town, to grab a copy of the *Washington Post* from a newspaper stand, unwatched by CCTV.

In town, parks. Takes a copy of the newspaper and then steps into an alley where weeds are breaking though the concrete. Under a streetlamp, opens the paper to the classified ads. And there it is, a new message for her from Kaitlyn. The ad is, as usual, discreet:

LONELY GIRL. NEWS. GO TO YOURFAVORITEARTIST.ORG/YOURPASSWORD. MY SURNAME OPENS DOORS. PEA AND HAM SOUP SOON. LUV U.

News? Her adrenaline spikes. Has someone found Warren? Oh, Warren. A frequent, unbidden fantasy image springs to mind: of standing on a runway, her hair being whipped by the slowing blades of the helicopter, walking into his embrace, her cheek on his chest warmed by a beating heart. She gets her life back. A life with Warren.

"Oh, honey," she says aloud.

She steps out of the alley, mounts her bike, and next thing she knows she's pushing open the door to the 7-Eleven, still wearing her helmet. Buys a burner flip phone with new cash she picked up at Kaitlyn's. Headphones, too. Then gets out of there, lickety-split. The street empty.

On the edge of town, where there's still a decent signal, she fires up the phone. Two bars. Anonymizes the browser, then enters *www.georgiaokeeffe.org/Tomyris* into the bar, her thumbs feeling fat and slow, her vision, through the narrow frame allowed by the helmet, blurred. Blank. Then on-screen a still of a video file emerges, thickly grained at first, resolving to HD. She plugs in the headphones. Studies it. It's Cy Baxter standing in what looks like some sort of forest, though the perspective seems weird. Pressing play makes another password box open up.

She thumbs in *Day.*

But it's not Kaitlyn.

"Sam."

Cy's voice is warm. Her heart catches at hearing him speak to her directly.

"First of all, congratulations on what you've achieved during this beta test, exceptional. Second, as you know, we found Kaitlyn and your message. Wow. I mean wow! That took some processing on our side." He pauses and shakes his head.

She remembers watching this man throw his tantrum outside the cabin. She bites her lip. He sounds sincere, unscripted. Hope bubbles inside her. A roiling nauseous mess in the basements of her being.

"Also, I have been moved by everything I've now learned about Warren. I can't imagine the pain of not knowing where he is, alive or dead, and also suspecting that the truth is being, well, criminally withheld from you, not to speak of America's abandonment of him. I share your anger. And, in line with the deal that you offered me in your thumb drive video— nice job—I have been making inquiries and I can confirm, I have news. I know where Warren is."

In response, Sam feels her lips twitch into a smile. *Knows where he is?* That means he's alive. Thank you, God. Thank you, God. Thank you, God.

"But you have to give yourself up, just like you said. That's our deal. You tell no one. You meet me, let us bring you in, and you get everything we know about Warren. So let's do this. Okay?"

Sam dares not even blink. The CIA *has* been hiding what it knows, and now Baxter is her ally, as she'd always hoped and wildly planned he would be, a vital powerful ally, and the only one she and Justin could think of who had the necessary powers to go around the denials of the U.S. government.

A sense of relief close to joy floods through her as the steady image of Baxter offers a proposal.

"So let's meet at the National Gallery in DC and end this. I don't know where you are, but you're nothing if not resourceful. I'll be there, tomorrow afternoon, that's day twenty-eight in Go Zero time, at three o'clock. And don't worry. Just me. I really, really hope you'll be there, too."

Will she do it? Can she afford to take such a massive risk? But it's everything she wanted, isn't it? Yes, it could be some kind of a trap, it's Baxter after all, but she will take precautions and she simply must meet this man whom she has, it would seem, successfully forced to uncover the truth about Warren.

With this question settled, she takes out the battery, casts it into the wilderness of sagebrush and dirt. With her good foot, ably kick-starts the engine. Twists the throttle hard—"Ning-nings," her Dad calls these off-roaders, and anyone with ears could tell you why. Two miles back up the road, uses the new cash to buy gas from a station that's too filthy and flea-bitten to have CCTV at all, then turns back for the campsite, borne up by hope's abrupt revival.

3 DAYS, 3 HOURS

FUSION CENTRAL, WASHINGTON, DC

ERIKA'S OFFICE IS SMALLER THAN Cy's and, symbolically, beneath it. Also, her windowless wall is, by comparison with his, just a wall, but she has her own en suite and a flat-screen television plus a sofa she can sleep on. Right now she's looking up all emails involving Cy and her and Virginia Global Technologies on her tablet. Merely an address to exploit tax benefits on European sales, no more. Innocent enough. Apple does it. Google. Amazon. They all do. None believe paying tax a duty or even of value. But she is now made aware of a certain amount of recent high-value trade via VGT: there it is, transactions to China and Russia, unspecified sales but generating some of the large profits that have regularly excited their boardroom, driving WorldShare's stratospheric stock price even higher. And yet, from what she can tell, these sales—sales of *what* is suspiciously *un*clear—took place *before* Russia, with its lunatic invasion of Ukraine, returned to being the object of international condemnation and sanction. Everyone used to deal with Russia back then. And from the only emails she can find, there has been no obvious trade with Russia *since* the February 2022 invasion and, as for China, little since then also.

Still, her chest feels tight as she leaves her office and turns her fragmented attention to the Void, spinning with activity as the clock runs down on the failing pursuit of Zero 10.

It's the fear, the fear she can't suppress, that Cy has a secret life, that this secret life has now made her complicit in a grievous international crime.

Even if irrational, even if the product of Justin's absurd accusations—that the real purpose of VGT is to defy international sanctions and arm America's enemies—images seize her of arrest, of cold detention, of court cases, of public vilification, of handcuffs, of bars, of orange prisoner clothes and perp walks, of prison time, all blooming now in her mind. Could Cy, the Cy she knows, or thought she knew, have engaged in such transactions? And what should she do herself right now, in this moment?

She *had* decided, after leaving Justin's, that she must report him to Burt Walker immediately, must reveal that this CIA employee has been actively working *against* the beta test, helping Samantha Crewe remain on the loose—and she must also reveal *why*. But not yet, not right this moment, she decides, at least not with her suspicions still alive that a fuller inventory of what Cy's been up to might yet lie in wait for her.

With Justin's claims now turning into a mental obsession, and with cooling coffee in a recyclable paper cup held to her chest amid this cyclotron of data and of streaming images to rival her own streaming, cyclonic mental state, she realizes she may need to do something very bold, very dangerous, very out of character, if she is to save all this, and save herself also. She might just have to briefly experiment, in other words, with being someone other than Erika Coogan.

Headset in place, she voice-dials WorldShare's accounting department.

"Erika Coogan here. May I ask with whom I'm speaking?"

"Uh . . . Dale. Dale Pinsky."

"Hi, Dale. I see all recent activities and transactions through one of our shells: Virginia Global."

"O . . . kay." A slight hesitation on the other end of the line.

"Everything from the last five years, Dale. Contracts. I'm with Cy, and he wants to bring me up to speed with all our VGT deals. So internally email me everything. Invoices, receipts. New deals in progress. On the books, off the books. Okay? Dale? Highest urgency."

"Yeah. And . . . Cy's asking for this?"

"Yes, and he doesn't have long to wait, Dale. You know what he's like."

2 DAYS, 7 HOURS

OUTSKIRTS OF BERKELEY SPRINGS, WEST VIRGINIA, 7:02 A.M.

SOMEONE IS OUT THERE. OUTSIDE her tent. There's been no blare of sirens, no high-pitched buzz of a drone or drumbeat of a helicopter granting a forewarning, just footsteps, the clear crackle of a boot on a dry twig nearby, then silence.

In her tent she feels the intruder close. Quietly she slides her feet into her boots and picks up her flashlight, heavy enough to serve as a weapon. Getting into a crouch, she waits until the noises abate; then she quickly parts the flaps and steps outside, to see . . . a male figure, bent over the ashes of last night's fire, setting a Zippo to a fresh pile of moss and twigs before snapping shut the lighter, *clack*, then standing, pulling off his woolen hat.

"Jesus, you scared the shit out of me!" she gasps.

"Coffee?"

He opens his arms. She goes to him. He hugs hard, almost too hard, then pushes her away until at arm's length they look into each other's eyes.

"Warren's alive," she tells him. "Cy Baxter told me."

"Told you? How?"

"We connected through Kaitlyn. He says he knows where Warren is."

"I bet he does."

"He's gonna tell me. I'm gonna meet him. Later today."

Through the woodsmoke he can only stare at her.

HALF AN HOUR LATER AND over coffee, the fanciest cup she's tasted in a month (bottled water makes a real good brew), he is still trying to talk her out of it. "I won't let you do it. I don't trust him. I think he's just gonna bag you, and you'll get nothing."

"I have to risk it."

"And if he *does* tell you where Warren is?"

"I turn myself in."

Justin realizes that, in this respect, she is far outside his purview. But there is a bigger shared issue to discuss: "But then we still bust him, right?"

Both hands cupping the tin coffee mug, she lowers her voice. "Maybe . . . but I might need to ask you to hold off on that as well. We might have to get Warren home first."

Justin's eyes, reflecting the firelight, blaze. "We had a deal."

"I'll still need Baxter's help after today."

"Sam, you can't ever believe whatever Cy Baxter tells you today about Warren."

"Let's see. This is all about Warren now."

"What about me?"

She turns to him. "What?"

"Erika Coogan knows I'm the mole, the one helping you."

"Oh, Justin."

"She figured it out. So I won't have a job." He shrugs. "Fine. But my point is, it's not just your decision what to do now, it's *ours*."

This journey has always been a shared one, but Sam can now see, and for the first time, a division in the road ahead. "What do you want from me?"

"Honor our deal. We have an historic opportunity here. You and me. It's fucking enormous. We're talking about stopping a new age of feudalism here in America and around the world—"

"Oh, Justin—"

"An era of servitude to the corporate-military industrial complex—"

"Justin—"

"With irreversible powers to coerce, indoctrinate, and suppress. This shit's what Orwell warned us about. It's on us to respond. And if not us, *who*?"

She can only sigh. Dear, outraged, good, embattled Justin, fighting tomorrow's wars today, a lone warrior on the barricades, a radical who has emerged from within the body of the institution he opposes, apparently eager now to make the ultimate sacrifice, his identity tied to his burning sense of mission: not unlike Warren in this regard.

"What I care about is Warren," she declares as she tosses the last of her coffee into the fire, where it hisses on the logs.

"You once told me, Cy needs to be stopped. Direct quote: That man needs to be stopped. You were as angry as I was."

"*No one's* as angry as you are. Now I need to change and go and meet a multi-billionaire." With this she goes back into the tent.

When she comes out again, Justin hands her the sheaf of papers. "If you find yourself in a moment where you need to, show him these. Tell him they're copies. Which they are. Tell him you have the originals. See what it does to his expression."

She takes the pile with both hands. "One question," she says. "We're still in his laptop, aren't we? Your little spyware thing."

"Mm-hmm. Every keystroke."

"And he has no idea?"

"Not yet, no."

She smiles, thanks God they maintain this secret advantage over Baxter, a brilliant move on Justin's part, and how beautifully it worked, with Kaitlyn winding Baxter up in true Kaitlyn fashion, infuriating him with her recitation of the periodic table, teasing him, making him crazy, and only then giving him the thumb drive, so that Baxter, plugging Justin's thumb drive (holding her video message) into his laptop, clicks away his usual protections so that the trespass and the spyware remain undetected to this day: a perfect example of it taking a thief to catch a thief.

"So you'll continue to snoop on his activities?"

"What do you think I do all day?"

"Love you."

"Love you back. Sam, when you approach him, here's what you do—"

"I know what to do," she interrupts. "I have an idea."

"What a relief. So it's goodbye, then."

"Justin . . . if something goes wrong, where can I meet you?"

"She finally admits to this possibility."

"Where?"

"I'm sticking to my part of the plan. The next location on our list. I'll be there."

She gives him the smallest kiss on his cheek. "Have a little faith."

He watches her walk away. Calls, "Got any to spare?"

1 DAY, 23 HOURS

NATIONAL GALLERY OF ART, WASHINGTON, DC

SOMEHOW, CY DOESN'T REALLY THINK Samantha Crewe will show up. Can't fully believe anyone will be so trusting, no matter what Sonia says about Sam's psychological profile.

He feels antsy, on edge, and was certainly of no use at Fusion Central, where Clear-Voyant is still failing to get a grip on its target. Its difficulty, it seems—the bug in the machine and not just when it comes to Samantha Crewe—is mortal randomness itself: noise, mutation, the anarchy of emotions, spasms of unpredictable behavior, disruptions that don't coalesce into another pattern, or in short, the shocking irregularities that define human nature. What chance could an algorithm have? And yet that remains the crucial challenge of the future, to bridge the gap between the calculable and the numinous, between the machine and the soul of man, and to this he will commit all his resources and the remainder of his life.

The gallery rooms in which he wanders are fascinating. Each bears the name of dead tycoon. Grand, imposing, they were funded by the Gilded Age titans who believed their souls and reputations would be redeemed and given a spiritual eleventh-hour pass if they pumped their ill-gotten gains into something "for the people" in their waning months before meeting their maker. Am I any different, he wonders, longing for immortality and self-justification, just not in bricks and mortar, but ones and zeros?

He has his earpiece in and a sweetly engineered mic the size of a baby's thumbnail on his collar. His special eyeglasses let Sonia and her discreet alpha subteam, based two blocks away, see what he sees. He's not dressed like a cybermonk today, to cut down on the chance of being identified and hassled by the great unwashed public seeking signatures, selfies, advice, benediction. Just jeans and a button shirt. Looks like he's practicing to be his own Dad. Or Tintin cresting forty. Carries a folder, a notebook, a pen.

The gallery guards in each room give him the once-over as he fakes interest in the paintings on the wall. He had no bag to search. Looks white enough, wealthy enough with the glasses, to be watched only lightly. The central hall is forested with thick green marble columns circling a fountain with a naked boy on top. Boy has wings on his heels. Mercury, messenger of the gods. Cy realizes there's a copy of the same one in his rented back garden. Or maybe it's the other way around. Mercury, he muses, he could be the patron saint of what Cy does: carry messages from the all-powerful to the powerless, and vice versa.

Turns right and sits on the broad central bench, where it is quiet. He is supposed to use this seat to stare in rapt fascination at the giant oil painting opposite him. It's fine, if you like that sort of thing, but Cy prefers photographs: clear views, no impressions, stick to the facts.

He picks up his phone while watching a teenager peering at an altarpiece. Then a sudden bubble of noise starts in the hall, the chatter of starlings, and the room suddenly fills up with a party of elementary school kids, all wearing bright yellow T-shirts and shepherded by half a dozen women with long straight hair streaked blond and looking harried. The kids hold hands in pairs, stare around them, their mouths, swear to God, actually open *in wonder*, mouths forming an eternal, infantile *Wow* as if new arrivals on the planet are beholding the collective works of man. Their chaperones usher them through into the next room, and Cy watches them, envying their naked excitement. Where has his own innocent wonder gone? What has come of it? When was the last time he found himself struck in the contemplation of an enchanted and inexplicable moment that surpassed his capacity to explain it or his desire to possess it?

"Are you Warren?"

He turns around. A teenager in a baseball cap, an Iowa State University sweatshirt, is looking at Cy, then at his watch, then at Cy again, confused now, as if something doesn't make sense.

Warren? Cute, Sam, real cute. "Yeah. Why?"

"Lady gave me fifty dollars to wait here until three and then give you this."

Cy snatches it out of his hand. "When? Where?"

"Outside, like an hour ago."

"What was she wearing?"

"Wearing? I dunno. Jeez, like sunglasses. And a baseball cap. A white one, I think." He leans forward and peers at Cy. "Hey, Jeez . . . are you, like, Cy Baxter?"

"No, I'm Mark Zuckerberg."

Cy is gone, back in the fat marble forest of the hall before the kid gets any wiser. Pulls out his phone and flicks open the note at the same time.

> 560 Eighth Street NW parking garage. Take the ramp down to basement level 2.
>
> Ten minutes. Come on foot.

What is this now, a scavenger hunt?

"Cy." Sonia's voice in his ear. "We'll send a car."

"There's no time."

He passes the guards, heads outside fast.

1 DAY 22 HOURS

PARKING GARAGE, 560 EIGHTH STREET NW, WASHINGTON

A FAST-EVOLVING CORNER OF TOWN. Half-built towers with attendant cranes, silent on this federal holiday Monday, infrastructure exposed, steel girders and poured concrete foundations. A world, normally, of workers in hard hats and dust. In the concrete bunker of an all-new underground parking garage, with megatons of cement above and below them and where no signal can possibly get out or in, Sam steps out from behind one of the thick pillars and sees . . . a pretty normal looking guy.

Face-to-face they stand, with Sam perceiving at long last her tormenter, her hunter, but also, potentially, her savior, too, a man several inches shorter than his reputation and power might lead you to imagine, with a still-young face as if nature is conspiring to have him not grow up as the rest of us must. An exception to the rule, then, in so many ways, and now standing in half shadow before her, the once vast distance between them reduced, almost, to zero.

Before he can speak she holds to her lips a silencing finger, then taps would-be pockets on her own breast and hip. Understanding the meaning of this mime, he draws his phone from a breast pocket and offers it to her. She removes its battery, then gestures for more of his devices. With a resigned shake of the head, he removes his earbud, also the speaker on his collar: these are dropped by her on the ground, where she stamps on them.

"Those were expensive," he notes.

But she is not yet finished. Directed by her eye, he heels off his slip-on shoes, then unfastens first his Rolex Daytona—"It's a classic," he warns, so she merely pockets it—then his wallet and then the eyeglasses (cast aside, skittering beneath a car). Jesus Christ, even his cufflinks!

"Really? Are you gonna let me tell you what I know or not? I'm starting to get the feeling you don't trust me. But okay, I'll let you have this moment."

"And contact lenses," she finally demands. "Heard you wear contacts."

"I can't see well without them."

"But I won't talk well *with* them."

"We can't put a camera in a contact lens yet."

"How would I know that?"

Agitated, he removes, with right index finger, first one then the other, saying, "You seem to know a lot."

When these are passed to her, and then thrown over her shoulder, she's ready to talk. "Warren. Where is he?"

"If I tell you, you'll still give yourself up? 'Cause I'm starting to get weird vibes here."

"That's still the deal, but I need to know what you know first."

"Well, I'm very pleased to hear that."

"Where's my husband?"

"Iran."

A breathless moment for Sam. "I knew it was either Iran or Syria; it had to be."

"It's Iran."

"You're sure?"

"That's the latest intelligence we have. From the CIA."

"And he's alive?"

"He is. He's being held by their government. I'm working on finding exactly where. So you were right."

She could cry. What she knew, in her heart, has just been proven, and all the mutinous conjecture of two years relegated now to ghostly static.

"So come," he says. "Let's walk out together."

He raises an arm, indicating the exit ramp, but she hesitates.

"What is it?" he asks. "Samantha?"

"I need . . . I need to know, where he is, where he's being held. If it's a prison, I need to know where. Who is holding him captive? And why . . .

why is our government denying knowing anything about it? And why are the Iranians not saying anything, either?"

"Come with me, and I'll help you find out. Okay? Let's go."

She stands there. She's really thinking it over. It would be nice to go with him in some way. But finally, she shakes her head. "No."

"No?"

"You have one day still. Find out *why*. While I'm worth something to you."

When he takes a step forward she takes one back, keeping a good six feet between them, reflexive social distancing.

"Sam," he says firmly, but when again she shakes her head, he looks less worried than he should be. "I have Capture Teams all around the building. You won't get a hundred yards."

"We can beta-test that."

With this, his voice becomes firmer, loses all diplomacy and patience and the charade of caring. "Now, I told you where he is. We have a deal. So be smart about this. I can find out more about your husband, but you need to come with me, right now."

"Twenty-four hours. You have one more day."

"I'm calling in the teams."

"Do it. But before you do"—she takes the sheaf of Justin's printouts from her backpack—"you might want to look at these."

She had flipped through the pages herself, pages she is still only just beginning to comprehend: full of unencrypted emails between Cy and someone called Iram Kovaci, chairman of Virginia Global Technologies GmbH.

He takes the papers, begins to turn the pages, seeing correspondence about his Basel-based shell company—hundreds of millions of dollars in contracts from companies in Russia and China, despite the trade bans of 2018, 2019, 2020, 2021, 2022—Cy Baxter and Iram Kovaci, former head of technology development program at WorldShare, the main correspondents.

To her, these papers read mostly like Greek, but some pages yielded greater sense when they described the covert rollout of "statewide surveillance systems" to "monitor every person from the moment they leave their doorstep to the moment they return to it, their work, social, and behavioral patterns recorded, analyzed and archived." Cy Baxter helping China and

Russia, establish surveillance systems on all their citizens, contracting out of a shell company in the Caymans so that he can defy sanctions.

"Creepy stuff," she tells him, taking back the papers. "Very Fusion."

He blinks fast, licks his lips as he reads, then looks up at her. "I don't have my glasses."

"You've broken the law, Mr. Baxter. A *lot*. You must be really glad no one else is listening to this conversation."

It takes him some time to reply. "Where did these come from?"

"You, apparently."

"Not what I mean. I'm a global businessman, I have global clients. So does Boeing. So does Walmart. So does McDonald's."

"So you won't mind if I tell the CIA, then?"

He barely reacts. "What makes you think they don't know already?"

"Good point. Then how about I tell the public? And I guess there's always the Senate. And the *Washington Post*. Unless you prefer the *New York Times*?"

She can see that his jaw is working, the muscles of his face tightening, the fine tendons of his left eye flickering.

"Or . . . or you can help me. Twenty-four hours. Otherwise, I'm sure I'll find some use for three million bucks while I look for Warren. Oh, and nail you."

He lowers his voice, his confidence clearly faltering. "If . . . if I were to help you . . . and I want to help you . . . then I would need to know who gave you these papers. Give me a name."

"Oh God."

"Does God have a last name?"

"Yeah. But he doesn't like people to know it. It's a comedown from 'God.' Find my husband, Cy, and I'll forget everything in those papers. As you can guess, those are photocopies. I have the originals."

"You expect me just to take your word you'll drop it?"

"What choice do you have?"

With this, she drops the stack of papers onto the filthy concrete floor. *Clomp.*

"Your husband's been missing three years," he says. "Twenty-four hours isn't long enough."

"Incorrect. For three years the CIA has been hiding Warren's whereabouts."

"Why should they tell me now?"

"They won't. But you have the power, the access, the tradecraft as Warren would call it, and I hope now the motivation, to find out. Go into their files."

He smiles, but bitterly. "You don't know what you're asking."

"I really think I do."

1 DAY, 21 HOURS

FUSION CENTRAL, WASHINGTON, DC

CY BLASTS UP TO HIS office past large teams still scrabbling for purchase on the slippery slopes of Samantha Crewe.

Sonia is the first to knock on his door.

"She didn't show up for the rendezvous," he reports, in a fugue state of warring thoughts.

"She didn't show up at all? Smart."

"I waited twenty minutes in a fucking underground garage. I'm busy right now. Do you mind?"

She doesn't move and he doesn't look at her, erasing their previous intimacy.

"Have a second?"

"What?" Still not looking at her.

"I found something."

Finally looks up from his laptop. She's holding her tablet with both hands. He should probably fire her, offer this to Erika as proof of his contrition. But what if she sues him? He needs to make a couple of calls, handle this with an NDA and a payout. "What is it?"

"I know we're not supposed to be looking for Warren Crewe . . ."

"Go on?"

"Well, before I knew *not* to look in that direction—"

"Just tell me."

"I ran every database we have on him, and I went into his deep

1 DAY, 20 HOURS

FUSION CENTRAL, WASHINGTON, DC

AFTER CY APPEARS IN THE doorway of her office, Erika doesn't deign to look his way. After he tells her (most of) what happened in the garage, she just observes, "Smart girl. What now?"

"I've decided to help her anyway. Find out everything the CIA knows about her husband."

"Oh really?" she asks, acting vaguely surprised but actually thinking, Russia-China; thinking, Undisclosed Swiss shell company sales; thinking, Sonia Duvall over the desk; thinking, I hate you; thinking, Get the hell out of my office . . . but saying nothing at all. From now on her real thoughts, real feelings, true intentions, will go underground.

"I'm going to help her find out what the CIA knows. . . . She'll turn herself in, and Go Zero will be a success."

"Bully for you."

"You don't believe me?"

Her look of complete faithlessness is ample reply.

"I don't blame you," he concedes. "I lost my way. You're right about me. I am my own worst enemy. But you're my lighthouse, my beacon. I need you, Erika."

"Yuck."

That didn't work.

friendship groups and the system just got a match . . . with an individual
to whom we've granted our top security clearance. Appears he's friends
with Warren. *Old* friends."

"With someone . . . *here*?" Who? A team leader? Who? His mind flashes
with candidates: Zack Bass, who underperformed on purpose? Lakshmi
Patel, the underchecked FBI placement? Erika herself, so confrontational
on all fronts of late?

"No."

"Then who?"

"Justin Amari. Burt Walker's guy."

The name . . . the name itself, like a freak wave, seems to rise up from
the surface of the turquoise ocean on the digital wall in front of him.

"Close the door."

Sonia is delighted to do so. When he reaches out his hand, she steps
forward holding up her Void-issue tablet like a handmaiden with an offering to an icon.

Cy takes it, enlivens the screen. And there it is: a wedding photo, two
newlyweds, and on the edge of frame, Burt Walker's irritating aide, that
pesky naysaying fault-finding fucker, but as he was back then, a grinning
overgrown frat-boy type too big for a cheap suit.

Cy experiences a moment of complete, piercing clarity. A whole cascading Tetris game *click, click, clacks* into place. He closes his eyes, takes
air deeply into his lower regions, then says, at little more than a whisper:
"Sonia, I love you," and then, in a true whisper, "Motherfucker."

When he opens his eyes, Sonia is incandescent. "It's good, right?"

"Mother. Fucker."

"Right?" She is grinning now, perfect teeth below shining blue eyes.

Cy gets it now. Can see it all. There, in magnificent high definition,
is the missing piece in the puzzle that resolves the entire mystery. It's an
end to everything not making sense. And how good this feels! How good,
to once more have the better of one's enemies, and for the advantage to
return to him. Whatever happens from this point on, whatever the future
sequence of events, even as he is yet to compute how to use this vital information, he now knows he will come out on top.

"What would you like me to do?" she asks.

He rises, begins to pace, then stops at the wall brimming with those blue-green waves, his famously fast brain in overdrive, making calculations as she watches.

Finally: "First, this stays here, just between you and me. Understood, Sonia?"

No problem there, not with Sonia.

"I want you to do something for me. Extremely important. I want you to find . . . to *establish* any connections you can between Justin Amari and some controversial organization. Okay?"

"Controversial?"

"Anything. A BLM rally he once went to. A donation he gave to a radical organization. Left-wing. Right-wing. Anything that even hints he's got any extreme views. If he's ever downloaded any material on al-Qaeda, Proud Boys, Ku Klux Klan, Hezbollah, the Kurds, anything, I don't care. And bring it to me. Will you do that, Sonia?"

"Of course."

"Because I can only trust *you* with this. You're the best I have now. It's you and me at this point. Okay? Are you game?"

She nods, seeming stunned to have entered so rapidly an extraordinary new level of intimacy beyond the merely physical. "Of course."

"And find out where he is right now. Actually, do that first. Go with a team to Justin's apartment. If he's there, call me. If he isn't, get in and see what you can find."

That's not part of any Fusion protocol. He can tell this makes her nervous, this summa-cum-laude girl who knows nothing about the real world, and so he rises, goes to her, embraces her, feels her heat through cashmere.

"Thank you," he whispers into her nice-smelling hair. "Now hurry."

1 DAY, 15 HOURS

INTERSTATE 81

SAM RIDES HER MOTORBIKE TO the edge of town as planned, hides it off the road, and starts to hike through the outskirts to the place Justin has picked out for their next meeting.

She drinks, then screws the cap back on her water bottle, looking at the closed-up diners and shuttered stores in the purpled dusk, businesses that aren't coming back. Where is everyone? At home, of course, ordering food in, their faces washed blue by their phones at the dinner table.

Looks at her watch. She hasn't the energy or time for much more running. Will Cy Baxter really help her now? Does blackmail ever really work? Maybe Justin is right and he's just a monster and this, this shut-down strip mall, this is the setting for her last act as a fugitive.

Oh, Warren, please come home. She recalls how he once told her his theory of why human beings had never met any aliens. "All over the universe," he'd said, "civilizations like ours appear and grow up and get smart, and around the time they get close to really transcending their brute origins, they start inventing the means of their own destruction. Bombs. Chemicals. Viruses. Gases in the atmosphere. This triggers a planetary disaster. Anyway, when one person can gather enough power over these destructive forces that can fuck up half the planet, eventually that person will use them. It's the entropic principle but accelerated. *Boom*. Then everything goes back to the Stone Age and we're back at the start, looking for someone who knows how to make a wheel."

Be alive, Warren. Please.

Sam, waiting at the appointed time and spot (behind a warehouse, second loading dock from the end). She raps on the metal shutter with her knuckles. A few seconds of silence, and the door cut into the shutter opens.

Justin.

He steps out and hugs her, peers past her into the darkness to check that she hasn't been followed.

"What is this place?" she asks.

"Remember video rental stores?"

1 DAY, 14 HOURS

I ♥ VIDEO, ROUTE 81

THE BACK ROOM OF THE defunct store (one Justin had worked in for several high school summers when he was a fan-boy movie geek who could name the directors of a thousand movies) is a fan-cooled concrete box with an abandoned couch, kettle, and fridge, a couple of trestle tables snaked with thick black vines of power and internet cables. Many boxes of old movie videos lie everywhere—the original *Die Hard*; *The Bodyguard*, with Kevin Costner and Whitney Houston; *The Godfather*, parts I–III; *Hell Up in Harlem*—as is enough of Justin's computer equipment to open a store. It's Batman's lair, Superman's Fortress of Solitude, a dork's paradise, fragrant with obsolescence.

With Cy Baxter and Erika Coogan now under pressure, both from the clock and from the power of the evidence against them, Justin and Sam settle down to wait and see if either will come through for them.

With his computer undetectably linked by spyware to Baxter's long-infected laptop, Justin resembles a bent-backed fisherman waiting for a twitch on the line.

Watching him, Sam realizes that her affection and gratitude for this man have not stopped growing. Yes, he has his own agenda here, his own priorities, his long war against Big Tech with its overrunning powers of coercion and influence and opinion-grooming and misinformation, all of that, but what he has done out of love and loyalty for Warren, and for her in some part, is nothing less than to detonate his career, blow it sky-high, out of the essential goodness of his own heart.

Dropping onto the sofa, she updates Justin on her conversation with Cy, the trap Justin had predicted and that she escaped only with the help of Justin's cache of pilfered emails, and then, also, about the latest on the deal with Cy: that either he helps her find Warren's exact whereabouts or these emails go wide, drop into the public domain, and vaporize his reputation and maybe his company.

Justin, for his part, manages to say neither that he her so nor that he'll believe it if he sees it. "Dude's a dog, what can I tell ya. But if a miracle were to happen, if we've forced him into helping us, it'll be today. Cy cares too much about winning." Picking up two old cell phones, he adds, "Oh, and something for you, lost property. Unlocked. Both still under other people's names. So we can talk if we have to, I dunno, split up."

As she watches, Justin resumes his patient wait-and-see work, hoping either for Cy to go look for Warren's classified file in order to save his own ass or for Erika to get her hackers to do the same in order to save Cy. He whistles tunelessly to himself, while Sam, drained dry, finally gives in and, with a still faintly aching right ankle, lies on a battered chaise longue like some supine subject for a Pre-Raphaelite painting. She doesn't even know he's taken a picture of her—snapped her lying there like a corpse—until she sees it later on the desktop of his chosen workstation: her blond hair scattered over a torn red velvet cushion, the frame edged with browned and wilted blooms. She guesses this is how she will look dead.

In this place, in this way, the night hours pass, as Monday becomes Tuesday, with Sam on the couch, in and out of sleep, praying that Cy, sixty miles away, is hard at work on Warren's behalf.

1 DAY, 3 HOURS

FUSION CENTRAL, WASHINGTON, DC

CY HAS CHOSEN AS HIS backdrop this morning the Niagara waterfall, megatons of cascading freshwater seeming to sluice over him, as he fires up his laptop and rapidly avails himself of the necessary security clearance and passwords and, importantly, cloaking software to secretly access, at the precisely appointed time, the secure network, which contains in its labyrinths the combined databanks of the NSA, the CIA, and the FBI, a cache of almost infinite size and of astronomical worth to the nation.

His fingers work fast. Although never a hacker per se, he knows about digital back doors, about security patches, about anonymity and self-destruct safeguards, about how to turn lines of code such as exploit/admin/smb/ into a crucial key to unlock a trove, a library, a universe.

Cy—protected from detection—will take every precaution (for you never know whether, as you hack, you yourself might be *being* hacked, followed, shadowed) as he enters unseen this virtual kingdom of official records, a library of intimacies that if made material would, as shelves, rival in size *six* New York City blocks.

And that's how it goes. My God, the thrill, the omnipotence he feels when he realizes that he is *in*, in the combined NSA and CIA classified database, inside the greatest secure library in the world, something close to the seat of all knowledge as it pertains to information on so many of its citizens, as well as on an enormous number of foreign nationals. Billions of souls are here, their records, their stories, their transgressions and mistakes, such as have warranted investigation, with Cy enjoying—as he never has until now—access to it all. The rush, the feeling, the idea that, were this godlike privilege something to be permanently enjoyed by him, that he would *know* . . . know almost everything about almost every person that his country has ever taken a special interest in. Surely this is the ultimate aim of his own ambitions—why this once-friendless kid trades in personal data in the first place—and it humbles him, reminds him that for all his present influence, it's these ancient government intelligence gathering agencies who horde the true mega-treasure of our secret lives.

He must work quickly though in this King Solomon's mine to find what he wants without being detected in real time.

But then, while typing scp-r/path/to/local/data—the actual command to steal/move data—a new thought strikes: Now that he's in, isn't it simpler perhaps and likely more effective to just take it all, copy it, then search later and with less time pressure for the file he needs? Of course it is. But is that even possible, to download so vast a database, this catalog of every person ever investigated for some misdeed by the U.S. government? God knows how much data that would be! More than teraflops, for sure; there would be more like peta- or exa- or zetta- or even yottaflops of it. Just how criminal is America? Historically, how many its citizens are wrong-doers? And how unbelievably tempting to find out! My God, so much data, so much knowledge, so many secrets and with them so much inherent power, a little more than a click away! Plus, he has all the links he needs right now to vast data farms where he could route and hide a downloaded copy.

And then? And then?

A new idea. An even better idea, an even more Baxterian idea. After he takes the whole fucking shebang, he can, on behalf of Fusion, notify the government that there has been a catastrophic data heist. Tell them their systems have been compromised, on a massive scale, all their records, all of them stolen. And by whom? The prime suspects . . . Well, that would have to be Justin Amari, a CIA mole, and his nefarious accomplice, one Samantha Crewe. Pin it all on his enemy, the whole thing, and let the FBI take Amari and Crewe out of commission, let *them* apprehend and then gag and bind these dangerous enemies of the state, distrust every word they say thereafter the way no one heeds a single word said by any terrorist rogue at Guantanamo Bay, while he, he, Cy Baxter, saviour, patriot, protector-in-chief, quietly and over time figures out what to do with everyone's secrets.

What a notion. What a gas. What a giant tech hard-on.

While his fingertips are poised above the keyboard, his mind streams with calculations, with cost-benefit analyses, with far-ranging projections of possible and probable outcomes, gaming all this out from opening gambit to midgame to endgame, so that, with the seconds running down to Zero Hour, he finally decides and does what he has always done: decides, and decides big. And idea too good to *not* act upon is acted upon. A once-in-a-hundred-years idea is set in motion. The genius of Cy Baxter asserts itself—he's always been able to make a knight's chessboard leap where others advance pawns—and so he begins to copy the entire combined databases of the NSA, the CIA, and the FBI all in one vast glut.

A progress bar appears on his screen to measure his success.

23 HOURS

CIA, OFFICE OF PUBLIC AFFAIRS, WASHINGTON, DC

"THANK YOU ALL FOR COMING at such short notice," Cy begins, sober, scholarly, not a hint of rapaciousness, facing a room packed with senior figures as he reads from notes he prepared in the back seat on the ride over. "I address you this afternoon on an urgent matter of national security, confirming that Fusion has today intercepted computer activity that suggests, we believe, that the NSA's data center based at Camp Williams in Utah was attacked and compromised at around nine-thirty this morning during a regular maintenance service."

CIA officers don't gasp, but there is a collective shifting of weight in chairs.

"We have further confirmed that the attack was the work of an American national and CIA aide, Justin Amari, familiar to many of you. Some of you I have briefed already on this situation. Some are hearing this for the first time."

"What the fuck?" croaks a senior NSA representative, as if on demand.

Burt Walker's face is ashen.

"Mr. Amari has also been identified as being an associate and friend of one Samantha Crewe, whom we know, at Fusion, as Zero 10, a current participant in our ongoing Go Zero Beta Test, for which this committee had provided cooperation and oversight. This participant is furthermore the wife of one Warren Crewe, an individual who is now missing. The CIA has repeatedly denied to Mrs. Crewe that her husband has ever been employed here. But it now appears that Mr. Amari, in an effort to assist Mrs. Crewe in her search for her husband, has used his intimate knowledge of the national security databases to exploit a routine security repair this morning in order to gain access to the Utah Data Center's servers and . . . and has now, we believe, downloaded vast numbers of classified files in an attempt to secure information on the missing Mr. Crewe."

"Cy, if you'd provide for the room some context as to the extent of the breach?" Burt Walker is clearly still trying to collect himself.

"We believe the hack was in the order of exabytes."

"Exabytes?"

"Potentially many millions of files."

"Millions?"

"We estimate that the entirety of files of those who have ever been of particular or unusual interest to have warranted investigation by the CIA or the FBI since Eisenhower." This horrendous news hangs in the air.

Burt takes over: "I notified the NSA of this breach an hour ago, so that its agents could immediately assess the scale of this emergency, and my staff has notified the White House. Law enforcement across the country has been supplied with the identities of Samantha Crewe and Justin Amari, and has been put on alert. We have reason to believe they may both still be in the Washington area."

Cy has no need to consult his notes to deliver what he says next. "It's Fusion's belief that this threat to our national security cannot be overstated. Also, one further detail: My teams at Fusion, working around the clock, have learned that Mr. Amari possesses several registered firearms, among them a military-style assault rifle, and so must be presumed to be heavily armed." This is almost true: Sonia uncovered an old assault rifle purchase record in Amari's apartment, though he sold the weapon after his gun license expired five years before. No evidence found of other guns. "Also, he has recently searched black sites for how to make explosives and so must be treated with extreme caution." Untrue again: Cy personally planted these searches, then backdated them. But overstating a danger was always preferable to understating it.

22 HOURS

I ♥ VIDEO, ROUTE 81

AT HIS KEYBOARD JUSTIN HAS been silently monitoring, hour upon hour, whether Cy's compromised laptop will come alive and be set to violent work by its owner. And now, at 3:00 p.m., he relays the news to Sam: There *were* forty-five minutes of frenetic activity on the laptop around nine o'clock this morning—this much was trackable by Justin thanks to his spyware—but, thus far, he hasn't been able to learn a thing about the actual nature of this activity.

"He could have been doing what you asked him to do, *could* have been . . . but something happened, I stopped being able to tailgate him. Probably employed some cloaking software, which is good and bad. Bad, in that we can't see what he found, good in that whatever he was up to, he took unusual care to cover his tracks. I'm still inside Cy's laptop, and I can tailgate him again, but that forty-five minutes is lost to us. If I had a team of hackers, real pros, maybe I could've burst through those new firewalls to see what he was up to, but I can't do that on my own." He holds up both hands, surrendering.

"So you're saying you think he went into government files? He did it. He did it, just as I asked him to."

"Slow down. It's *possible*. We have a gun to his head, so yeah. But let's not get too excited." Here, however, Justin cannot suppress a smile when looking into Sam's radiantly hopeful face. "Look at you. Like the cat who got the bird."

22 HOURS

FUSION CENTRAL, WASHINGTON, DC

ERIKA FINDS CY AT HIS desk, on his laptop, in a mood far too good for the moment.

"It was you," she says.

"Hello, my love."

"You were the hack. You hacked those databases."

"And what, my darling, would make you think that?"

"Burt just called me about the briefing you gave. Of course, he presumed I already knew about it. You're framing them."

Cy turns from Erika to the digital screen. "These two people, they're bad people. Very bad. And now they've done a very bad thing. A tremendously bad thing."

She steps in front of the screen. "Why are you doing this to them? Why? You have to tell me. You owe me that."

"They're criminals. Clearly."

"I don't believe that. Neither do you. Bullshit. Guns, explosives? It's a fiction. You're going to get these innocent people hurt, Cy. Perhaps even killed. You realize that? You're doing a fucking *swatting* prank on them!"

"It's true that they may be in some danger now."

She feels something close to a broken heart. "Tell me. This is your chance. I'm giving you this last chance. To tell me everything. For me. For Michael. Actually for *yourself*, . . . because I really do believe your soul is on the line here."

She stares into his face, trying to read it for telltale signs, hoping against hope he will speak the words she badly needs to hear. Cy, oh Cy, say it, tell me the truth and rescue that still redeemable part of yourself. And for a second she thinks she has reached him, connected on their old wavelength, that dorky boy she first met, the young man she fell in love with, the business partner until so recently she had complete faith in.

But then that boyish expression hardens before her eyes, and from the mouth so often kissed, in passion, in love, in admiration, only the words: "Baby, take a break. Go home. You're losing it a little bit. I love you. But go home."

With that, he leaves the room.

And something slips irrevocably into the past.

I have lost him, my green-eyed boy, lost, she thinks, as her eyes rest on the wall, on a lone polar bear adrift on a floating raft of ice, bear as doomed as the ice. Then she moves to his desk, on which sits his beloved, seldom-deserted laptop, left here in his haste to escape her.

MILO AND DUSTIN AREN'T BASED in the Void itself. They are brilliant enough, but they have too many indictments (sealed, later dismissed) for hacking in the past, plus a penchant for bongs and facial hair that make certain others uncomfortable. Instead, they work in the basements below the Void to the hum of a thousand cooling fans. The carbon offset on the network of cooling systems necessary to keep all this tech at optimum operating temperature is eye-watering, toe-curling. And that's just the onsite system. The data drawn down here requires server farms across the country; they've just built one in Alaska, laid in cabling systems that look like the Large Hadron Collider unwound, just to keep the cooling bills down.

Milo and Dustin's job is to make sure the data gets where it needs to go and to check the system for leaks and the digital sulfur-stench of unauthorized hacks. They have noses for such work, so they serve as Fusion's border patrol and enforcement guys against rogue incursions. In essence, they man the portcullis and drawbridge and arrow slots of this magic kingdom, a Rosencrantz and Guildenstern of the present age. And they're very, very good at what they do, and very well paid too.

A significant amount of their time, however, is spent just talking shit.

Dustin: "Someone just invented it."

Milo: "No way."

"A smart condom."

"And it—what, you wear it? It has, like, connectivity?"

"Tracks thrust velocity. That's what it says. Thrust velocity."

"Jesus, is that information anyone actually *needs*?" Milo has pulled up the specifications on-screen. "Heart rate, calories burned, and other stats during intercourse. Wi-Fi connected. Great, so the whole family can get real-time updates, nice, nice."

"Does it tell you if she fakes it?"

"Ah, *now* he's interested. Be a disaster for *your* relationship, dude."

That is what Erika finds Milo and Dustin discussing as she enters the room. Milo leaps up and gives her an unsolicited bear hug. "Erika!"

Dustin smiles but doesn't make eye contact. Dustin is shy.

Milo still has a strong Polish accent, even if he's a native in code. "Jesus bloody hell. What's been happening up there? This Justin Amari thing? No way. He seemed so cool. Got sweet tattoos, though."

These two remind her in a small way of a decade ago when WorldShare was just her and Cy and a dozen hire-a-nerds like this. The memory hurts her.

She takes a deep breath and sets Cy's laptop in front of them.

"I need to know what's been going on here, guys. And we don't have long."

Milo says: "Erika . . . whose machine is that?"

She opens the laptop as they watch and types in a password, not her own, but familiar to her.

21 HOURS

I ♥ VIDEO, ROUTE 81

THE DAY WARREN LEFT, SAM was reading at the kitchen table and the room smelled of ground coffee and the stock bubbling on the stove, ham bones slow to surrender flavor. Sam liked to cook.

She had looked up from her novel as he came downstairs with his travel bag over his shoulder. He never took check-in luggage, just a carry on, his small bottles of shampoo already in clear plastic, his travel laptop wiped every time he came home, and the burner cell he never fitted the battery into until he was taxiing to the stand in a foreign airport.

"I don't want you to go," she said. He had set his bag down by the door, was leaning against the frame, watching her, hands in his pockets.

"You always have a bad feeling, and it's always been fine."

"It's worse this time."

"I'll see you on Tuesday."

"Promise?"

He walked into the room and put his arms out. She stood, took the embrace, rested her head on his chest.

"Yeah. Put on your apron and make me some cookies."

She snorted with reluctant laughter. A taxi horn beeped outside.

"Be careful. Like, way more careful than usual, please."

"The most careful."

He lifted her face so he could kiss her properly, then turned for the door. She followed him so that she could wave him off from the porch. He slung his bag into the back seat, turned, and waved, and she waved back. That was it.

On Tuesday morning she baked cookies. Kind of a joke, kind of not a joke. Warren didn't come home. At midnight she ate all the cookies, then threw up. Life became hell.

LOUD MUSIC WAKES HER. SITS up on the sofa. "Long Cool Woman" by the Hollies is playing on an old-fashioned CD player. Justin is hunched over the laptop, staring at the screen, his body rigid with new tension.

"Sam!"

"What?"

"Something . . . something's happening here. . . ."

"What?"

"On Cy's laptop. The walls . . . I think the walls have come down."

21 HOURS

FUSION CENTRAL, WASHINGTON, DC

MILO AND DUSTIN HAVE CY'S laptop between them; they've wired it into their own machines and are working on it simultaneously. They don't make more than an occasional grunt for twenty-odd minutes, but suddenly they look at each other with quizzical expressions.

Erika looks at her phone. She's asked Cy's secretary to ping her when Cy is back in the building. The first thing Cy will look for, the *first and only* thing he'll notice is missing, is this laptop. "Guys, talk to me. Where are you?"

"We're . . . ," Milo begins. "Okay, Okay. So we're through the internal firewalls. Exposed the SSL encryption, and it looks like he . . . like Cy . . . like he just pulled some kinda . . . well, a super-massive amount of data from a government server in Utah around—"

"Nine-thirty this morning?" predicts Erika.

"Nine thirty-four to be exact."

Erika doesn't seem particularly surprised.

Milo asks, "We're not going to get into trouble for this, are we? 'Cause you're talking to two guys who've been there before."

"Several times," Dustin pipes up. "Didn't end well."

"Where is the data now?" she asks.

Milo, more reluctantly: "A server . . . in . . . looks like . . ."

"Manila," offers Dustin.

"Manila," Milo confirms. "I guess he has a personal server in Manila?"

"Can you access it?"

"Actually, we already have."

"Can you search it? The data?"

"We haven't tried yet. Will we get in trouble, Erika? Really?"

"Let's just say I'd really appreciate it if you'd search it, and I'd remember that."

After Milo and Dustin exchange nervous but also excited looks (both know they were born for moments like this), Milo asks, "Search . . . for what, exactly?"

"One name: Warren Crewe."

I ♥ VIDEO, ROUTE 81

Justin's hands are shaking, hovering above the keyboard. He looks completely paralyzed. "We're in."

"In? In what?"

"Inside some personal server . . . somewhere. He's not using the cloaking software now. Just his usual security walls. We're tailgating him . . . can see his keystrokes, exactly what he's doing . . . where he goes, we're along . . . along for the ride."

"So where's he going? What's he doing?"

"Not sure yet, but it's—it's like he's got eight hands. It's crazy. Attack code after attack code. He's gaining access . . . to something. . . ."

FUSION CENTRAL, WASHINGTON, DC

"Talk to me!" Erika says. "What have you found?"

"We're in *something*," Milo replies. "But the cache is so . . . fucking . . . vast. A huge single data dump all bundled incredibly tightly together. I mean, this is hundreds of thousands of pages . . . millions of pages. "

Erika thinks, Oh, Cy, what have you done? But she knows already, knows exactly what they're looking at here: the fruits of the biggest data breach in history. Cy did it, hacked into the agency's famed libraries full of a trillionfold secrets. Has lost his way, to the point that he has allowed himself to do this. And in order to achieve what? She knows this, too: to frame as dangerous criminals two people who know *his* secrets, could incriminate *him* with huge crimes.

Her phone pings. Cy's secretary! Cy's meeting across town, canceled. Someone got Covid. He's being driven back now. ETA, half an hour. Half an hour?

"I need you to pull the Warren Crewe file," says to Milo and Dustin. "Can you search for just that one file? Extract one file only?"

"The extraction of . . . of a single file? Man, that would take time. Other layers to crack. How long we got?"

"How long? How long would it take?"

"Hours."

She looks at her watch, and then at Cy's laptop, tethered to other, bigger machines. She urgently needs to get it back onto Cy's desk. "What can we do right now? Come on, guys!"

Milo looks at Dustin, who finds his voice. "We have a choice."

"Between?"

"Extracting nothing, or . . ."

"Or?"

"Copying it all."

"Taking it all," translates Dustin. The whole *thing.*"

"Can you even *do* that? Copy it *all*?"

"We're one click away from download."

"Literally," Milo says. He moves the cursor into position, then waves his index finger over the return button on his keyboard. "Your call. But . . ."

"But?"

"This is big. . . ."

Erika looks at the keyboard, then at her watch. "I have to get this laptop back upstairs, guys. Like five minutes ago."

"Then we stop now?" Milo asks. "Pull the plug?"

"If we copy it all, could you then go through it for me later? Find The Warren Crewe file, erase the rest?"

Dustin: "We'd still need time. But yes."

She nods. Decisive. Then it's clear. "Step outside. Both of you." The hands of both these hackers ought not to be on this terrible action, she reasons. It's her call. Her responsibility. She has to do it.

When the young men are gone, she moves toward the keyboard. Life is short. Regrets are long. Here goes everything. A life. A love. A living. She taps. DOWNLOADING . . .

Pale, she turns and opens the door, revealing two even paler young men. Says to both: "You can come back in now."

19 HOURS

I ♥ VIDEO, ROUTE 81

AWKWARDLY FEEDING A CIGARETTE INTO and out of the unvisored pane in her helmet, Sam examines a poster stuck freshly onto the store window: SLEEPY CREEK MUSIC FESTIVAL. Starts tomorrow. BARS AND FOOD STALLS. Nice, she muses. MUSIC, READINGS. Oh my God. POETRY, PHILOSOPHY, ENVIRONMENTAL LECTURES. Evidence of the other America, those other Americans, the children of the Age of Aquarius, the dropout, Earth-loving crowd, keeping alight the fires of humanity's original values. She'd love to go there, to Sleepy Creek, with Kaitlyn, with Warren, to just listen, to learn, to dance, to partake of that lost world, to sleep, yes, most of all to sleep. But that is a forlorn hope right now.

Steps out the cigarette. Returns, for the hundredth time, to look over Justin's shoulder. Beside them, a workstation of linked hard drives, still hot from imbibing all the stolen privacies copied from Cy's distant download.

"There must be something about Warren there," she says.

Justin has spent the time sifting thought this vast contraband for any and all files on his best friend. Nothing so far.

Sam has spent the time alternately pacing, sitting, making coffee, drinking coffee, asking Justin if he wants more coffee, then asking Justin if he's sure he doesn't want more coffee, and all the time muttering things like "Whatever we think of Cy Baxter, he did as he promised: He went into the files to look for Warren, and surely at great risk to himself. He did what he said he would do, and I have to be grateful for that at least. Right?

Justin? Justin?"

Finally, four and a half hours into his investigation, Justin is ready to summarize.

"All I can find here," he tells her, "confirms their story. It looks like they once paid Warren for six research papers on things like opportunities for investment in Eastern Europe. There's nothing here on Iran. Not that I can find. Nothing that remotely suggests Warren ever officially worked for the CIA. And nothing on his whereabouts. There's some stuff in his file on your activities, though, your accusations against the agency, claims of a cover-up, the history of their denials, but not one file suggesting that the CIA has been doing anything other than telling the truth all along."

"Then his file wasn't in the download."

"Possibly. Or they scrubbed the file, deleted it, rewrote history. Or there was not file."

"Can you look again? There *must* be something. Something extra."

"Sam."

"They're lying. I know they are."

"I wouldn't be at all surprised, but I don't know how to find it here."

Tears come to her eyes as they look at each other.

"There's only one thing that stands out to me. . . ."

"What?"

"There's an affidavit the agency secured, from a . . . from an Anne Kulczyk. Have you heard that name? A woman in her early forties, address in Foggy Bottom"

"And?"

"This woman denies . . . denies that Warren ever worked for the CIA, and she categorically denies ever knowing him."

"So?"

"Well, who asked her? She's a nobody. Why get a nobody who never knew Warren to give an affidavit swearing she knows *nothing*?"

18 HOURS

ANNE KULCZYK'S RESIDENCE, FOGGY BOTTOM, WASHINGTON, DC

IT'S FIFTY-FIFTY BY NOW THAT the motorbike has been flagged on the system. Sam had ridden it into Washington for her meeting with Cy, and knows she's seriously pushing her luck with this trip. Still, helmeted, she cruises on two wheels into Anne Kulczyk's neighborhood. There are too many cameras in this part of town to risk walking more than a few yards, not with her hobble. She turns into Kulczyk's drive, kicks down the stand.

Neat lawn, ordered flower beds, flesh-colored underthings on a rack on the porch. It looks like a horror movie waiting to happen. The woman who answers the door is fixing her earring, head at forty-five degrees, looks annoyed, embodies brisk mistrust of unsolicited visitors.

"Yes?"

"Anne Kulczyk?"

"You're delivering something?"

Sam feels Anne's eyes taking in the motorcycle helmet, the tight jeans and boots. De-helmeting, she offers: "No. I'm Samantha Crewe. Warren's wife."

Anne straightens up, the earring forgotten, and stares at her, a stare that confirms to Sam's mind immediately that her sworn affidavit was a lie.

"May I come in? I need to say something important to you."

"I've never heard that name in my life."

"I know you knew Warren. Please. Five minutes."

Anne lets Sam in and takes her through to the living room.

The room is dull in a good-taste sort of way. Everything very neat. Small. She's a woman who lives alone, but she has no cat. Yet.

"I told you. I've never heard that name. I don't see what else we have to discuss."

"Miss Kulczyk, I bet you're a good person. A decent person."

"How would you know that?"

"You let me in your house. You let me sit on your couch. I need you to tell me anything you know about my husband. I beg you."

Anne fidgets. Crocheted doilies adorn the glass coffee table, and knitting needles impaled into a skein of wool rest on the couch beside her. Hobbies fill voids. Sam knows this, too. She studies Anne. This woman, this stranger, so ineffectual looking, so anodyne, pale and solitary, how much power she has over her in this moment, the power to thwart her hopes, to make or unmake her world.

"I've seen your affidavit. You lied, under oath."

"I think you should go now."

"You know where he is."

"Please. Go. Or I will phone the police. I shouldn't have let you in here."

"Part of you wants to help, I can tell. How did you know my husband? Did you work with him?

Sam can begin to see the arguments raging inside this woman, a years-long struggle that goes to the center of her sense of herself, of her estimation of her own decency, which is eventually decided with the offer of a single word: "Yes."

"Bless you."

"I don't want your blessing."

"Please, can you help me? Anything you tell me will stay between us. I give you my word. I'm trying to save Warren's life."

The woman's laced fingers tighten in her lap. "What do you know?"

"I know the CIA is denying he ever worked for them."

"Are you wired? Would you mind opening your shirt?"

As Sam obliges—unbuttons; reveals naked shoulders, belly, bra; then rebuttons—Anne Kulczyk turns on a digital radio, and only then sits again, this time at Sam's side.

"Officially, he didn't. That's where the problem starts. He worked with us, for the analysts. I was an analyst back then. Analysts don't hire spies."

"He was a spy?" Sam's heart leaps.

"He was an agent. Who did research. But there's often, as in this case, no difference. How much do you know?"

"Assume I know nothing, and you won't be far wrong."

"Warren was collecting information on . . . on the Iranians. He was useful to us analysts, but we aren't allowed to hire agents in the field. Only operatives do that. So Warren worked off the books for us, at finding intelligence on corruption within the Iranian government. That was his specialty. Sniffing out the money trails. But he also got interested in the state of Iran's nuclear program. Dangerous stuff. And he got paid through us analysts, unofficially. The bigwigs knew it. His reports were widely read inside the agency. They just couldn't admit it because he hadn't been officially vetted and approved. So when Warren went missing, it was easier to say that they had no information on his whereabouts and that he was never an agency asset. This was not true, but that's when the ridiculous cover-up began. It snowballed. Thailand, and all the rest, suddenly this evidence appearing from thin air that he went to Bangkok. It was a mess. And Warren was the victim of it. Remains the victim of it. He was doing good work for us."

Sam has tears running down her cheeks. Anne rises, comes back with a napkin for Sam.

"And the Iranians? Why didn't they—"

"Crow? About catching a CIA agent? Because Warren had more value as a secret bargaining chip. You have to understand the calculus of prisoner swaps—prisoners are being swapped all the time, totally under the radar for the most part. Sometimes low-value prisoners are exchanged for high value ones, deals that the public would be outraged about. That's the advantage of secrecy. Warren was a complicated case. He was of low value compared to the prisoners the United States mostly bothers to hold. But Iran was looking to swap Warren for a much higher-value figure, a bombmaker say, a real incurable extremist held by the U.S. government somewhere around the world, but the United States refused to do the trade, *couldn't* do the trade, because it wouldn't even admit Warren was working for them! And so the weeks, the months, and now the years go by. He becomes a problem too hard to fix." Anne bends to Sam, looks her directly in the eyes. "I don't know how much this can help you. But I'll tell you something else. When I heard that Warren had gone missing, well, first I went to the bathroom and threw up . . . but then I reached out to his Iranian contact. I received a coded message back. Dawud was sure the Iranians had stopped Warren at the airport trying to leave Tehran, and that they sent him to—to a military prison."

Sam can't immediately reply. Military prison, spy, Tehran, Iranian contact? Oh, Warren, why? Why not the normal life? Why aren't you mowing the lawn right now, stopping to go pick up a can of two-stroke gas?

"Which prison?"

"I could never find out." A silence. And then: "But I think the Iranian contact may know. He has since defected. He's living in Washington and if anyone knows anything he may. His name is Dawud Khuzani. And that's all I can tell you."

17 HOURS

WASHINGTON HIGHLANDS, WASHINGTON, DC

DAWUD KHUZANI'S WIFE LEADS SAM through a low-rent living room where a TV is playing, toward a kitchen in back of the house overlooking a bare, grim yard: very poor housing, she thinks, for the government to place a defector in. A man, heavy-stomached, turns at the stove where he is making coffee as his wife explains to him, in rapid Farsi, all that Sam has just informed the woman in English at the front door. Sam expects resistance but instead the man's face softens into sympathy and sadness, his eyes on Sam the whole while. Finally, the man himself speaks.

"Welcome."

She is functioning now purely on the fumes of her rage. What she really needs is a bed, preferably one in a hospital. "Thank you," she replies.

"Would you take some coffee with me?"

"Yes, I would. Thank you."

As the man's wife excuses herself, he bids Sam to sit in the kitchen's single chair.

"Please."

She sinks into it, her elbow resting on the Formica tabletop and studies him: receding hair, short-sleeved shirt tight over his belly, the buttons, under pressure, inclined. By the smell, the man likes his coffee strong.

He begins his monologue. "You will want to know if Warren is alive. I believe he is. Warren spoke to me of you many, many times. We spent many hours together in Tehran. We decided we were very lucky men to love our wives and to know it. Such blessings are rare."

Sets the coffee in front of her. Stirs cream into his own coffee.

"He was fearless. Quite fearless. Among other things, he was trying to find out information on the nuclear program for the CIA. I said I would help him if I could. Later, I was told an American was detained at the airport when trying to leave—this sort of thing goes around—and I knew it must be Warren. They will have interrogated him. At some point he may have confessed that he is CIA. And if he admitted that, then he would have been sent to a black site, not an official prison where the inmates are logged, but a secret place where the prisoners are nameless, just a number, where no official light shines. So Warren, if he is still alive, will have a number. That is all I know. I'm sorry. The Iranians will continue to deny they hold him, keep him in the shadows, perhaps to produce him suddenly as if by magic, a brokering chip if they should ever need to swap another secret prisoner. This is the unknown work of nations. And the United States does not appear to be ready to admit its mistakes or involvement or do anything we know about, to get him home. This government, right up to the president, has forsaken Warren, and the agency will do anything, it seems, to forestall any investigation of its role." Dawud turns to look out the window on his own backyard world. "But all that is behind me. I'm an American citizen now. I sell cars instead of secrets." Drinks his coffee.

"The name of this prison?"

He doesn't turn to face her.

"I will keep your name secret."

"The world has changed," he says. "There are no secrets anymore. We all walk naked, under a burning light."

"The name?"

"It's near Isfahan. Possibly. A site just south of Isfahan. That is the one place I know of. He could be there."

SAM, HELMET BACK ON, HOBBLES toward her motorbike in a state of advanced nervous exhaustion. As she does so she notes a car parked super close behind it. A standard-looking rental, but fancy for this neighborhood. As Sam approaches her bike, a woman climbs out of the car. Comes toward her.

"Please don't run."

Sam gets on the bike and turns the key. Warren, Warren, Warren . . .

The woman's voice rises in appeal. "Samantha."

Should she run? Is it over? The woman has a phone in her hand, and Sam knows exactly how fast these people can blanket an area with drones and cars, and there aren't any subway stations to get lost in around here, so she dismounts, slowly.

"I'm Erika Coogan."

"I know who you are. Was it the bike?"

"Lotta cameras round here. But don't worry, officially I dismissed its significance. At Fusion, I mean. I came alone."

"Did Cy send you?"

"No. Cy is not going to help you. He never was."

"He already has."

Erika shakes her head. "Uh-uh, sorry."

"I made him look for Warren; it helped us."

"He's not trying to help you, Sam."

Erika says this with such assurance that Sam cannot doubt it. Then she begins to see this woman properly. Erika looks like *she's* been on the run and hasn't slept in a week, as if, under the corporate pantsuit and the careful makeup, she's held together by duct tape.

Erika asks: "Will you give me five minutes of your time?" When Sam looks around for cameras, Erika adds, "We're good here."

Sam's whole nervous system is screaming at her to run. "How do I know a Capture Team isn't on its way already?"

"I traced you going into that house over twenty ago. They're still not here, are they?" If I'd wanted you caught, you'd already be in the back of one of our SUVs."

Sam has to accept this also.

"Here's what I need to know first," Erika says. "What was the deal you made with Cy?"

"We . . . we have information on you guys, illegal technology sales, defying sanctions. We're willing to trade it for information on Warren."

"At this point, he's not going to honor that deal. But I'll help you."

"I don't trust you."

Sam turns away, but Erika grabs her arm.

"He's not only *not* going to help you, but he's officially accused you and Justin Amari of conducting a cyberattack on this country . . . of committing a massive hack into the NSA's data center and of stealing millions of pages of classified information."

"We did."

"You *did*?"

"Well, we only did what he did. We followed his laptop."

"Followed his laptop?"

"We had access to his personal laptop. From the thumb drive I gave him. So we were able to follow him, monitor him when he went to his hiding places, and download the same huge amount of data he downloaded. We have it only because he has it."

Erika now understands. "Listen to me. You have to destroy that data. All of it. You cannot have it. Your lives are nothing beside the value of this data. Cy has already convinced everyone that you're both dangerous, possibly armed. That it was you who hacked the NSA database and that you're attacking this country. Right now, the full might of American law enforcement is looking for you. It's about to come down on your head. You aren't in the world of ducking cameras and camping trips anymore. Go Zero is over. This is the real thing. You're being hunted with guns. Get rid of that data, or he won't even have to frame you. He'll be right. Right now you are a national threat."

It strikes Sam that this could be true, all of it, and yet she can think only about Warren, the cold prison near Isfahan that holds him.

"Let me help you," Erika pleads.

"You and Cy have been selling technology illegally to—"

"Not me. You can believe that or not, but it's true. I do know now what he has been up to thanks to Justin, and I want to stop it, too. I want to help you. Help you, and help you find Warren. But we need to move very fast. Okay? It's all about the next few hours. You need to stay out of harm's way till I can show the right people that you're not responsible for this cyberattack."

"Look, if you really want to help me, don't worry about my safety. Get me proof that Warren is alive. And tell me the name of the prison in Iran where I know they're holding him."

"Your safety first. Then I'll do all I can. Can you hide? I've heard you're quite good at that. Somewhere in a crowd. Safety in numbers. Surround yourself with people. Witnesses. Where you can't be targeted and harmed. And take this—it's a pager. No one is tracking it. I can communicate with you privately."

Sam looks suspiciously at the pager. They still make those? By now, she is so used to fearing all devices, but her need overrides this impulse, and she takes it. To trust someone: she tries to remember what that's like.

16 HOURS

I ♥ VIDEO, ROUTE 81

WRINGING THE THROTTLE FOR SPEED, Sam rides the sixty miles straight back to Justin, tells him everything she's learned. They're both being hunted. That's a bad status to have in today's America.

"She said we have to destroy all the data we took. Right now. All of this." She waves a finger over the stacked hard drives, brick on brick of stored sins, secrets, errors, crimes, omissions, scandals—decades' worth.

"Oh I bet she did."

"Let's do it, Justin. It's putting us in real danger." When she sees his reluctance: "What *now*?"

"It's evidence. It's the evidence we need. To take Baxter down. That's why she wants us to destroy it. You see that right? This? All of this . . . it's a nuclear bomb. Which means we're a nuclear power. They don't like that. They can't allow that. Us holding all the secrets." His eyes are wide. Hasn't really slept in forty-eight hours. "Wonder what the world would look like if we detonated all that?"

"Justin, please."

"Would it make for a worse world, or a better one, do you think? It's an interesting philosophical question."

"I'm not even talking about this. Promise me."

"I am."

She sees how excited he is by this lethal fantasy, full again of that Justin Amari intensity. "People do need to know," he says, "just what their *government* has on them . . . that this capacity exists, and what harm it's doing to them. Look, even if they put Cy away, the agencies still have his ill-gotten data, and every day they find better ways to harvest more of it. Where's it gonna end? What does *that* society look like? I'm just saying. We need a system reboot."

She steps away from him at this point, jabs her finger at the drives, her voice rising in intensity. "Erase it. Now. Justin, I don't know how to do that. You need to do it."

"Too late."

"What do you mean too late?"

"I already have a copy. Actually, *copies*. Bounced everything we've got off to a couple of remote servers, two different counties, for safekeeping, and all I have to do is post the IPs and *boom*."

"Boom? Boom what? What is boom?"

"Data bomb. The biggest data dump in history. It's our protection. It's our leverage, just to make sure they do the right thing. And this baby will make Wikileaks look like the midweek gossip column in the *Fuck Knuckle Times*."

She runs her hands through her hair, can feel the static of his revolutionary zeal in its strands. Senses also the itchiness of his trigger finger to fire the weapon he now possesses.

"That's not our agreement, Justin. This was about Warren. Remember? Always about Warren and about Cy Baxter. Not blowing up the world. Erika is going to help us find out exactly where he is, and take down Cy. We just have to stay off the radar a few more hours, until she tells us that we're no longer in danger. And then we win."

"Win what? The prize money?"

"As soon as she says it's safe, we can get out of here. We know where Warren is, what happened to him. That's huge. For me." Tears appear in her eyes. "He's at a black site in Iran. We'll find him. We did it. I know he's alive. And now we can go to the press with everything we know, expose the lies about Warren, expose Cy, force the government to take action. We *won*, that's what I mean. Now, please destroy that data. Otherwise it's gonna get us killed."

He weighs this, then gives a shrug. "If that's what you want, okay."

"Justin. Do it. All of it, even the copy you've saved. Do it right now."

As Sam watches, Justin sits again at his computer and, with reluctant actions, after a series of tapped commands, tells her that the erasure has begun, wiping the hard drives of all the megadata until, in under ten minutes, this particular nuclear arsenal is but a stack of impotent invisible bricks once more. Only then does Sam feel the relaxing of the invisible hand at her throat.

"Good," she sighs, when something deep in her pocket beeps. The pager. Erika's pager.

"What the hell is that?"

"From Erika."

"Jesus, Sam!"

The pager slow-scrolls a message: *Leave now. They're coming to video store.*

"They're coming," she tells Justin. "They know where we are. We have to go."

"Erika fucking Coogan? Telling us what to do now?"

"Are you finished erasing everything?"

"Yeah."

"Everything?"

But when Justin doesn't react immediately, looking at the hard drives and computer instead, Sam implores: "What? *What?*"

"They win. In the end, they win. They always do."

"We have to go!"

And with that, Justin picks up their two burner phones and follows her out the door.

14 HOURS

FUSION CENTRAL, WASHINGTON, DC

CY WALKS AROUND THE BACK lot of the video store. Not in reality, of course. In his fury he has to stop himself from virtually kicking things, turning over furniture, wrecking the joint. Left behind, after his prey's easy escape, the physical proof of their occupation in the form of a pile of hard drives, nice evidence certainly, come to think of it, of an attempt to store a very large amount of data. Yes, to all appearances Justin Amari and Samantha Crewe are indeed cyberterrorists, and how supportive of his made-up depiction of them all this abandoned tech is: he couldn't have furnished their hiding place any better if he'd tried.

"What do you want to do with the hard drives?" he is asked by a team member onsite.

"Get them back to Fusion. Make sure everything on them is erased. Immediately. Everything."

With that, he leaves, is whisked back to his office, where he finds Erika in his chair, wearing her coat. Her right hand rests on his laptop.

"They have a copy," she tells him.

"They? Copy of?"

"Justin and Samantha. They compromised your laptop. Back in the forest. When you inserted Kaitlyn Day's thumb drive. Spyware. They tailgated you. *They've* been monitoring *you*. All this time."

"I don't believe you."

She pushes his laptop toward him across the glass table. "Check."

"And how would you know this?"

"They were there. When you illegally downloaded all those NSA and CIA files. Guess what? They got a copy. You provided them access. They got everything you got. Stole every file you stole."

It takes him a moment to process all this, but he soon does, and even seems pleased with this news. "Then . . . I was right. They *are* a threat to national security."

"Only because you allowed them to be so."

"They stole the nation's secrets, Erika. They now need to be stopped."

"Only after *you* stole them. Only *because* you stole them."

"Except I pose no threat to the nation."

"Says you."

"They were blackmailing me; I was all part of their plan. Surely you see that? They're terrorists."

"Who now possess everything the CIA knows about you." Her eyes are cold, her manner even colder. "And me. And WorldShare. And the Caymans. And the illegal Russian sales of spyware. And the Chinese sales, and God knows what else. Justin and Samantha have it all. In short, it's over. You ruined it."

"Nothing is over. In fact, it's perfect that they copied the files. They've only succeeded in making themselves public enemy number one and two, with a big target on their backs. The heat's on them, baby, not us. Nothing is ruined. Nothing they say now, or do, no information they have, can impact negatively on us. This is incredibly great news actually. We're off the hook."

She stares at him, shakes her head. "Michael used to say something to you, when you were like this. Remember what it was?"

"What?"

"Go fuck yourself."

With this, she is gone.

Sitting behind his desk, looking at his laptop and thinking briefly of his mistake in inserting that thumb drive—an error that has now paid such unforeseen dividends—a new thought arrives, and not one his hyperactive mind has ever yet produced: that this day might conceivably now end, spectacularly, and surprisingly, with Justin Amari and Samantha Crewe being zipped into body bags, and how terrific that would actually be.

2 HOURS

OUTSKIRTS OF BERKELEY SPRINGS, WEST VIRGINIA

THE PLAN IS A LITTLE counterintuitive, but that, perhaps, is its strength, and it goes like this: Until Erika Coogan can send word that law enforcement has stood down, and that they're in no physical danger of being met by lethal force, they will hide out in the middle of the largest phone-filled crowd they can find, the theory being that if law enforcement should now wish them dead, their best protection is *other people*—witnesses in other words, a defence force of instagramming phones that will ensure that any arrest, if it comes to that, will have to be a peaceful one.

So that's how they end up driving the video store owner's old truck, with I ♥ VIDEO still on the sides, toward the Sleepy Creek Music Festival (twelve thousand paying attendees), being held at a private campground near the Potomac, about ninety minutes, or a hundred miles, from Berkeley Springs.

She looks out the window. A full sky. Cloud-free morning. Other cars pass close by. Sees through double glass, hers and theirs, a young woman surely headed to the same place they are, carefree, flowers in her hair, high on life, singing along to some mute song that enlivens her heart even more. Sam, while still sick with fear, is aware that there's something new in her as well: feels high from a certain piquancy that perhaps only comes when you know someone wants to take your life. Every moment is just that little bit more precious now that your life may be far more finite than you ever imagined. Stay alive: all she has to do now. Just like everyone here is doing. Stay safe, and stay alive by whatever means. After so much hiding in the wilderness, cleave now to other people. And when it's safe to do so, only then can they turn themselves in, amid the music and these hope-filled people. Mission accomplished.

As the car slows to line up for the festival gates ahead, Sam lowers her window to take a program of events from a passing festival official with a beauty queen's diagonal sash, then reads aloud the attractions to Justin: bars and food stalls, Discovery Area for shops and artisans, Sustainable Green Fields, The Center for New Consciousness, yurts for readings and workshops, music, art, poetry, face painting, breathing workshops. They begin to laugh, for the first time in days.

"Kaitlyn would love the shit out of this," Sam says.

She glances at Justin, seeing a Mona Lisa smile on his lips.

"Sounds like she designed it," he replies. "The Center for New Consciousness? We'll bone up on the Hard Problem of Consciousness, finally figure out who the fuck we are."

"Okay, how about this?" she says. "They've printed out the UN's Universal Declaration of Human Rights . . . Want to hear one of the articles?"

"Why not."

"'No one shall be subjected to arbitrary interference with his privacy, family, home or correspondence, nor to attacks upon his honor and reputation. Everyone has the right to the protection of the law against such interference or attacks.'"

"That settles it. We're fine, then. And to think that for the longest time I've been worried."

With this, he reaches out and lays his hand, palm upward, on her leg. She looks down, surprised to have been touched—something jumps inside her—and then, swelling with unacknowledged feeling for this all-sacrificing man beside her, she places her hand, palm down, on his. Their fingers entwine, tighten. They don't look at each other. Don't need to. They have looked at each other enough times. But now a new circuit is created, one that does no injury to Warren and yet is not entirely innocent, either: a charge that is entirely private, and as unique as a password.

"First thing we do, after we park?" she proposes softly.

"What?"

"Get our faces painted."

1 HOUR

FUSION CENTRAL, WASHINGTON, DC

HEADSET ON, WINDING UP A call.

Sonia Duvall. In the doorway suddenly. Tablet, miniskirt, high heels, cheeks aflame, shining with good news.

He nods for her to close the door and winds up his call.

"Justin's servers," she tells him. "We found them all. He uses unlisted cloud servers located in a data storage facility in Amsterdam. We attacked it, got in, wiped everything, masses of stuff."

"Everything?"

"Vast amount of recent material in there from this afternoon. Millions of new files."

"Wiped?"

"Entirely. And we now have full control of the servers."

"Did anyone see the files before they were wiped?"

Shakes her head. "Of course not. I did exactly what you said."

"Then you've stopped him. You just disarmed a terrorist. *You* did, Sonia. That's massive. This is incredible."

She nods, smiles.

"How does it feel," he asks, "to have saved your country from tremendous damage?"

Her eyes widen. She swallows. "It feels great."

Smiles: "Just great?"

Her own mission statement now emerges: "I want to be excellent at everything I do."

He approaches her then. "May I?"

She nods. He embraces her. With her head resting on his chest, he smells her shampoo, kisses the top of her head.

"Great job," he says. "Now let's get back to work."

As she exits—that incurved back, that taut skirt, those indented buttocks—he feels a delicious throb. His eyes fall on the enchantment of a white digital dove taking wing from the long lateral limb of a forest giant. Flap, flap, flap, and away, until the last single pixel carrying its image blinks and goes green. I love Erika, he thinks, no question, always will. But this is fun.

At this very moment, his headset unleashes Lakshmi Patel's voice: "Mr. Baxter? We have them."

He descends quickly to the control floor.

"Visuals up," he instructs, never more like the captain on the bridge of the starship *Enterprise*.

Burt is there. And appearing from her office, Erika also.

Magically up on the big screen: an aerial shot of a Ford Tundra in slow traffic, on Route 9 heading northwest from DC, vast machines now working in perfect harmony–tracking, plotting, charting–learning in real time how to make predictable the shocking anarchy of human behavior.

"It's them?"

"Justin used to work for the truck's owner. The link was the video store."

By drawing a radius around the video store, they have been able to slave that area's CCTV coverage and so log and identify the vehicle and its direction of travel. The images are now on the big screen, all courtesy of a deployed drone.

"Medusa over target."

"Let's pull up a Predator, too," Cy orders. "Burt?"

"Okay with you?"

It's now Burt Walker's turn to make a call of his own, a real-time mission control/situation room call on a critical matter of national security. He looks at Cy. Looks back at the screen. Then at Cy again, then at all the Voiders staring at him in silence, waiting, before he nods his assent.

"You heard the man," Cy translates. "And give me an ETA on that."

"Predator requested."

Cy is delighted by the addition of an armed drone. The Predator is the real thing. With its laser and Hellfire missiles, a necessary tool. Pictures of the fugitives are all very well, but the power to actually stop these terrorists in their tracks, obliterate them if need be, and to order such a thing from Fusion's control room, that's power, and that is what is needed now. Real prime-time American power. Old-school might, where the bad guys don't know what just hit 'em. And in command of that power, that might, that vengeance, that justice: Fusion.

"Ground teams, where are we?"

"Traffic heavy. Twenty minutes for the DC team."

Further imagery up now of the DC Capture Team in convoy, sirens blaring, eight black SUVs streaking up a highway's hard shoulder.

"Target waiting in line of vehicles for entrance to the music festival."

"Where's the festival?" Cy asks.

"Sleepy Creek."

"Have we notified festival security?"

"Sir, they have a description of the vehicle at all the gates."

"Is the festival security armed?"

"Yes, sir."

"Get me whoever is in charge of security there. They need to know the exact threat level they're facing."

Back in his office, the call is patched through to him. He pulls on his headphones to deliver the sobering news to some security chief that extreme caution must be exercised in any dealings with these armed fugitives, and that they should call in extra local law enforcement, and perhaps the National Guard, but he is quickly reassured that the festival's own robust and armed security has been reassigned to concentrate on the exact gate Fusion has identified as the truck's entry point.

1 HOUR

ROUTE 9, OUTSKIRTS OF BERKELEY SPRINGS, WEST VIRGINIA

"FUCK," JUSTIN MUTTERS, EDGING FORWARD in the tightening line of cars approaching the festival gates, roughly twenty vehicles back from the security cordon. Ahead, clearly visible, the serial sequencing of red-white-blue cop-car light bars. "Not good."

Sam sees the same problem. "What do we do?"

Erika's pager then beeps in her pocket. Rapidly, she reads the incoming: *They are on you. Peacefully surrender.* She reads this to Justin. "So that's it. It must be the all clear. We've got to surrender now. Ready? This is it. It's okay. It must be safe to surrender. She's telling us it is."

"Let me think. Wait."

"What?"

"Wait."

"Think what? Erika says to surrender. We have to trust her. Let's just get out and walk to festival security and give ourselves up. It's over. Justin? It's *over*."

Justin leans forward, peers up into the cloudless sky. "Okay," he replies, then taps into life the GPS on the SUV's dash to permit an overview of where exactly they are.

"Okay *what*?"

"Okay," he repeats, tapping the screen.

But then, as Sam exerts upward pressure on the door handle, Justin wrenches the wheel, throwing Sam sideways into him as he plants his foot on the gas and, with a roar of eight cylinders, launches at giddying speed back up the same road they've just been inching their way down.

"What are you doing?!"

"I dunno. Hopefully, the right thing."

Already sixty miles an hour.

"Are we . . . ?"

Seventy.

"You believe that . . . ?"

Eighty . . . And then, surpassing ninety, and now ignoring Sam's continual protests, and as a helicopter appears in the sky overhead threshing the air, and as more flashing lights become visible in the distance ahead, sirens *wee-haw*ing—he heaves a second time on the steering wheel and barrels into the woods, the car lurching and leaping over the uneven unsealed road, gunning through a tight cloister of trees until, emerging out the other side into wide-open fields, he swings again toward the horizon, pursued, with every maneuver, by objects seen and unseen.

Disabled by panic, Sam cranes forward to see the chopper above and, in a desperate effort to end this, reaches for the handbrake, but he beats her to it. His right arm, his grip, is far too strong and will not relent. Looking into his face for answers, his profile fixed on some destination, she is stunned by his mysterious calm, as if he's prepared for this, knew all along it was going to happen.

"Talk to me!" she shouts over the roaring engine. "Tell me what this is!"

"I gotta expose them all. The whole deal."

With the field in front of them coming to an end, and behind them only a tornado of dust, Sam braces for impact as Justin chooses to plow through a wire fence instead of an iron gate, then swings—trailing wood and wire—onto another a two-lane blacktop heading east.

"There's a tunnel up ahead," he says. "You're getting out. You have that phone?"

"What are you talking about?"

"The phone I gave you at the flower shop. *Do you have that phone?*"

"Yes."

"Then get ready. You're getting out."

"Don't do this."

Ahead, as he and the GPS predicted, a tunnel. "Listen to me. Listen to me okay? I linked our phones. Open the browser on your phone and it'll take you to a live stream. Then you'll see what I see. Understand? You'll be my witness. We can stay in touch."

"I'm not getting out."

"You're getting out!"

The tunnel is coming up fast.

"I'm not leaving you." Sam's chest is clogged with fear. Grabs hold of his arm, shakes him.

"We need to do this fast," he tells her forcefully, passionately, "or they'll know I stopped. Are you ready? Open your door."

As they reach the narrow cover provided by the overpass, she hears behind them the growing whine of sirens. Above, the helicopter. They enter the tunnel at speed and then everything vanishes in the enveloping darkness until her eyes readjust.

"Sam, open your door! Open it!"

Her hand reluctantly finds the handle again, lifts it obediently, but she is shaking her head. The door opens a crack. "What are you going to do?"

"Keep the phone on. Get ready."

Inside the short tunnel, Justin jams on the brakes hard. "Go! *Go!*"

Assisted by a push from him, she lands in the dark, a phone in her hand, smelling gas as she hears a roar and watches . . . watches . . . watches in distress as the SUV becomes a small silhouette in the tunnel's bright mouth before disappearing.

Hardly able to see and with no time to think, she hears the trailing sirens behind increase to a shrill scream. She pushes herself back into a dark recess moments before one, two, three, four chasing patrol cars sweep by her. Only when they're gone, when even the sound of them has faded, does she start to feel her way back down the tunnel toward the circle of light.

Emerging, she slides over a barrier, then with her last energy climbs the wooded incline away from the road, up toward the top of the overpass, pausing to hide under thick cover as a second parade of patrol cars—one, two, three, four—whiz by beneath her in hundred-mile-an-hour pursuit.

A HILLTOP, ROUTE 9

When she makes high ground, her heart is punching through her rib cage. She collapses under a new tree in heavy leaf and turns on the phone, opening up the livestream. He's broadcasting, as promised, filming everything now as he drives . . .

Flashing images on that tiny screen describe a huge scene: the SUV's path ahead entirely sealed off by squad cars fanned out across the road, a blockade being approached at high speed, as if the cameraman-driver wishes to plow straight into them, eliciting from her a terrified, helpless "JUSTIN!" directed at the phone, before the truck's suicidal onrush mercifully slows and dwindles to a stop.

The camera then flips and gives her Justin's face, insanely relaxed still, his sense of mission allowing him to surmount the terror of his situation, addressing her: "Well, you can't say I didn't try."

She's given, next, his rear view, out his back window, showing a phalanx of other patrol cars arriving, cutting off his backward escape. They have him; he's caught.

I'm thankful, she thinks, because at least you're safe now, my wild friend. Our mad ride is over.

POLICE ROADBLOCK, ROUTE 9

The cars ahead all have their doors open. Behind the doors, crouched, are police officers, their guns raised, aimed right at Justin. And as he sees them (these cops, their lethal weapons) *she* sees them too through her phone, as if the guns are equally aimed at her. And to oppose these weapons, Justin aims his phone, turning this moment into an event with an online audience of Sam and God knew how many others.

As Justin moves toward his captors, the sound of their warning shouts rises: "Do not move!" "Get rid of the phone! DO NOT MOVE!" "PUT THE PHONE DOWN." "Get rid of the phone or we *will* shoot! Get rid of the phone and get down, facedown!"

But he'll be damned, damned to hell, if he's gonna give away his only protection, because it's this phone, and the phone only, that's keeping his arresters honest.

"PUT DOWN THE PHONE! PUT DOWN THE PHONE NOW!"

"I'm filming you!" Justin shouts.

Part of him always knew it would come to this, to him, alone facing police weaponry, being told to stop or they'd shoot. But at least he's done enough, hopefully, almost, to give Sam a chance to continue the fight, and bring down this whole house of cards.

"LAST WARNING! PUT DOWN THE PHONE!"

"I'm filming you! Your actions are being livestreamed!"

If the word *livestreamed* holds any meaning to the officers, it does not quiet them.

"PHONE DOWN! PHONE DOWN! NOW! RIGHT NOW!"

"The world is watching!"

"NOW! PUT THE PHONE DOWN!"

But he won't give up his only advantage. He calls back, "I surrender! I surrender!" and moves, with arms raised, closer to the waiting, poised, hard-aiming police with their silent flashing car lights and sharpshooter stances.

And then a single gunshot signals the beginning of the end: It strikes Justin in the right thigh. He doubles over, shouts in pain, then drops onto his other knee on the highway. Blood wells from the plug hole.

Calls again: "I surrender!"

But another shot rings out, striking his right arm at the shoulder. The phone is dropped. There will be no arrest here today.

Ignoring the police warning, he retrieves the phone with his good arm, raises it directly to his face to say into the screen: "Your call."

And with that his thumb swipes the blood-splashed screen and dispatches a preset message and server link that passes into the ether, where it will hopefully, if there is any justice in the world, pass to Sam and that, if she plays her necessary part in it, will set in motion a planned and devastating sequence of events. *Whooosh.*

A HILLTOP, ROUTE 9

Sam screams. Drops the phone Justin gave her as if she herself has been shot, as if the fusillade she hears off-screen is now entering her body, an assault that has no mercy. But she is not harmed, she is not shot, and all the terrible things, the terrible things in the world that are happening right now, are simply what she can hear through a fallen phone.

Please, she prays, as the sound of an incoming message arrives on her phone, be alive, be alive, Dear God, be alive, an old prayer, much practiced, much used for Warren, directed now for Justin.

As seconds elapse, and when no further sounds come, and when her need to establish if this prayer has been answered becomes unbearable, she picks up the phone again to see that the video link has been severed. She has lost him, her friend, and in his place, instead of Justin's living transmission, one final mystery.

A message. From Justin. Two words: *Your call*. And then a link to some other site. The name of the link: *Tomyris*.

FUSION CENTRAL, WASHINGTON, DC

Cy saw Justin Amari's injured body resurrect itself, rise back to its feet, to magically defy its destiny, but it was an illusion and in the next instant he was hurled backward as more bullets peppered him, each striking with the force of a punch, his limbs made to jerk as if he were a puppet on drunken strings, before falling for the final time.

With his adrenaline enormously high, still intoxicated by the culmination of the Justin/Samantha situation, Cy is again able to think. One down, one to go. But this gamer sentiment fails to deliver the expected relief. As he stands at the handrail of the gantry looking down on his stunned and silent staff members below, who have been following the real-time horror show on the big screen, real time American justice straight out of the movies, he hears a verdict being rendered: *Murderer*. The accuser? *Himself*. The thought of being directly responsible for this death takes hold of him. And with it, perhaps his own life is ruined also. If the stunt he pulled is ever found out, he is in great trouble, dire trouble, terminal trouble. A panic takes hold and only intensifies as he watches new images on the big screen, of his own Capture Team arriving at last on the scene and, via their bodycams, delivering the added news that the Ford Tundra does not hold Samantha Crewe. Not only is she *not* shot, but this lady, very much alive, has escaped capture again.

That's not good.

As he watches the images of the truck being searched and, on other screens, security forces advancing with weapons leveled on the lifeless body of Justin Amari, he tries to reassure himself—Justin was the brains of the operation, and at least he is gone. *He* was the loose cannon, the one I could not bargain with, while *she*, on the other hand, will still do anything to find out if her husband is alive and where in Iran he is being held. So single-minded is she, I'm sure she'll keep her mouth shut about me, if I can come through for her. She came up with the deal terms herself: her silence for information! An easy exchange. Her idea, not mine. So if I can just find her, I can renew and deepen this pact. And I *will* help her. That's the solution! And by normal means, working *with* the CIA, now that he has deleted the stolen files and also Justin's copy of those files. The genie is back in the bottle. The greatest database of secrets in the world is once more secure. And so the new mission, the simple one, is exactly the same as the old: Find this woman, this trickster, this slippery, reckless, unnaturally talented fugitive, and do it before anyone else does, and make sure nothing about Virginia Global Technologies sees the light of day.

All will be well, yes it's fine, he tries to convince himself. But these platitudes don't entirely console or convince him. A core panic remains, undiminished, and even grows. This woman *can* destroy him. She is smart. Knows a great deal, has his emails. She will know he was the one who initiated the download! She knows! She knows! She knows! And now, her accomplice, her helper, her friend, is dead. She will want revenge. She'll be planning it already. What cyclic madness! In the onset of some panic attack, he feels feverish as he watches the big screen. What has he done? What on earth has he done with all that he has built, with all that he has made of himself? A terrible error has been made. Surely he can't have thrown it all away. Surely Fusion can still find one woman, pluck her from the human mass, and strike a deal with her, score a happy resolution?

Damn it, where is Erika? He needs Erika. Cy steps back from the railing as the walls of the Void seem almost to pulse and that single accusing word returns to take hold again of his thoughts: *Murderer.* No, no, no, he argues. The police fired the shots. They made the decision. Justin should have put down that phone. And still the thought returns: They will catch me; I will be exposed. There is enough information to lead them back to me. Where is Erika? She should *be* here!

Back in his office, he slumps into his chair, drinks a mouthful of water as his eyes fix on the magic wall: a sunlit South American rain forest, tropical birds, gigantic fruit. Maybe he should leave the country for a while? Go zero. But where can you go and truly not be found? Where can anyone go anymore?

What the hell is happening to him? He can barely breathe and his heartbeat is not right. Why is he feeling this way? Just because Justin Amari is dead and Samantha Crewe is *not*? No, what just happened happened, that's it—the guy could have surrendered peacefully—and all Cy did, and all he *is* doing, all they can prove he did, was make sure that his poor, much-maligned, embattled country is safe for another day.

For many seconds he can only stare at his laptop, this compromised machine, this all-betraying unfaithful weapon on his desk that Justin violated and took ghostly ownership of. Opens the lid. Light illumines his face. Cy's privacy has almost been restored, but until Samantha has been caught and silenced, then he will continue to feel naked, unclothed, dispossessed of every intimacy.

In such a state, he is interrupted by a voice from the open door.

"Good afternoon."

In the doorway, Deputy Director Burt Walker, grim-faced. And then, appearing behind him, Erika, sharer of his professional life and bed for fifteen years.

Cy looks back at his laptop but makes no move to type a single thing, and when he looks up again it's not at Burt; it's Erika he sees, her sorrowful face sending him a coded clue, from which he can start to fathom the riddle, discern the enigma, piece together the puzzle that is the future, whose ambassador he had—until this very moment—believed he was.

ONE FLOOR BELOW, THE REVERSING clock originally with a month to mi-
nus but now with only seconds left, slips digit by digit toward the climactic
Zero, which, when reached, garners no great reaction from the stunned
staff on the floor, no applause, barely any attention. A single round 0
flashes, a symbol of collective failure, chastising everyone, because near
it, on the big screen, the resolute portrait of Zero 10 remains undimmed,
the sole outstanding fugitive in the gallery of the captured.

THE FUTURE

It should have taken weeks to put together a story like this, since there are so many moving parts to it, but they assemble most of it in less than three hours. The first installment anyway. There will be more, much more, to come, months of it in fact, months in which serious questions will be raised about a secret program known as Fusion, which partnered with the CIA and WorldShare; about the wisdom of the Go Zero Beta Test; about the hidden domestic ambitions of the CIA; and about the trustworthiness of Cy Baxter and other Silicon Valley elites as stewards of private information. But for now reporters everywhere race to get this early chapter out ahead of the lawyers for WorldShare and the government, who are saying little.

CIA SPECIAL ASSISTANT JUSTIN AMARI,
UNARMED WHEN KILLED BY . . .

SERIOUS QUESTION RAISED ABOUT
THE POLICE KILLING OF . . .

WHO WAS JUSTIN AMARI? WHAT WE KNOW . . .

The cables around Cy Baxter tighten continually, as if by a winch. Stiff-mouthed, a month after the killing, a photographer catches him getting into a waiting car in DC, off to face questioning by the Senate Committee on Commerce, Science, and Transportation, where he sits for three days, eyes wide, defensive, with so much he doesn't recall but promises to look into, pledging to be helpful, pledging his fealty to America, deflecting all criticism.

> **NEW CALL FOR CY BAXTER TO BE INVESTIGATED BY THE DEPARTMENT OF JUSTICE...**

> **FEDERAL INVESTIGATION OF WORLDSHARE'S MISHANDLING OF USERS' PERSONAL INFORMATION STALLS...**

> **BAXTER ACCUSES GOVERNMENT OF "DEMONIZING" SOCIAL MEDIA...**

> **CY BAXTER CLEARED BY DOJ OF ANY INVOLVEMENT IN JUSTIN AMARI KILLING...**

The public, distrustful of Cy, continues to demand he face criminal charges for the killing, which people feel is directly connected with Fusion and Go Zero, but the pressure comes to nothing when the government announces that it is dropping its probe into Baxter and WorldShare. As cofounder, chief executive, board member, and largest stockholder in the tech giant, Cy promises critics that he will "reorient" the company to concentrate on "privacy-focused" operations.

> **FTC CONSIDERS BUT BACKS OFF PROBE INTO WORLDSHARE SALES OF TECH TO...**

> **"FAIR AND APPROPRIATE RESOLUTION" FOUND BETWEEN WORLDSHARE AND FTC...**

> **GOVERNMENT CONFIRMS BOLD FUSION PROJECT: MAKING AMERICA SAFER...**

> **CY BAXTER ORDERS $500 MILLION SUPERYACHT WITH HELIPAD AND...**

And so the latest attempt to regulate the internet and curb the powers of the private interests who control it comes to nothing. As WorldShare's share price not only recovers but hits all-time highs, Cy Baxter survives the greatest challenge yet to his career and reputation. Emerges largely unscathed with the added cache of being a survivor. Attends Paris Fashion Week with his new love, WorldShare employee Sonia Duvall. Drops sixty-two million dollars on a penthouse in Manhattan. And the internet, in the meantime, quietly evolves in the only way it can; just like the universe, driven by forces not fully understood, ever-expanding, forever flooding with new elements, actions, and counteractions, a growth beyond exponential, a system commensurate only with human complexity itself. The last chance at stopping or even slowing this expansion came at the moment of creation. After that, it was always only going to be something to be beheld, accepted, observed with powerless awe, like stars, like the earth's spin, like oysters opening under a full moon to provide a glimpse of a pearl.

THE FUTURE

LANGLEY AIR FORCE BASE, HAMPTON, VIRGINIA

IT'S A NEW WORLD: OR, if not entirely new, then vastly altered from the one Warren Crewe remembers leaving behind just three and a half years earlier.

As he descends the thin metal steps of the military aircraft, squinting against the light—all light now takes on the quality of torture—he rates as a triumph each step that delivers him closer to good old American tarmac, so that, when he finally reaches it, America that is, he pauses to turn to his escort for the flight, one Staff Sergeant Channing Bufort, to say "Home sweet home" before getting down on the ground to give that blessed macadam a good and proper kiss.

Bufort is smiling when Warren gets back to his feet. "Been a while, huh, Murphy?"

"Too, too long."

Sergeant Bufort, grinning, knows Warren only as "Murphy," on account of the name tag on the green flight suit they'd randomly given him back there at Al Dhafra Air Base in Abu Dhabi, and only just now switched for civilian clothes. Warren doesn't give a hoot what anyone calls him as long as it's not a number.

HE IS MOVING SLOWLY. WHY? she wonders but is afraid to find out. His skinny legs, long unused and too long abused, no longer appears to have their old strength. But it might also be that with each step an anxiety grows in his chest that might just be some version of PTSD, or it might be that he's simply nervous as a cat about seeing her again, hoping like hell things they both haven't changed too much.

As he approaches, she notes civilian clothes too big for him, jeans, T-shirt, bomber jacket.

Here he comes. Closer. Closer . . . Jesus Christ, Warren! Four years! Four years. And how ill you look, my darling. Hardly recognizable from the man who gave me a goodbye wave from the curb, then got in a taxi, only to vanish. Gray hair now. Beard. She cannot bear to think of all the horrors he's been through, the shaming, the perversities he's endured.

But he is here, regardless, back on U.S. soil, a free man as a result of her elusive antics and Justin's genius and life-surrendering commitment, actions that finally drew attention to Warren's predicament at the very highest levels of government. At least for a time. Erika Coogan helped, too. Using Fusion's capabilities to the fullest—from analyzing satellite photography to sieving internet traffic and calls, to employing spyware that miraculously got them inside Iran's own national computer systems—the searchlight fell on a single Iranian black site south of Isfahan holding an unknown prisoner with U.S. citizenship. Enhanced satellite photography of the prison exercise yard, and even the stealth slaving of the prison's own security cameras, confirmed that Prisoner 1205 was indeed Warren Crewe. From there, Burt Walker's help galvanized political will to pressurize Iran to admit what was now obvious, which left the White House with no choice but to finally accept an offer for a (highly unequal) prisoner swap: an Iranian terrorist plotter in exchange for poor, broken Warren. Sam's government finally did what it could and should have done on day one: the right thing.

He looks ten years older. Perhaps more. And what *deeper* damage has the last four years done? Just as she has mightily changed, in ways numerous and profound, with new sides to her, inner injuries capable of causing her a ton of trouble down the road, that is nothing to how he will have been transformed by indignity and trauma. Both of them have passed through so many lives, too many struggles, to reach this rendezvous unaltered. There will be a half dozen new sides to both of them they will not know or recognize or ever be able to truly fathom. New demons they will each have to wrestle with. How, for instance, can she ever truly convey her guilt about Justin's death, which haunts her every waking hour? How to hide her rage at a society that would let Cy Baxter do what he did, and then exonerate him, let him walk away scot-free? This rage of hers—a child of Justin's rage—is growing in her, rather than shrinking. Justin's sacrifice— she tries to telepathically explain to Warren—must not be allowed to stand for nothing. It cannot. Perhaps only you, dear Warren, could understand this, fully. Only you. Only you will be able to appreciate and support the measure I may be about to take, if my courage holds. Won't you agree? Because I'm going to ask your permission. What will you say? How will you reply? After all this time apart.

WARREN'S ESCORT STOPS, LET'S HIS charge advance the last few steps alone until, at long last—a miracle—he is in her arms, she in his. She closes her eyes, head against his chest. It's easier this way. Eyes closed means they both can be anywhere and everywhere at once. They can even be strangers again, if they wish, meeting for the first time at a party at a friend's house, dancing to Van Morrison as plastic punch cups bob on the illuminated pool, talking on and on. Or they can be at the lake house in those first breathless hours after they wed, when they couldn't let go of each other. Or they could just be any couple entwined at any airport in the world, free of context, two people holding on. Chest to chest, his traumatized heart races along with her own.

Pushing her away, he examines her good and long. She moves a strand hair from her face to permit it, pins it behind her ears. And in return she looks into his face. Takes stock of him, the damage the days have done but also the things that have not changed, until she smiles, all strangenesses fading into the familiar, into the remembered, as if to say that what counts, all that counts, is that they are here together, and that once again they have time.

"So," she whispers, through a smile, through tears, "what kept you?"

THEY TALK MOST OF THE night until his eyes close and fathomless exhaustion carries him into sleep.

But before then, they managed to tell each other as many stories as they figure the other can bear, kiss tentatively, and assess and crucially feel out the changes in each other. He admits to feeling ancient. A wreck. *Systematically ruined* is the phrase he uses to describe himself. He has the shakes. His hair is spun with gray. Has a nervous condition also. Is he still himself at all? he asks her. Of course he is, she tells him, bestowing kisses as he breaks down, then sobs in her arms.

For her part, she needs him to understand her present state of mind, and also the steps in her thinking that have led her here. . . .

First, there was her decision to turn herself in.

After Justin was killed, she hid for another day but then began to engage in secret talks with Erika Coogan, who gave her assurances that no harm would come to her. It was in no one's interest to make a martyr of her.

And so Fusion, with the agreement of the CIA and the FBI and the U.S. attorney general, was able to offer her, in exchange for her full cooperation, complete immunity for what had become known as DataGate. Justin Amari in his grave would alone carry full responsibility for the hacking of the NSA, a theft that, in the final analysis, had done no damage at all to national security, thanks to the swift work (and deadly aim) of law enforcement.

So she had been able to return to her old life, even resuming work in ER at Boston General, seeing a lot more of Kaitlyn Day also, reliant as never before on her counsel, her friendship, her madness, her wit, her soup. At the same time, in exchange for Sam's silence and cooperation, orders were given at the highest levels that ultimately resulted in Warren being found and returned.

But what she doesn't tell this man, before he falls into sleep, is what she is thinking of doing next.

She put off making a final decision until Warren was safely home, because only with his rescue and repatriation can she know her own true mind. But after talking half the night, explaining to him as best she can her own state of mind, *does* she know any better what her next move will be?

In the kitchen, this home, this dear home, with morning light pinking the clouds outside, she thinks: If I do this, as I believe I have to, I'll be a criminal again. And a *major* criminal. Sought by everyone. If I'm caught— and why wouldn't I be eventually?—the price I pay will be enormous. If

I do it, go through with the plan, if in other words I do exactly as Justin asked me to with his dying entreaty—*Your call*—and finish the task he began, I might never find my way home again.

So that's the choice. Stark. Brutal. On the one hand, there's Warren— reclaimed husband and home at last—on the other, a life of chaos, of living rough, of hiding, of insomniac nights and curtailed days, of going zero, as she has learned well enough how to do.

But she's already made up her mind. In truth, she is not wrestling with her decision in this moment. Warren, unaware of her exact plan but sensing, as he always has, that there's something she's withholding, has already told her that the great wrong that has been done here cannot be allowed to stand. He said this to her. That Justin's killing and Baxter's exoneration cannot be allowed to stand. His words. Was it a coded signal? For a man whose adult life has been built around a desire for justice, she's hoping he will understand. Standing in the kitchen, wearing her all-weather jacket and hiking boots, a backpack stocked with essentials strapped already on her back, she pauses not to give in to second thoughts, but only to mourn the life she has just decided to say goodbye to for a while.

On the breakfast table, two burner phones. One is for Warren. She picks up the other, this small detonator of information into which she has just inserted a life-giving battery. It's time. Yes, finally, it's time.

A half dozen thumb taps bring up a message inbox, and inside this, long since prepared by Justin, a link—one that owes its name to an Iranian queen who, in response to a very great treachery, led her armies to defend against the attack of a corrupt king.

Her thumb pauses over the tiny screen, which, once tapped, will release Justin's giant backup copy of Cy Baxter's data hack into the world. The biggest leak in history, it will be, of many if not all of the most secret files of the CIA, the FBI, the NSA. Everything on everybody who has ever done anything wrong. And among the vast list of the unpunished, Cy Baxter himself. As she cannot extract just his file, she must release them all.

As Justin knew, such a wave of national embarrassment, of sudden public nudity, of hypocrites exposed, of credibility so painstakingly cultivated over twenty, thirty, fifty years capsizing with a single headline, may redraw public life in significant ways, ushering in a season of shame, of shock, of incredulity and remorse and apology, of litigation and resignation, of reputational executions in the town squares of the nation, of enforced humility. Who knows? It might even bring about Justin's ultimate dream of a system reboot. All this is possible, she guesses, but in her mind it's still Cy Baxter she's after.

Her dead friend's words return to her in this critical moment: *They win. In the end, they win. They always do.*

Yeah, she thinks, perhaps, before adding, aloud to no one, unless to Justin, to sleeping Warren, to herself: "Until they don't."

A single tap.

Woooosh.

It's done. And with this she tightens the straps on her backpack and exits the back door, shutting it so softly behind her as to be undetected.

Gone.

ACKNOWLEDGMENTS

TO COME. LEAVE 4 PAGES

ABOUT THE AUTHOR

TO COME